ABOUT THE BOOK

Two alien species. One threat to Earth.
But who is the real threat and who can be trusted?

Twelve-year-old Flipper didn't believe in aliens — until he was kidnapped by one. When he wakes up one morning on the planet Vetrix he is trapped in the midst of an inter-planetary war. As Flipper struggles to survive and find a way back to Earth he discovers he may be a descendent of one of the warring species and that his intervening in the war may be his destiny, if destiny is decided by a computer program.

On Earth, Allison begins having dreams that turn out to be real experiences. When she watches a purple man disappear with her cousin, Flipper, no one believes her. Allison's best friend Josh agrees to help and together the two sixth-graders begin their own investigation that leads them to the truth behind the Roswell Incident of 1947 and current alien activity on Earth.

As they try to figure out how to expose the secret colony of aliens and their plans to destroy the human race, Allison attempts to use her dreams to locate and rescue Flipper.

ABOUT THE AUTHORS

Bill Bush grew up in Yates Center, Kansas, and is a graduate of Yates Center High School and Tabor College, where he earned a Master's degree in Accounting. He is a CPA and runner as well as a writer, is author of several collections of short stories, and has written a column in the Harvey County Independent since April, 2013.

His desire to write comes from his mom, Phyllis Roth Lewis, who was a published author and wrote numerous short stories, poems, and books.

Bill lives in Halstead, Kansas with his two teenage children, who are the inspiration behind many of his stories. You can learn more about Bill at www.billbushauthor.com.

Blake Bush is a fourteen year old eighth grader in Halstead, Kansas, who also takes three high school classes.

For several years he has attended Space Camp at the Cosmosphere in Hutchinson, Kansas. He loves video games and is a self-proclaimed Nintendo nerd. His next favorite activity is to annoy his older sister.

Blake is a member of the Halstead Middle School cross country, track, and Scholar's Bowl teams.

More information: www.snaderpublishing.com

To the Youngs,
Thank you for the opportunity
to do the book signing.
Welcome to Vetrix!

Bill Bush

VETRIX

Blake Bush and Bill Bush

Blake Bush

Flipper, Allison, and Josh, Book One: Vetrix
published by Snader Publishing Company, Halstead, Kansas, USA
This book is also available as eBook.

First published 2017

© 2017, all rights remain with the authors
© 2017, cover design by Deb McLain

printed On-Demand Publishing LLC, 100 Enterprise Way, Suite A200, Scotts Valley, CA 95066, USA, www.createspace.com

ISBN-13 978-1-945871-22-1

More information can be found on the publisher's website:
http://www.snaderpublishing.com

For my children, Sydney and Blake.
You inspire me more than you will ever know.

TABLE OF CONTENTS

CHAPTER 1

Flipper was a normal twelve-year-old kid, or so he thought. Little did he know that a war several million light years away between the Gudes and the Snaders was about to change his destiny. Then again, the Gudes and Snaders didn't realize Flipper was about to change theirs either.

***

"It's Friday *and* Halloween." Allison, who was dressed up as Athena, lamented. She wore a long flowing toga and a crown on her head. She loved reading about the Greek gods, and her favorite author was Rick Riordan. Allison had even named her dog Anna, after Annabeth in the Percy Jackson books. She continued, "I don't think teachers should be allowed to assign major projects when they know everyone's going to be squirrelly. I mean, the school encouraged us to dress up and they still expect us to be able to concentrate in class?"

Flipper sat next to Allison in Social Studies thumbing through his notecards before the bell rang. He was dressed as a Nerd. His short-sleeve, button-up shirt was partially untucked and he had a pocket protector and pens in the front pocket. His jeans were pulled up way too high. Flipper wondered how anyone actually wore them like that all the time. He had tape around the middle of his glasses and his normally straight, blond hair was black, greasy, and combed with a center parting. He had come to school with a sign on his back that said *Kick Me*, but a teacher made him take it off when everyone kept doing just that.

"Allison, you're in sixth grade now. It's time to grow up. Try to be more like your older, more mature cousin." Flipper patted his chest as if Allison didn't know who he was talking about. "Calm, cool and collected."

She rolled her eyes. "Good grief! You're eleven months older than me."

"Yes, but a person matures a lot in eleven months. You'll see."

Allison chuckled. Flipper could always make her laugh, even when she was stressing at school. She changed the subject. "Do you have your presentation ready?"

"Yes, but I can hardly think about it. I'm too excited about going to Carlsbad Caverns tomorrow."

They lived in Roswell, New Mexico, only an hour and a half away from Carlsbad, yet Flipper had never been there. He recently did a report on bats for school so his parents had promised they would take him to see the caverns. People sat outside the caves every evening to watch as the bats flew out, just over their heads. Flipper couldn't think of anything that sounded more exciting.

"Too excited?" Allison asked sarcastically. "What happened to calm, cool and collected?"

Flipper gave an uneasy smile.

"Hey, guys!" Josh said, coming into the classroom. Josh loved to dress up which made Halloween his favorite time of year. He was wearing an alien costume that had over-sized feet. His seat was right in front of Allison. Josh was tall for a sixth grader and his bulky costume made it difficult for him to slide into his seat, which was connected to the desk.

Allison and Flipper both giggled. They knew Josh didn't mind them laughing at him. He liked to be silly and make people laugh. Josh was thirteen but still in the sixth grade. His dad was in the military and when he was in the first grade they moved three times. He had to repeat first grade, which meant he was older than most of the students. He was also bigger, which gave him an advantage when playing sports.

"Okay, class," Mrs. Smith said, standing up from her desk. "It's time for our presentations. Josh, you're up first."

Getting up turned out to be harder than sitting down. Everyone in the class laughed at Josh's struggle to stand. Flipper was sure Josh was smiling, though no one could see it underneath the papier mâché alien head he wore.

Eventually, Josh made it to the front of the class and gave his report in a muffled voice. "My report is on the Roswell Incident. On the evening of July second, nineteen forty-seven, several people said they saw a disc-shaped object flying through the air. This was during a thunderstorm. The next day a local rancher outside of Roswell, New Mexico, claimed to have found a piece of what he said looked like an exploded aircraft. On July eighth, the Roswell Daily Record reported that the Air Force base in Roswell had captured a flying saucer. Although the Air Force claims that the flying saucer was simply an experimental weather balloon for a top secret project, many people today believe the United States military found a UFO spacecraft, captured the aliens, and covered up the truth.

"Now, every year, Roswell celebrates a UFO Festival during the first week in July. People from all over the world come to visit the museums, talk about aliens, and tour the crash site. My parents told me about the festival in nineteen ninety-seven, which was the fiftieth anniversary of the crash. Hotel rooms were sold out as far away as Albuquerque and Lubbock, Texas. Several celebrities, including Oprah Winfrey, were here. The theater at the mall had a pre-release showing of Men In Black and Will Smith was there signing autographs.

"I don't believe the crash was a UFO with aliens. That doesn't make any sense to me. It was storming and people wouldn't have been able to tell what they really saw. Besides, there is no real evidence to prove it was aliens. But, I think the city of Roswell is smart to promote the festival and for businesses like McDonald's and Wal-Mart to put aliens on their buildings. It helps them make a lot of money. The end."

Some of the kids clapped quietly.

"Thank you, Josh," Mrs. Smith said.

"Good job!" Allison and Flipper both told Josh, patting him on the shoulder as he sat down.

***

As Allison walked between Flipper and Josh after school, her waist-length bright red hair bouncing behind her, she looked at Josh, who was still wearing his alien head. "You know, Josh, I believe the crash in nineteen forty-seven really was an alien spaceship."

Although it was still a couple of hours away from sun set, the dark clouds gave the afternoon a dusk sort of feeling.

"Really?" Josh said with surprise.

"Yeah. There is so much we don't know, both in outer space and here on earth. My parents told me the government keeps a lot of secrets from us. Who knows, maybe there are aliens living here in Roswell." She shrugged her shoulders.

"I think Principal Hermann is an alien," Flipper's serious tone made it hard to tell when he was joking. "Have you seen the way she walks around all hunched-back? And she never smiles. If I was an alien from another planet, I wouldn't ever smile."

Josh shook his head. "My dad's been all over with the Air Force. He told me there was no way the military could be hiding aliens without him knowing."

"Maybe some people are good at keeping secrets," Allison said, dismissing Josh's argument. "What do you think, Flipper?"

He pushed his glasses up. "I don't know. It doesn't seem very likely. I mean, to keep a secret like that for this long. I think someone would have said something. But maybe, if…" Flipper stopped speaking as Allison stiffened and tightly grabbed his arm. Josh kept walking; with the alien head still on he didn't notice they had stopped.

Allison was staring across the street. Flipper followed her gaze. She seemed to be looking at the empty lot. In the back corner stood an evergreen—the kind that looked like a large Christmas tree—looking a bit out of place in the barren field. He saw sparse patches of tall weeds, lots of dirt, and a tumbleweed blowing across in the light, steady wind. He didn't see anything worth looking at, let alone to be frightened by.

He looked back at Allison. Her eyes were glued to the lot and the vein in her neck was bulging. He could tell she was scared but didn't know why. He suddenly felt cold and uncomfortable.

"Are you okay, Allison?" His voice betrayed his nervousness.

Other than her quick breaths and heaving chest, she didn't move or speak. Flipper's arm was throbbing from Allison's tight grip, but he did his best to ignore it. He felt desperate to help his cousin. "What is it? I don't see anything."

"I-I-I… I don't know," she finally stuttered. She blinked rapidly like she was coming out of a trance. Her eyes remained directed across the street and her speech was labored. "I didn't see anything either, but I could feel something. It was like a strong presence, like someone was across the street watching us."

Flipper looked again. "I still don't see anything."

Allison took a deep breath and relaxed. She let go of his arm, looking down as she did so. "I'm so sorry, Flipper!" He was bleeding where her nail-bitten, jagged fingernails had dug into his skin.

"Holy cow, Allison!" Josh walked back toward them. He removed one of his alien gloves and gave it to Flipper. "Here, use this to wipe the blood."

"I don't want to mess up your costume." Flipper tried to hand the glove back to Josh.

Josh waved his hand in refusal and said enthusiastically, "Putting blood on it will make it that much cooler."

Flipper hesitated, then held the glove over the cuts. "Thanks."

"What was that all about?" Josh asked, concerned.

"Allison thought she saw something," Flipper said with skepticism.

"Actually, I thought I kind of sensed something," Allison tried to explain again. "I had a strong feeling that someone was watching us—the most intense feeling I've ever had." She glanced back at the now obviously empty lot. "I don't know. I guess it sounds crazy. Maybe it is crazy."

"Maybe it was an alien," Josh said, raising his hands and walking towards her—more like a zombie than an alien.

"Stop it," she said, playfully pushing him away. Allison laughed as they began walking again. "But maybe it was an alien and only I can sense it because only I believe."

"Sports teams send scouts to watch players they might want to recruit," Josh said with rising enthusiasm. "Maybe you're being recruited."

Flipper laughed so hard he had to stop walking. "Does that mean she's an alien?"

Josh laughed with Flipper while Allison stood with her hands on her hips, visibly irritated.

"Remember, if I'm an alien, you're an alien. We're related."

Flipper stopped laughing. Josh laughed even harder.

***

"Flipper, is that you?"

Flipper, Josh and Allison had just come into the house after trick-or-treating later that evening. "Yes, Mom."

Flipper's mom hurried into the room. She was full of life and loved the holidays, but this was the first year she had let Flipper go trick-or-treating by himself. She had given them very specific instructions about where they could go, what they could do, and when they had to be back. They each carried a cell phone. But still, his mom worried. "How did it go?"

"It was okay," Flipper said without enthusiasm.

"Yeah, I think we are outgrowing the whole trick-or-treating thing," Allison said, slumping onto the couch.

"But not the candy," Josh said, dumping his sack onto the floor, eager to go through it.

"I'm just glad you're home safely," Flipper's mom said. "And not too much candy. I agreed that Josh and Allison could spend the night since they are going to Carlsbad Caverns with us tomorrow, but you promised you wouldn't stay up late."

"Yes, Mom." Flipper and Allison dumped their sacks on the floor and began eating and trading candy.

Two hours later Flipper, Josh and Allison were in their sleeping bags on the living room floor. Although they were only a few feet apart they could barely see each other. The burnt out streetlight left only the dim moonlight shining through the large front window to see by.

Flipper was giddy about their trip the next day and talked about it non-stop until Josh fell asleep and began to mumble about playing basketball and being stuck in quicksand.

Flipper went quiet and then looked at Allison. "Do you really believe there might be people on other planets? Or were you only teasing Josh?"

"I don't know. It's hard to look up at the sky and not think there are more people out there somewhere." Allison paused before deciding to

15

continue. "But mostly I sense there are others out there. Sometimes I sense they are close—in Roswell. I haven't really talked about it because it sounds crazy. I know we were joking about it earlier, but sometimes I do wonder if I'm not from another planet."

Flipper laughed. "That would explain a lot."

Allison laughed too. "Yeah, I pretty much walked into that one."

Flipper smiled at her. "Good night, Allison."

"Good night, Flipper."

***

Allison's dreams that night were intense, and she didn't feel like she was dreaming. She felt like she had gone back in time—was reliving the previous day—but there was something quite different about this repeated experience, like a long déjà vu.

She was back in Social Studies class and Josh was giving his presentation on the Roswell Incident. Everything looked the same as it had that morning, but this time she was overwhelmed by the same strange sensation she had felt when walking home. She felt like she was in the presence of someone important; kind of like when she met the mayor at a dinner she went to with her parents. Except this felt like she was in the presence of someone much more important than a mayor.

Allison turned and looked behind her. In what had been an empty seat in the back row that morning sat someone she had never seen before. He was older than the students and had a slightly amused expression. His hair was rumpled and his skin was... She blinked, hoping her eyes would clear. His skin was... Allison gaped at him until he noticed her stare and looked her way. She jerked her head back to Josh, droning on about the Roswell Incident.

She felt the presence ease, so she looked back. The man was gone, but she couldn't get his image out of her mind.

His skin had been purple. Brightly, unapologetically purple.

Instantly, she was with Flipper and Josh, walking home from school. She froze sensing the same overwhelming presence as earlier. But this time, when she looked across the street at the lot, she saw the purple man from the classroom standing, watching them.

This time, she locked eyes with him for several moments. The purple man tilted his head, looking at her, puzzled. The look of confusion on his face mirrored what Allison felt. She looked at Flipper and saw her hand clamped on his arm. She looked back across the street but the man was gone.

Allison tossed and turned as her dream intensified.

She began having flashbacks to their evening of trick-or-treating. Everywhere they went, the purple man was there, watching, following. The sense of his presence intensified with each sighting. Finally, she couldn't take it any longer and started running towards him. She didn't know who he was or what he wanted, but she couldn't stand the feeling any longer. She was scared and angry. She screamed, "Just leave me alone!"

Allison startled awake and sat straight up, sweating, breathing heavily. She was awake, but the intense presence she had felt in her dream was still with her. In fact, it was even stronger. She jumped to her feet and turned around. The purple man was standing in the room with them, holding Flipper in his arms. Flipper was still asleep.

"What are you doing?" Allison demanded.

"We are trying to protect you. Blake… Flipper… has been chosen to save us all."

And with those words the man and Flipper vanished.

CHAPTER 2

Twenty-four hours earlier:

"Jake, I have an idea how your dad can keep the Snaders from attacking us," Chezlor said as they walked into the kitchen.

Jake's dad was a General for the Gudes, a species with violet skin that lived on the planet Vetrix.

General Jaxxen lived on the military base. Jake and Chezlor heard explosions in the distance. Soon they would be able to smell the smoke from what they assumed was another training exercise common in the middle of the day.

Jake had black hair that lay straight back and never seemed to be out of place. He was as calm, cool and collected as Chezlor was awkward, goofy, and disorganized.

"He needs to stop them soon," Jake replied. "I'm afraid it's only a matter of time before they attack our capital."

Although they were both twelve years old, Chezlor looked to Jake as an older brother. Maybe it was because Jake was usually so serious, making him seem much more mature than his age suggested. Chezlor, on the other hand, avoided being serious, usually with a prank or flippant remark. He felt immature.

Chezlor jerked his head back, trying to flip his shaggy, purple hair out of his face. He flipped enough away to see out of one eye. Good enough for now as his hands were full. He turned to face his best friend. "Hold out your hands, palms down."

Jake held out his four-fingered hands (four fingers was normal for Gudes) and Chezlor placed a glass full of bright red juice on the back of one of his hands. "Is that too heavy?"

"No." Jake was confused by the question.

Chezlor set the second glass full of red juice on top of the back of Jake's other hand. "Now, is that too heavy?"

"No, it's fine."

Chezlor saw how hard Jake was concentrating to keep the glasses balanced and knew he had him. "Well then, good luck," he said as he walked away.

"Where are you going?" Jake asked in a panic.

"I have chores to do." Chezlor closed the kitchen door.

"Chezlor!"

Chezlor laughed and shouted, "Yes! Got him!"

"Got who?" Alya appeared from around the corner. Her smooth violet face and shoulder length light lavender hair gave her a gorgeous two-toned look. She wasn't quite twelve, but she was close. She was average height for her age, but Chezlor seemed to tower over her, standing at least six inches taller.

Chezlor's face suddenly felt warm and his cheeks turned red. "Um, I, uh…"

"Did you do something to Jake?" Alya demanded.

"Well, he may be in a little predicament." Chezlor smiled and looked toward the kitchen.

Alya glared at him with her hands on her hips. "What did you do?" She had a way of sounding just like his mother used to.

Chezlor shrugged his shoulders. "Nothing he didn't volunteer for."

Alya opened the door to the kitchen and chuckled. Jake stood in the middle of the room, a glass on each hand, unable to move without spilling the juice. He couldn't grab them with his palms facing down. She looked at the red juice then down at the light-colored floor.

Jake had fallen for another one of Chezlor's pranks. Chezlor noticed the perplexed look on his face, and his clenched jaw told Chezlor that Jake was furious. Chezlor watched to see what Alya would do. She liked his sense of humor and often helped him pull his pranks but he thought she was overprotective of Jake, who, he had to admit, was his most frequent and vulnerable target.

As he expected, Alya's soft heart won out and she walked into the kitchen to help Jake. Just before she reached him she saw movement out of the corner of her eye. She looked to her right and saw a two-foot tall tarantula walking toward her. She screamed, grabbed Jake and spun him around so he was between her and the tarantula. The glasses tumbled, spilling red juice all over Jake, Alya and the floor.

Chezlor laughed hysterically. Alya was still screaming when he picked up the tarantula with one hand. "Relax, it isn't real." He held out his other hand, revealing the remote that controlled the large spider.

"Chezlor Daniels!" she hollered, slapping his arm.

"I knew you wouldn't be able to resist helping Jake. My prank worked to perfection." He took a bow.

Suddenly, Jake's older brother Fox came running into the room. "Jake! Chezlor! Alya! We are under attack! The Lizards are on their way. We have to get to the shelter now!"

***

They were not being attacked by actual lizards. War had broken out decades ago. After Mounticek Jaxxen became the Commanding General, the Snaders assassinated his wife, in what Jaxxen called the ultimate act of cowardice. He started calling them Lizards, the lowest form of life on his planet. Besides, he thought they looked like lizards anyway—red, slimy skin, long, forked tongues. He never insisted anyone else use the term, but those closest to him naturally called them Lizards too. It had become a habit for them.

Jake, Chezlor and Alya were in the shelter with Fox. Fox was ten years older than Jake and a Commander serving under their dad. Fox didn't look as much like their dad as Jake did. General Jaxxen and Fox both stood six and a half feet tall. Fox was not skinny, but he didn't have the muscular build that General Jaxxen and Jake both had.

The underground shelter had been built to protect the highest commanding military leader during times of attack. General Jaxxen had occupied the house above the shelter for almost ten years. This was the first time he had to use it. The commons area in the shelter was a large and comfortable room and could easily fit thirty people without them feeling confined. There were four long couches, several chairs, three tables and an open area in the center. The smell of smoke from above had been replaced by that of must. The smell was strong enough that most people commented on it when they first entered. The adults had been in the shelter numerous times practicing 'worst case scenario' drills. The children had never been down there.

Jake, pacing, cast an angry look at Chezlor who was relaxed in one of the reclining chairs. "Why don't you take this situation a little more seriously?" he demanded.

"What are you talking about?" Chezlor asked.

"You're relaxing when our planet is in danger!" His arm movements were equal to the volume of his voice. "And you were playing pranks at the same time our capital was being taken over."

"He didn't know the capital was under attack," Alya tried to reason with Jake.

"It wouldn't have mattered," Chezlor interjected. "I still would have done the prank."

Alya shot him a look that said he wasn't helping.

"I can't believe you!" Jake turned to walk away.

Chezlor stood, giving up his comfortable chair to meet Jake on equal footing. "First of all, we aren't trained soldiers. There isn't anything we can do to help against the attack. Second, if we have to change who we are and quit having fun, they might as well just go ahead and have our planet. If we can't enjoy ourselves and play pranks, then what are we fighting for?"

It wasn't that Jake had to admit to himself that Chezlor was at least partially right that annoyed him the most at that moment. It was how Chezlor continued to smile like he was calm and happy. "We should still be thinking like soldiers since that's what we're supposed to be preparing for." Jake didn't mean to but subconsciously shot Alya a look as he spoke. Gudes were usually sent away for military training when they turned twelve, which Jake and Chezlor had done months ago. Alya was still eleven. Jake wanted to begin his training the day he turned twelve but his dad refused to let him go, telling him they had to wait until Alya turned twelve so the three of them could go to training together. Jake knew it wasn't Alya's fault and felt bad when she hung her head. He didn't say anything though.

General Jaxxen entered the shelter with Majors Zowsky and Styler, his two War Consultants. They were the strategic brains behind his success. Major Zowsky, or Sierra as the kids called her, was a hard-line, by-the-book, take-no-prisoner thinker. Major Nicole Styler, on the other hand, was more of a risk taker, and spent most of her time thinking outside the box. Jake knew his dad liked the dichotomy.

"Dad, what's going on?" Jake asked.

General Jaxxen spoke to the children as if they were part of his War Council. "The Lizards caught us off guard. We weren't expecting them to attack the capital this soon. Unfortunately, we weren't able to put up much of a fight. It was like they knew our every move before we made it. We suspect someone high up in our command chain tipped them off. It could be someone from either our military or our government. It was probably someone from inside the capital, but at this point I don't have any leads on who the mole is. I don't know who I can trust outside of this room."

General Jaxxen had never shied away from talking war and strategy in front of his sons, except on a few occasions. He believed that letting his sons listen in was the best way for them to learn. Jake enjoyed knowing what was going on, and felt important that his dad trusted him. General Jaxxen turned and spoke directly to Jake, Chezlor and Alya. "We are safe for the moment. This shelter is deep, secluded and well-guarded. The Lizards won't be able to get to us. Even though they seem to be constantly one step ahead of us right now, we are well prepared to survive an emergency like this one." His eyes met Jake's. He wasn't good at giving comfort, but when he spoke he had a command to his voice that made him easy to believe.

General Jaxxen turned to Nicole. "Did your computer program finish running?"

General Jaxxen and his advisers knew over a year ago that they were in danger of losing the war. In their desperation, Nicole came up with a plan to develop a software program that would analyze possibilities to stop the Snaders and turn the war around. The program was complete and had been running for several days. She had abstracted data from over two dozen planets, including every person living on them. The computers the Gudes had developed didn't have any problems storing that amount of data. The challenge was to program the computer to analyze as many scenarios as possible (at least in the octillions) and find the most likely (if there was one) way to defeat the Snaders.

"Yes Sir. The computer program showed only one way to defeat the Snaders permanently." Nicole handed General Jaxxen, Sierra, and Fox each a piece of paper. "The computer concludes that we need to get Blake Brick here as soon as we can. He is the key to defeating the Snaders."

General Jaxxen took the paper and scanned the summarized results. He laid the paper on a table. "Major Zowsky, what do you think?"

Sierra seemed anxious to give her input. "Sir, the program has never been used and we can't trust its reliability. It's beyond reason that one person could defeat an entire army. This Blake Brick is far away, untrained, and as far as we know oblivious to how the Snaders think and fight. Besides, we don't know what his skills are or if he would even be willing to help. What can one person do? We need a sound military strategy!"

"With all due respect, Sir," Nicole piped in, "the program has been used. Admittedly, not on such a scale as this, but it was one hundred percent accurate in all the tests. Blake Brick is far enough removed from this war that he hasn't had contact with the Snaders and should be trustworthy. The program factors that in." Nicole looked straight at Sierra when she said this. "One of our largest challenges is that we don't know who we can trust on our side, which makes any strategy risky at best. Although it's a long shot, we should at least bring Blake in and find out what he has to offer. The computer is programmed to figure out things we cannot see, discover, or understand. I believe we should trust it."

Jake picked up the piece of paper his dad set down. He scanned it, quickly reading the bio of Blake Brick. He had never interrupted his dad while he was talking military strategy, but he felt a strange and intense feeling about Blake. "Dad, I think we should go get Blake. I can tell he will help us."

"Jake, this is a decision for those trained to make it."

"But Dad…"

"That's enough!" his dad commanded. "We have serious business to discuss here and I don't need any distractions right now."

Jake felt his inside compress, squeezing life from him. He often felt more like a distraction than a son. His face burned as he felt Alya and

Chezlor looking at him. They had been his closest friends for years and knew how important his dad's words were to him. He wanted more than anything to please his dad, but had failed again.

"Has anyone else had access to that computer?" General Jaxxen asked Nicole. "How sure are you that the computer or the results haven't been tampered with?"

"No one else has access, Sir. I trust these results completely."

Sierra spoke up again. "Sir, may I remind you that we don't know if traveling is possible right now, let alone safe. Especially at the distance we are talking about. And we have no way of determining if Blake is capable of traveling safely."

General Jaxxen turned and looked at his oldest son. "Fox?"

"Yes, Sir," Fox said, coming to attention.

"What do you think about the possibility of retrieving Blake Brick safely?"

"It's risky, but I believe it is doable. It will take someone with traveling experience and the abilities to pull it off." Fox continued to look his dad in the eye, reading the unasked question. Fox had traveled as much as anyone in the last few years. He was a spy, and a good one. General Jaxxen knew Fox was the best choice for the mission, and he trusted his son's judgment.

"Yes, I can do it," Fox said.

"Okay," General Jaxxen determined. "Fox, be ready to leave as soon as possible. Nicole, gather as much information on Blake Brick as you can and get it to Fox so he can locate him easily and quickly. Sierra, contact the other generals. We need to discuss what is going on and see if we can determine who the traitor is. For now, not a word of this to anyone."

"Yes Sir!" all three said.

CHAPTER 3

Twenty-four hours later:

When Flipper disappeared with the purple man, Allison freaked out. She drew a deep breath and let out short, piercing screams over and over and over again that woke everyone in the house.

Josh's ears hurt. He began yelling, "Allison, What's wrong?! What is it?! Allison, calm down!" His initial concern for her was waning and quickly turning to anger. Every time he told her to calm down she would panic even more.

Flipper's parents were downstairs in a matter of seconds. His dad turned on the lights while Aunt Dee went to Allison, grabbed her arms, bent down and looked her in the eyes. Allison was on the verge of hyperventilating. Josh was thankful that calming Allison was no longer his responsibility.

"Allison, it's okay. Everything's fine. Your Uncle Dennis and I are right here. Please try to calm down." Flipper's mom was slowly able to get Allison to relax with her smooth, calming voice. "You're safe. We're all safe. Now, what's wrong? Did you have a bad dream?"

Allison tried to speak but in her distress it came out as incoherent stuttering. She looked at the ground as she took several long, deep breaths. Finally, she screamed out, "Flipper's gone! Somebody took him and they disappeared!"

Josh had to swear on his Grandpa Ben's grave three times before Dennis and Dee were convinced they weren't pulling a prank.

As Aunt Dee cradled Allison and gently rocked her back and forth, Josh noticed her darting eyes and contorted mouth didn't exuberate the calmness that her voice portrayed to Allison. In fact, the longer Flipper was missing the more her voice began to crack.

Flipper's dad, Dennis, searched the house and yard. He snapped his flip phone shut as he entered the room. Aunt Dee eagerly stood in anticipation as if she hadn't been lovingly comforting Allison all this time.

Dennis stopped, took a deep sigh, and shook his head in the negative, then ran forward to catch his fainting wife.

***

Allison sat on her mom's lap, with her Aunt Dee beside them. They were all crying. Her Uncle Dennis and her dad were walking around the neighborhood, looking for Flipper. Two police officers sat across from the ladies, patiently waiting for Allison to tell her story.

Allison did her best to recount the day's events. She told the police about the man in her dreams—the same man she saw disappear with Flipper. "I was scared, but the man said he was trying to help. I was confused. I didn't know what to say. I should have said something, or screamed sooner. But I just stood there and stared."

She buried her head into her mom's shoulder and cried some more. Her mom stroked her hair. "It's okay, dear. You're safe now."

One of the officers said, "I know this is hard, but the more you can tell us, the sooner we'll be able to get your cousin back."

"O-o-okay."

"In which direction did the man leave the house?" the officer asked.

"He didn't."

"What do you mean, 'he didn't'?"

"He didn't leave," Allison explained. "He disappeared."

The two police officers looked at each other. Allison could tell they didn't believe her.

"And what did the man look like?" the first officer asked, trying a different tact.

"He was tall. He looked like he was old enough to be in college, or a little older."

Allison looked at her mother for reassurance. Her mom nodded at her, and she continued. "All his clothes were black. And… and… and… his skin was purple and he had webbed feet."

***

Josh sat in stunned silence as he tried to accept that Flipper was gone. They had been best friends for the last three years. They did everything together. He just couldn't believe what was happening.

The two police officers sat on the other side of the room from Josh talking to Allison. Two more police officers were searching the room. Josh guessed they were looking for fingerprints or other clues as to who took Flipper. He watched them absentmindedly. That is, until they found something on the floor.

"Harold, look at this," the one officer said as he squatted, pointing towards the floor.

"What is it?" Harold asked.

"I don't know. I've never seen anything like it. Some kind of purple goo."

"Take a sample and we'll have the lab run tests," Harold said.

The other officer carefully scooped the slimy substance into a plastic tube and sealed it. He wrote something on the tube and put it in a bag marked Evidence.

***

Some time later, Allison was calm and sitting beside her mom. Her aunt talked to the last two police officers by the front door.

"Ma'am, it was dark and Allison woke up from an intense dream. She could have easily mistaken the kidnapper for the man in her dreams. Alternatively, it's Halloween and someone may have used a costume as a disguise. Or maybe she didn't see anyone at all. The kidnapper couldn't have just vanished into thin air as she said, so it's difficult to discern how much of her story is true. What does your son look like?

Dee looked down, fighting back tears. "Flipper is five feet tall and weighs about eighty-five pounds. He has thick blond hair and blue eyes."

"What was he wearing?"

"He sleeps in sweats and a tee-shirt. He had, um, I think gray sweats on. And, oh yes, he had on his UFO tee-shirt. It was gray also, with long-sleeves, and has a picture of a green alien standing beside a spaceship."

"I assume Flipper is a nickname?" the officer asked.

"Yes, his dad and I started calling him that when he was little. He was always walking around flipping things in his hands. He still does it, mostly when he's thinking. He kind of goes into his own little world, deep in thought. It's an annoying habit at times, but it was so cute when he was little. We tried to break him of the habit, but have never been successful. It's really more of an obsession for him. Anyway, the name Flipper just stuck and now everyone calls him that. He seems to like it."

"Um, ma'am. What's his real name?" the other officer asked.

"Oh, yes, I'm sorry," she said. "His real name is Blake. Blake Brick."

CHAPTER 4

"He's back!" Nicole announced. She stood beside Fox in the commons area. They were both looking at a pale, tranquil creature, asleep on the floor, when Jake, Chezlor and Alya emerged from the kitchen.

They stood for a moment, staring at the thin, human body.

"What are these?" Chezlor unfolded two black sticks attached to two nearly square pieces of glass.

"And these?" Jake picked up two soft, oblong items. He looked inside of one and quickly dropped them both. "Whoa! They smell horrible."

Fox laughed. "Those are called shoes. Humans wear them on their feet."

"What for?" Alya asked as she curiously examined the feet of the strange-looking being.

"Human skin is not as thick or tough as ours. They wear shoes to protect their feet while they walk. And those," Fox said as he took the u-shaped spectacles from Chezlor, "are eyeglasses. Some humans need to wear them in order to see clearly." He carefully folded the eyeglasses and set them neatly on top of the socks and shoes.

General Jaxxen and Sierra came out of his office.

"Fox, who is this?" The General asked, confused.

"Sir, this is Blake Brick," Fox answered as he received astonished looks from his six companions.

General Jaxxen was incredulous. "Are you sure?"

"I'm positive. I followed him all day to make sure I had the right person. There is no doubt that this is the one Nicole's computer program selected to defeat the Lizards."

"I expected him to be a little more, um," Sierra cleared her throat. "Older."

"If the computer selected him, then he must be the one," Nicole said, though she sounded less sure of herself than before.

Sierra turned to look at the General. "Sir, this is a joke! He is just a boy! We don't have time to waste on this nonsense!"

"We don't know anything yet," Nicole said defensively. "Let's find out a little more about him before making a rash judgment."

"Fox, you observed him for a day. What do you think?" General Jaxxen asked.

Fox thought a moment before answering. "I didn't see anything that would indicate he was unique. He seemed like a normal kid from earth." Fox paused. "He didn't seem special at all, but his cousin Allison, she was remarkable. She could tell I was there. In fact, she saw me."

"Are you sure?" General Jaxxen asked with concern. "We've never had a problem remaining invisible to the humans."

"Yes, I'm quite sure. There was something extraordinary about her."

Sierra looked at Nicole and spoke with disdain. "Maybe she was the one the computer meant. Maybe it made a mistake."

"No," Nicole said. "The computer could not have gotten them mixed up. It's just not possible."

"Blake, Allison, it doesn't matter," Sierra said. "Neither one of them are going to be able to help us in a war. We need someone older than ten to fight against the Lizards. And we need more than one!"

"I'm twelve." Everyone stopped and looked down at Blake. He unfolded and placed the eyeglasses on his face then proceeded to put the socks and shoes on his feet before he stood.

"What did you say, young man?" General Jaxxen asked.

"I'm twelve years old."

Nicole stepped toward Blake and squatted, looking him in the eye. "Blake, I'm Major Styler, but you can call me Nicole. How are you feeling? You have traveled a long way."

Blake flinched when she first approached him. The purple people scared him. Even so, this gentle sounding one brought him some comfort. He looked at her and tried to block the others out. "Everyone calls me Flipper."

Nicole smiled. "Okay, Flipper. How are you feeling?"

"I'm okay, I guess. Who are you people? And where are we?"

The warm, fuzzy feeling Flipper received from Nicole quickly disappeared when the older angry-looking man with a white moustache spoke. "We are the Gudes and we're on planet Vetrix, the nearest inhabited planet to Earth. We have been Earth's protector since its inhabitance. The Lizards are an evil species originally from the planet Rex. They are attempting to take over the universe and have been very successful so far. Their next targets are Vetrix followed by Earth. You were selected by a very sophisticated computer program as the one person who could put an end to the advancement of the Lizards and end this dreadful war."

"So…" Flipper started. He looked from General Jaxxen to Fox, to Sierra, then back to Nicole. He smiled sheepishly. "So, you're saying we aren't in Kansas anymore?" Fox chuckled like he understood Flipper's joke. Flipper wondered if he did.

"Boy, this is a very serious matter!" Sierra said with disgust.

"General, would you like me to return him?" Fox asked.

"No, it's too risky," the General said. "Besides, I can't afford to have you away more than you already have been. We need to regroup and decide on our next plan of action against the Lizards."

"You're being attacked by a bunch of lizards?" Flipper asked incredulously.

"No," Nicole said smiling. "Lizards is the nickname for the Snaders, our enemies from the planet Rex."

"General Jaxxen nicknamed them the Lizards years ago. He said he wouldn't give them the courtesy of calling them by their real name," Fox explained.

"Besides, some of them are rumored to have tails they can regrow," Chezlor said.

Flipper looked behind him and noticed the kids for the first time. There were three of them and they were about his age. The boy who hadn't spoken looked at him and Flipper felt a strange connection.

He looked around at everyone again. Their facial features were very similar to humans—two ears, two eyes, a nose and a mouth. Their bodies were also mostly similar—two arms, two legs, similar heights and weights as humans. And they were wearing clothes, like humans do.

There were two things that made them look different than humans. First, they had webbed feet. Their feet were wider and more round than human feet, and they only had four toes. If they are called toes, Flipper thought to himself. None of them were wearing shoes.

The second difference was their skin color. They were all purple. Most of them had purple hair too, although each was a different shade. The General's hair was so light it looked almost white. Sierra had the darkest—Flipper's art teacher would have called it royal. She also had the longest hair. It went more than halfway down her back.

"You're purple," he blurted out.

"We prefer violet," Sierra corrected him.

Although they acted a lot like humans, they were talking about aliens and being on another planet. I guess if I'm on another planet,

Flipper thought to himself, they aren't the aliens, I am. He had trouble wrapping his mind around that thought.

Nicole saw the troubled look on his face. "Blake, I mean Flipper, what's wrong?"

"You guys all look different."

"Our skin color is very different from yours," Nicole explained. "Beside a few other minor exceptions, we are very similar to the human race."

"I mean, you guys look different from each other. I thought all aliens would look the same."

The kids all giggled, and Fox and Nicole also chuckled. General Jaxxen maintained a serious look while Sierra looked irritated. Apparently she was. "Is that what you Earthlings think? Other species different from yourself are nothing but a bunch of identical mind-numbed robots?"

"I-I'm not sure," Flipper stammered, suddenly afraid to say more.

"And what is that picture on your shirt?" Sierra continued. "A green person with an over-sized head and large black eyes? I don't know of any species that is green. And a tall thin body with long, bone-skinny arms and legs. Is that how you Earthlings look? Like you haven't eaten for two months? You have no understanding or respect for our people! Why do we waste our time trying to protect your planet?"

Sierra paused. Flipper thought her tirade was over, but he was wrong.

"And what is that goofy looking aircraft? Round? Any good engineer knows a round aircraft would never get off the ground. The aerodynamics would make it impossible to fly."

Flipper's eyes were starting to tear up. He had tried to be strong, but now his alienation and fear were consuming him. He blocked out the rest of Sierra's rant. He just wanted to go home.

"Fox, I want you to take Flipper to the cell," General Jaxxen directed. "We'll lock him up so he's safe until we have an opportunity to return him to Earth."

"At least give him a chance!" one of the kids blurted out.

General Jaxxen turned toward the only kid without purple hair, but before he could say anything, Nicole spoke up. "General, the computer said Flipper was the one to help us defeat the Snaders. We can't just throw this opportunity away. Let's at least see what he might have to offer."

"What are you suggesting?" the general asked.

"What would you have us do, Nicole?" Sierra sneered. "Send him away for training until he's eighteen and old enough to fight? We can send a note to the Snaders that we want to postpone the war for eight years to develop our secret weapon."

"I'm twelve," Flipper said, feeling a little more at ease since the black-haired boy and Nicole seemed to be sticking up for him. "Can't Gudes count?"

Nicole continued without giving Flipper's comment any consideration. "Let's evaluate him."

"A test?" General Jaxxen asked.

"Let's try to find out what the computer saw."

"I have a suggestion, Sir," Sierra said.

"What is it?"

"Have him fight FireKing. Let's see what he can do in battle. Besides, if he can't beat FireKing he has no business trying to fight the Snaders."

"Wh-Wh-What? Wait..." Flipper stammered.

"Very well," General Jaxxen cut in. "Fox, prepare Flipper for battle. We leave in one hour. Sierra, Nicole, in my office."

"I've never been in a fight," Flipper said.

The adults ignored Flipper as they headed to the General's office.

"Who is FireKing?" Flipper asked as the three kids approached him.

Jake answered, "He's a twelve ton dragon."

CHAPTER 5

"No one believes me."

Allison sat across from Josh at her parents' round dining room table. The smell of homemade cookies filled the air as her mom baked in the kitchen. Josh dunked his third warm cookie into a cup of milk. Allison's remained untouched.

"I know it sounds crazy, but I know what I saw. It didn't feel like a dream. I relived the whole day. It was real. And I know I saw that man—that purple man—with Flipper. He spoke to me, almost like he knew me." As she finished she realized how it sounded. The confidence in her voice wavered. "Then they just disappeared."

"I believe you, Allison," Josh said, trying to reassure her.

"Thanks, Josh. I thought you didn't believe in aliens?"

"I don't, but I believe in you."

"Oh Josh!" A wave of tears flooded her eyes.

"What's wrong?"

Allison held a tissue up to her eyes. "That was so sweet! Thank you!"

Josh and Allison had been close friends since the fourth grade but their relationship consisted of Josh being silly and Allison teasing him. They were rarely serious. They sat in an awkward, uncomfortable silence. Josh quickly finished his cookie and started on another.

Finally, Allison blurted out. "Josh, we have to find Flipper!"

"That's what the police are trying to do."

"But they don't believe me about the purple man. They won't know where to look. We have to figure out what happened to Flipper and where he went. Then maybe the police can go get him."

"Okay, where do we start?" Josh asked.

Allison thought for a moment. "Maybe if we look around at some of the other places I saw the purple man we could find a clue."

"You said you saw him while I was giving my presentation at school," Josh said as he wiped the milk moustache from his face. "But it's Saturday, the school will be locked."

"I also saw him on the way home from school," Allison said with rising enthusiasm. "That's only a couple of blocks from here. Let's go!"

They took their cups to the kitchen and Allison told her mom they were going for a walk. Josh grabbed one more cookie. Josh was a good athlete and the fastest kid in the sixth grade, but he had trouble keeping up with Allison as they ran to where she had seen the purple man. Allison found the spot she had been standing the day before and pointed across the street. "That's where I saw him."

They darted across the street and looked around the yard. A few minutes later Josh called out, "Allison, look!"

He was on his hands and knees beside a bush. Allison got down on the ground beside him. She reached out and lightly touched the purple goo hidden beneath the shrub.

"This looks like the same stuff that the police found in Flipper's house!" Josh exclaimed excitedly.

"What is it?" Allison asked.

"I don't know, but we should take some with us. We need something to put it in."

"I can get something from my house."

Allison ran back to her house while Josh stayed with the goo. She found an empty container in the pantry. She grabbed a spoon and ran back. After getting as much of the goo as they could into the container they walked back to her house.

"What should we do with this?" Josh asked.

"I don't know. Should we give it to the police?"

"They already have some."

Allison jumped up and down. "I know! Let's take it to the UFO Museum. If anyone knows about aliens around here it should be them.

"Is the museum open on the weekend?"

"Sure. Remember when we went there on a field trip a few weeks ago? The guy working at the museum said they were open seven days a week."

"Oh, okay. Josh pulled his cell phone out of his pocket and looked at the time. "I have to be home for lunch in ten minutes."

"I'll pick you up after lunch."

***

An hour later, Allison knocked on the door and waited for Josh to answer. When he opened the door, she started laughing. "What are you wearing?"

Josh had on a cloth cap with ear flaps, a long, brown trench coat and held a large curvy pipe. He bowed and said, "Sherlock Holmes, at your service, ma'am."

"You look ridiculous."

"Check out this pipe," Josh said, ignoring her. He put it to his lips and blew; bubbles floated out.

"You are one of a kind," Allison said, still laughing.

"Thank you, ma'am." He shut his front door. "Now off we go to solve the crime."

Twenty minutes later, as Josh and Allison approached the UFO Museum on foot, Allison started to feel the presence, like she had felt in her dreams and when Flipper was taken. She stopped in front of the Museum and scanned Main Street, alert. Several cars drove by. People entered and left some of the downtown shops. The light, subtle presence remained. Wherever, or whoever, it was coming from wasn't moving.

She noticed Josh, who had stopped when she had and was watching her as much as the other people. "Do you sense something?"

"A little. At least, I think so. It's hard to tell because it's not really strong," she admitted.

"Let's go take a look in the museum." Josh opened the door and held it for her. "Maybe that's where it's coming from."

The inside of the UFO Museum was brightly lit but deserted. The large room contained mostly newspaper articles, old photographs, and exhibits of supposed UFO parts. The farthest corner of the room was dedicated to a gift shop. They walked around and looked at some of the exhibits. Josh read some of the old newspaper articles about the crash in 1947.

"It says here the UFO sightings were during a thunderstorm, just like I said in my report." Josh pointed to the framed newspaper hanging on the wall. "It would be hard to see anything during a thunderstorm. And the military said they were performing a weather balloon experiment and the weather balloon crashed."

Allison refused to read the article. "Of course the military said that. They wanted to keep it a secret."

"I don't know, Allison. It sounds pretty convincing to me."

As they talked, a man with a full, dark beard, wearing jeans and one of the museum's t-shirts, emerged from the back, stopping at the counter in the gift store. "May I help you, kids?" He almost shouted.

They walked back and Allison set the tub of goo on the counter in front of the man. "We need to have a substance tested to see if it comes from an alien."

"I see." The man smiled. "Did you see an alien?"

"Yes sir," Allison admitted. "I saw him several times."

"Well, we don't do the tests here, but we have a kit you can purchase and do the test yourself at home." The man pulled a box off of a shelf behind him. He slid it onto the counter towards them. Josh and Allison scanned the box, looked at each other and nodded.

"We'll take it," Allison said.

They paid for the kit and left the museum. "Josh, I have that feeling again. I feel like someone is watching us."

Allison looked again up and down Main Street but didn't see anyone that looked suspicious.

"Let's check out the back." Allison started walking before Josh could respond.

The UFO Museum was in the middle of the block and connected to the other downtown buildings. They looped around the buildings and made their way down the back alley.

"The feeling is getting stronger." Allison anxiously scanned the dimly lit alley.

Josh followed her eyes. "I don't see anyone."

Allison continued to walk, trying to follow the sensation. Ahead, a gray metal storm door sat at a slight angle on the ground about twenty feet behind the UFO Museum. She approached it. "The feeling is the strongest here."

Josh tried to open the door. "It's locked."

He knelt on the ground and laid his ear against the door. Allison did the same.

They both jumped when they heard a loud bang. Allison let out a slight scream before she covered her mouth with her hands.

Josh peeked down the alley. "Someone's going through the garbage."

Allison's voice trembled. "We better get out of here before someone sees us."

Josh nodded in agreement.

They quickly left the alley. As they turned the corner, Allison turned back for one last glance at the dented storm door. "I sure would like to know what's behind that door," she muttered.

***

"We can set up the kit in our garage," Josh said as he and Allison walked up the driveway to his house. The cars were both gone but Josh could tell his dad had been in there recently. His dad often spent Saturday afternoons in the garage drinking soda, working on a project, and watching football. He spotted a can of soda on his dad's workbench and there was still a game on the television. Allison opened the kit they had just purchased and dumped the contents on the counter. She picked up the instructions and began reading. Josh picked up a round glass object with a circumference about the size of a baseball and a lip about a half an inch high. He turned it around in his hands.

"What is this?"

Allison looked up. "Huh?"

Josh held up what he thought looked like a lid. "What's this?"

"That's a Petri dish."

Josh giggled. "So we pee in it?"

Allison slapped his arm with the instruction manual. "No, we don't pee in it!"

She snatched the Petri dish from him and set it in front of her. She scooped a little goo from the container and put it into the Petri dish.

"I don't know, Allison. It looks like grape jelly to me."

"I doubt you would want to make a sandwich with this stuff." She added to the Petri dish a teaspoon of a clear liquid from the bottle of Alien Identifier and several other chemicals included in the kit. Once she was satisfied she had added the correct ingredients, according to the instructions, she stirred them together until the substance in the Petri dish turned black.

She picked up the directions and read aloud: "If your substance turns to a bright glowing color, it came from an alien. If you substance turns black, it did not come from an alien."

"Darn it," Allison said, crestfallen.

"See, I told you it was jelly," Josh said.

"It is not jelly!"

"It looks exactly like jelly."

"If you think it's jelly then taste it," Allison said.

"Okay," Josh said.

When he didn't move Allison grabbed the container of goo, opened it, and shoved it at him. "Taste!"

Josh didn't want to taste the strange substance they had found on the ground. But like normal, he had spoken without thinking, so he wasn't about to back down now. He stuck his finger in the goo and scooped some up.

He put it in his mouth and almost immediately spat it out. "Oh, that's awful!"

He grabbed his dad's leftover can of soda and chugged. It was warm and awful, but anything was better than the taste the goo left in his mouth.

Allison giggled. "I told you it wasn't jelly."

"Okay, okay, you were right," Josh conceded.

Their conversation paused and the commercial on the television caught their attention. It was a commercial for Carlsbad Caverns.

Allison said what Josh was thinking. "We were supposed to go there today with Flipper."

She looked like she was going to cry. "I miss Flipper."

Josh felt the heaviness in the air. "Me too."

Allison looked at the test kit. "This seems to be a dead end. What do we do next?"

"You said you felt the presence behind the museum. Maybe we should go look around and see if there are any clues," Josh suggested.

"We can't snoop around now. Someone will see us."

"We'll go later, after dark, when no one will be there."

"Josh, do you think Flipper is all right?" Allison asked.

Josh wanted to be upbeat and positive, but he didn't have it in him at the moment. "I hope so. I don't know what I would do without him."

They sat in silence for several minutes.

"Josh?"

"Yes?"

"What if Flipper was really taken by an alien?"

"Then we'll have to steal a spaceship from the government to get him back," Josh said with a grin on his face.

CHAPTER 6

"How big is a twelve-ton dragon?" Flipper was desperate to avoid the test. Jake, Chezlor, and Alya were supportive, but they weren't able to help him talk his way out of fighting. He didn't care about this war. He just wanted to go home.

It was almost time to leave. Flipper wore a black uniform that he thought was made out of some type of plastic. It formed to his body and was very flexible. He liked it. At least it made him feel like he could fight a dragon.

"Really, really big," Chezlor spread his arms as far apart as he could.

Jake must have seen Flipper's eyes widen. "Don't worry—the bigger they are the harder they'll fall."

Flipper lit up, "We say that too. Did you steal it from Earth?"

"What are you talking about?" Jake asked.

Before Flipper could respond Alya entered the compound carrying a large round tray with star-shaped chips and a bowl in the center. She set it down on the coffee table. "I didn't have time to make you a meal but you should at least have a snack before fi...before you leave."

Flipper wasn't sure if he could eat but he was starving. He picked up one of the chips and examined it.

"Alya makes the chips herself," Jake said just before stuffing several into his mouth.

Flipper pointed at the bowl. "Is that cheese dip?"

"Yes, I made that too."

Flipper decided he better start eating before Jake and Chezlor had it all devoured. He had to admit the star-shaped chips looked neat, but they made it hard to scoop the cheese. He finally managed to get a decent amount of cheese and shoved the chip into his mouth. Immediately fire alarms went off in his head. He tried to hold the chip in his mouth but it was too hot. He cupped his right hand and spit the chip into it. He opened his mouth and waved his left hand in front trying to put out the fire. Why he forgot he wasn't alone he didn't know, but when he again became aware of the presence of Jake, Chezlor, and Alya they were starring at him in disbelief.

He felt embarrassed. "Sorry. That was really hot. Do you have any water?"

"Of course." Alya quickly exited and returned with a tall glass of water, which he gulped down.

"I'm really sensitive to spicy food," Flipper confessed.

"We thought you would be used to it." Alya said genuinely.

That was one of the strangest things these Gudes had said to him. "Why?"

"The spiciness comes from green chilies from earth." Jake explained.

"You mean Fox brought back green chilies grown in New Mexico?" Flipper was astonished.

"You don't think the only thing we bring back is people, do you?" Chezlor joked.

Fox came into the room carrying an armful of weapons and laid them on the table. He picked up the two guns.

"Here are your guns. They are synced and magnetized with the uniform."

Flipper scrunched his forehead. "What does that mean?"

"It means that these guns will only work for the person wearing the uniform you have on. It's rather an ingenious battle mechanism.

If you lose your gun or it gets stolen by your opponent, he won't be able to use it against you."

"Is a twelve-ton dragon really going to try to steal my guns and shoot me?" Flipper asked rather sarcastically.

"Well, I… No. But you get the idea."

Fox cleared his throat and quickly continued, "The magnetism element is really spiffy. It allows you to place the guns anywhere on your uniform you want. Then you have easy access to grab and use them when needed." He demonstrated by placing the gun on Flipper's uniform in several different places and removing it.

Flipper held the guns. He gulped as he thought about pulling the triggers. The only guns he had ever shot were when he played laser tag.

"How many shots does each gun have?" Jake asked.

Flipper was thankful for the question.

"You will have nine shots with each gun. I think it will only take three or four shots to kill FireKing."

"What do they shoot? Bullets? Lasers?" Flipper hoped it was lasers so he could pretend he was playing a game with his friends.

"They shoot tiny balls that stick to their target. After a few seconds the balls detonate," Fox explained.

"If it explodes do I need to be a long way away to shoot?" Flipper asked, confused.

"No. The balls are designed to explode into whatever surrounds it for optimum impact to the target. Now, here is your sword. Like the guns it will magnetize to your uniform so you can stick it anywhere. Plus, it is also synced to your uniform, so if FireKing steals your sword and swings it at you, it will go right through you without causing any harm."

Flipper noticed the hint of sarcasm in Fox's voice. He looked up at Fox and saw a grin on his face. Flipper smiled back and for a moment forgot he was about to go fight a beast that would be trying to eat him for dinner. Fox picked up the last item from the table. "This is your shield. You can use it to block the dragon's tail and, more importantly, his fire. You have to keep it up if he shoots fire at you. A dragon's fire will burn you but it won't kill you."

"Well, finally some good news," Flipper said.

"Not really. The fire will paralyze you and you will feel the pain, but you can't die."

"Oh, yeah, that's not such good news."

"You'll be fine. Just hit him with a few shots from the guns. The fight will be over before FireKing has a chance to even get close to you."

"It's time to go," General Jaxxen announced as he entered the room with Sierra and Nicole. "Is the boy ready?"

"Yes, Sir!" Fox said.

"We won't be able to teleport from here," the General said. "The Lizards have expanded the area to scramble our teleportation devices."

"What happens when the teleporting gets scrambled?" Flipper asked intrigued.

"We go adrift," General Jaxxen stated matter-of-factly.

"What does it mean to go adrift?" Flipper asked.

Nicole answered, "A couple of things can happen when the Snaders intercept us when we teleport. Most of the time we drift off into space where we suffocate or burn up."

Flipper gulped. "What's the other?"

Sierra spoke. "We simply disappear."

Fox added, "We believe that we teleport to another dimension, but no one has ever been able to prove what really happens. We lost a couple of men this morning who teleported from just outside this facility."

Teleporting didn't sound too exciting to Flipper.

"We can use the tunnel," Sierra said. "We should be out of range of the Snaders monitors when we reach the end."

General Jaxxen turned to his youngest son. "Jake, I want you and your friends to lock this place up tight after we leave, and don't go anywhere."

"But Dad, we were expecting to go with you to watch Flipper fight!"

"No," his dad said. "It's too dangerous. I won't risk having you, Chezlor and Alya out there. We may not be able to protect you."

"We'll be fine!"

"You'll be fine because you're going to do as I tell you. Stay here where it's safe."

"We can take care of ourselves."

"I said no and that's final." General Jaxxen turned to the others and said, "Let's go."

CHAPTER 7

After reaching the end of the underground tunnel, they walked a few more minutes before General Jaxxen decided they were out of the Snaders' range and it was safe to teleport.

"Nicole, teleport to the old arena and see if it's clear," General Jaxxen ordered. "Then come back and report."

Nicole knew there would not be anyone at the old arena. FireKing had taken it as his home after it had been abandoned over a year ago and no one had dared to go near there since. FireKing was the biggest and meanest of the dragons. Even the other dragons avoided him. She knew the scouting trip was more to test if they were far enough away from the Snaders to teleport safely. General Jaxxen asking her to go meant she was the most expendable of the group. But, she knew she had no choice but to obey.

"Yes, Sir," Nicole said quietly, then disappeared.

Flipper had never teleported before and was nervous, especially after learning the Snaders were trying to scramble the Gudes teleporting abilities. Well, technically, he *had* teleported from Earth to Vetrix, but he had been asleep so that didn't count. He wondered what it would be like to be in one place one moment and another place the next.

"Let me see your wrist," Sierra said.

He held out his arm and she put a band around his wrist. It looked like a watch with a different sort of face. It had digital numbers and symbols flashing, but none of it made any sense to him.

"This will allow you to teleport, but it's been programmed to only go from here to the old arena and back. We don't want you to accidentally end up in Timbuktu."

"Hey, we say Timbuktu on Earth too!" Flipper said excitedly.

"You know where Timbuktu is?" Sierra asked.

"No. It's a slang term. We say we are going to end up in Timbuktu when we mean we could end up anywhere."

"No, no, no," Sierra said.

Fox chuckled behind them. As Fox had spent some time on Earth, Flipper wondered if Fox knew what he was talking about.

"Timbuktu is our capital," Sierra explained. "We don't want you to end up there, or worse, adrift. Well, General Jaxxen and Nicole don't want you to. Me, I could care less."

"Thanks for being honest," Flipper said.

"You're welcome."

Flipper made a mental note to himself that Sierra didn't understand sarcasm.

Suddenly, Nicole appeared out of thin air.

"That is so cool!" Flipper exclaimed.

Everyone looked at him like he was a little odd, but he was used to that.

"Everything is clear, Sir," Nicole said.

"Flipper," Fox said, "you just have to think about where you want to go in order…"

Before Fox could finish, Flipper had disappeared.

"Let's go," General Jaxxen commanded.

Everyone teleported to the old arena, but Flipper wasn't there.

"Why isn't he here?" Sierra demanded.

"We all made it fine, he should have too," Nicole replied.

"Maybe his band wasn't programmed correctly," Sierra said. "He may have teleported anywhere."

"The band was fine," Nicole said defensively. "He could only have teleported to here."

"What if the Snaders jammed his teleporter?" Fox proposed.

"I don't see how…" General Jaxxen started to say.

Suddenly, Flipper appeared. "This is awesome!" he yelled before disappearing again.

Nicole tried to hold in her laughter because no one else seemed to think it was very funny. "He's going back and forth, just like his band is programmed."

Flipper appeared again, then disappeared. He did this several times as fast as he could before he stopped. "I have got to get me one of these!"

"Are you done now?" General Jaxxen asked impatiently.

"Do you think I can take one of these back with me to Earth?" Flipper asked.

"Don't be so quick to assume you'll be alive to return to Earth." Sierra really knew how to put a damper on things.

They were standing on top of a hill underneath an overhead shelter. Flipper looked down and could see the old arena below. It didn't look like much. The ground in the middle was all dirt and most of the seats around it were rotted and cracked. But it was huge. Flipper thought it was much bigger than the football stadiums he had seen. He guessed it could hold half a million Gudes.

The arena was in a valley surrounded by hills. Many of the hills had shelters similar to the one they now stood under. He could picture as many, or even more, Gudes sitting on the shelters. Fox had told him the arena was once used to conduct dragon fights between Gude soldiers in training and a dragon. He thought about what it might look like when it was new and full and wondered how they would have kept the dragon from attacking the crowd in the stands or on the hills. He looked beyond the hills. There was nothing in sight except the arena and the shelters. It was like the arena was in the middle of a desert. He wondered how all the Gudes would get there. Then he remembered they could teleport. Flipper tried to fit the pieces of the puzzle together in his mind. "I bet they built the arena in an area the dragons lived. They found a spot that allowed as many Gudes as possible to watch the fight, then they teleported to the arena to watch the battle. Maybe if the dragon attacked the crowd they just teleported away to safety. What a crazy scene that must have been…"

"Flipper, are you okay?" Fox asked.

Flipper had walked a few feet away from the others. He held his sword with both hands, flipping it up and down while he paced. He had been so deep in thought he had tuned out the others and forgot he was about to fight a dragon himself.

Fox repeated, "Are you okay?"

At that moment Flipper heard what he needed to disprove the ridiculous statement that there is no such thing as a stupid question.

Flipper was mad, but more than mad, he was in a desperate panic. "You kidnap me while I'm asleep because some dumb computer picked my name and now you won't take me home but tell me I have to fight a dragon even though I haven't had any training and if somehow I'm lucky enough to win my reward will be more fighting. How am I supposed to be okay with that?"

General Jaxxen spoke angrily, "I'll have you know Gudes begin their training for war when they are twelve and any of them would consider it an honor to be chosen for the test you now face."

"I'm not a Gude!" Flipper bellowed. "Besides, you already have two twelve-year-old boys that could be here instead of me but you haven't even let them start their training. My dad would call you a hypocrite!" He had never spoken to an adult with such emotion and disrespect. He didn't care. He was about to die.

General Jaxxen took a step forward and Flipper thought he was about to be hit. He closed his eyes then opened them after a few seconds when nothing happened. Fox was standing between Flipper and General Jaxxen. After several more seconds General Jaxxen stepped back and Fox slowly turned to face Flipper.

"I know in your world you do not fight at your age." Fox spoke with calmness but Flipper could tell he wasn't going to like what Fox said any more than what General Jaxxen had. "I can assure you that the General isn't going to allow you to return home without facing FireKing. I promise that if you can't handle it I will step in."

At least Flipper now thought he had a chance of getting out of there alive.

Flipper nodded, and for the first time in his life wished he was sitting in Mrs. Smith's Social Studies class. He slowly turned and walked down the hill towards the arena. He thought about Josh and Allison and his mom and dad. They would be worried sick about him. They would be even more worried if they knew what he was about to do. He heard what sounded like a train coming from behind. He turned around just in time to catch a glance of a dragon heading right toward him. He didn't even have time to duck before the dragon flew past him, missing his head by inches. The wind from FireKing passing by was so strong it sent him tumbling down the hill. Over and over he rolled until he came to a stop at the edge of the arena battle field. He coughed and moaned. He had swallowed a lot of dirt and every inch of him felt like it was broken. He knew he had to get up fast because FireKing would be back. As he stood, he mentally checked his body. All the parts still worked.

Next time I fall down a hill I have to keep my mouth shut, Flipper said to himself as he spat dirt out. He looked up and saw FireKing flying towards him again. He pulled one of the guns off his uniform and pointed it at the dragon. FireKing landed a hundred feet away and, as he did, Flipper felt the ground shake. They looked at each other, each sizing the other one up; both waiting for the other to make the first move. FireKing's body was almost fifteen feet tall, with a long neck that stretched his head another twenty feet high. His head alone was several times the size of Flipper. His wingspan was fifty feet. He had a rough, scaly body that was a very dark red or blue. Maybe even purple, it was hard for Flipper to tell. His tail was twice as long as his body and had a crooked bend, like it had been broken and never healed. FireKing stared at him, snorting heavily. Smoke poured from the dragon's nostrils. Flipper would have been fascinated by FireKing, if he hadn't been about to try to eat him. He didn't want the fighting to start but figured he would be better off not waiting for FireKing to make the first move. He aimed the gun at FireKing and pulled the trigger. At first he didn't know if he had hit the dragon or not. The two continued to stare at each other for a few seconds before Flipper heard the explosion. FireKing blew fire up into the sky then charged toward Flipper. Flipper walked backwards as he fired several more shots. As FireKing neared, he swung his head back and then forward toward Flipper. Flipper dove out of the way just in time to avoid it. As he rolled away, he heard the explosions from his shots. He was within a few feet of the dragon's body. He jumped up, lifted the gun and pulled the trigger over and over again. He hit the dragon five more times at close range before the first gun ran out of ammunition. He tossed the gun away and ran. The explosions from his shots rang through the air. He counted all five before he stopped to look. The angry dragon turned and glared at him. Flipper quickly looked over FireKing's body and couldn't see any damage. The explosions hadn't harmed him; Flipper knew he was in trouble.

FireKing opened his mouth and Flipper raised his shield. Fire came flooding from the dragon's mouth and engulfed Flipper. He ducked and closed his eyes. For several seconds he was surrounded by the fire, yet protected by the shield. The smell and heat of the fire was overwhelming. When it finally stopped, Flipper was amazed that he felt fine; he was unharmed. The shield had done its job! He peered over the shield just in time to see FireKing lower his head, as if getting a closer look. Flipper was gripped with fear as the scaly head was less than twenty feet away. He grabbed the other gun, quickly raised it and fired. He sprayed all nine shots towards the dragon's eyes. FireKing raised his head and roared in pain. Flipper didn't know if he had hit both the dragon's eyes but he knew he had at least got one of them. He turned and ran as the balls exploded. FireKing cried in pain, flopping his body uncontrollably. When Flipper was far enough away not to be hit by the flailing dragon, he stopped and waited for the dragon to calm down. He pulled off his sword and charged. He swung the sword at the dragon's wing. Blood came squirting out. He was covered with the dragon's blood and couldn't see. He wiped the blood from his eyes but before he could get his vision into focus, FireKing swung his tail around and knocked Flipper through the air. Flipper landed face down on the ground with the wind knocked out of him. He rolled onto his side in time to see FireKing open his mouth and issue another stream of fire. Flipper pulled his shield up just in time to guard his upper body. He was engulfed by the fire but realized immediately that he hadn't got his legs protected. For several moments his legs felt like they were logs in a campfire. He lost all movement of them. Flipper tried to crawl using only his arms, but he moved too slowly to do any good. He started to cry because he knew the fight was over. He was about to be toast—quite literally.

FireKing used his crooked tail to cradle Flipper and pull him close. He leaned his head down to within a few feet of Flipper. Flipper could feel the heat and smell the smoke coming from the dragon's mouth and nostrils. He was in enormous pain and he was scared, but most of all he was mad.

"You can fly, breathe fire, and are bigger than me. This isn't a fair fight. I'm just a kid!" Flipper shouted.

As FireKing removed his tail from around Flipper and lifted his head up and away, Flipper screamed at him, "If I had a super power you would be in so much trouble!"

FireKing stepped towards Flipper and lifted one of his front legs high in the air. Flipper was about to be squashed like a little bug. FireKing slammed his leg down for the crushing blow to Flipper's body. Just as FireKing's leg hit the ground, Flipper vanished. FireKing jerked his head down and lifted his leg back up. There was nothing there.

Flipper reappeared and FireKing slammed his leg down again. Again, Flipper disappeared. Flipper appeared suddenly in front of FireKing, who let out a stream of fire. Flipper disappeared and reappeared behind the dragon. He slashed FireKing's tail with his sword. FireKing roared and swung his tail around to hit Flipper, but he had vanished. Flipper appeared underneath FireKing. He stabbed one of the dragon's legs several times before disappearing again. This time he appeared on his neck, just below his head. He figured if he could slash his throat it might kill the dragon. The thing Flipper hadn't thought about was how afraid he was of heights. When he looked down and saw the ground thirty feet below, he dropped the sword and shield and held on to FireKing's neck as tightly as he could. Flipper screamed for help with his eyes shut—paralyzed by fear.

The sword cuts were taking their toll on FireKing. The enormous dragon stumbled and finally collapsed. Flipper screamed like a three-year-old girl, clinging tightly to FireKing's neck as he fell. Fortunately for Flipper, FireKing fell forward and did not land on him. Flipper slid off of FireKing's neck and onto the ground. He still couldn't move his legs, so there was no chance of running away. For that moment he was just thankful to be on the ground. The dragon was breathing heavily and trying to get up. Flipper looked around. He spotted his sword, but there was no sign of the shield. If he could get to the sword maybe he could finish off FireKing. He started crawling towards the sword, pulling himself with his arms. After twenty feet, he grabbed the sword and turned around to crawl back. When FireKing roared, Flipper knew he was through. FireKing wasn't able to stand, but he lifted himself high enough to turn his head and face Flipper. Their eyes met for a brief moment before FireKing took a deep breath to blow his fiery breath down on Flipper. Flipper didn't have the shield, was in extreme pain and was very frightened. A small part of him welcomed the relief that death would bring. Out of reflex, he ducked and covered his head with his hands, knowing they weren't going to provide any protection from the dragon's breath. As FireKing began to exhale, Fox appeared and grabbed Flipper. They both vanished before the fire reached their bodies.

The dragon stopped blowing fire and looked at the spot from which Flipper had just disappeared. FireKing really hated teleporting.

CHAPTER 8

Jake paced the commons room, still fuming that his dad hadn't let them go watch Flipper battle FireKing. As he paced one way, he saw Alya sitting at the table, drawing. When he paced the other way, he saw Chezlor leaning back in a chair with his feet propped up.

How can he be so relaxed at a time like this? Jake thought to himself. Seeing Chezlor relaxed fuelled Jake's frustration. He wished he felt as in control as Chezlor looked.

"I can't wait to hear how Flipper slayed FireKing," Chezlor had a faraway look like he was picturing the battle in his mind.

"How can you be so sure he'll win?" Alya asked.

"The computer picked him to help defeat the Snaders," he replied matter-of-factly.

"That doesn't mean he will defeat FireKing," Jake argued.

Chezlor looked at Jake. "He has to. He doesn't get to fight the Snaders unless he defeats FireKing. And he can't defeat the Snaders unless he fights them. So he has to defeat FireKing."

"There's no reason we couldn't be there to watch," Jake huffed.

"That would have been awesome!" Chezlor got another faraway look in his eyes. "I would love to see a battle with a dragon."

"Your dad is just trying to protect you, Jake." Alya usually had a way of calming others. Jake refused to let go of his anger.

"There isn't anything dangerous about watching Flipper fight," he said bitterly. "I'm tired of being treated like a kid."

"Well we aren't soldiers," Chezlor said sarcastically.

Jake snapped. "We should be training to be right now!" Again he shot Alya an angry look, but this time it wasn't accidental and he didn't feel bad about it. "We're capable of a lot more than he realizes." He paused, still pacing, now ripping the air with his hands. "I hope Flipper tears that dragon apart and shows him that kids are able to be heroes too."

Chezlor stood up and started towards the kitchen. "Well, I'm going to get something to drink."

Alya put her hand on Jake's arm and he stopped. "You'll get your chance someday. And when you do, your dad is going to be so proud of you." Dang, she made it hard to be mad at her!

He let out a big sigh, his shoulders dropping several inches. "Thanks, Alya. You always know how to make me feel better."

"Jake!" Chezlor called. "Come to the kitchen. You have to see this."

"Oh great," Jake's voice was slow and thick; his head hung low. "He's going to try one of his pranks."

"I remember when you loved Chezlor's pranks." Alya lifted his chin so Jake had to look at her. "You used to try to prank him back."

Jake chuckled. "Yeah, I remember. I could never get him."

"And you used to ask him to try to prank you because you loved the challenge of trying to figure them out."

Jake nodded his head; he remembered.

"What happened?" she asked.

Jake's eyes returned to the floor. "I don't know. Now I just hate them. I can never figure out what he's doing until it's too late. He always gets me."

"You have come close to figuring them out before. What did you used to tell us your strategy was with Chezlor?

Jake quietly mumbled, "Stay focused, study your adversary, and keep learning."

"Jake, you're smart. If you keep trying, you'll figure Chezlor out, then someday you can turn the tables on him."

When Alya gave Jake these pep talks he almost believed her. He wanted to, and tried to, but he just couldn't quite get there.

"There's that word again… Someday," Jake sulked. "It's always going to be someday." He took a couple of steps toward the kitchen. His walk screamed defeat.

Alya raised her voice, betraying her frustration with Jake. "Then why go in there? If you've given up trying, then why go into the kitchen at all?"

Jake shook his head. "Chezlor is my best friend. He's never going to stop pulling pranks. If I avoid this one he will get me later, and get me worse because I avoided him."

Alya tried to reason with him. "You know how this ends. You end up feeling discouraged or angry or both."

"What do you know about anger," Jake fumed. "You never get angry."

"I do too; I get angry about a lot of things."

"You never show it," Jake countered.

"Of course not. Nothing good comes from being mad." Alya argued.

"That's not it. You just have to have everyone like you. Even my dad likes you more than me."

Whoa! Where had that come from? He didn't know he was going to say that until he did. What did it matter? It was true.

Alya put her hand on his arm. "I'm sorry Jake. You're right. Part of me wants to be angry with you, but another part feels bad because you think your dad likes me more. It's easy for me to ignore anger."

Jake calmed. "You don't get angry enough and I get too angry. I guess that's why we're such good friends."

"Jake!" Chezlor's voice rang from the kitchen.

"You don't have to go in there."

Jake ignored Alya. He walked to the kitchen and opened the door, hesitantly. As he did so, a bucket of water came splashing down on him. Jake stood—wet and deflated. Chezlor rolled on the floor laughing.

***

Fox laid Flipper down on a bed in the medical room next to the commons area. Flipper was unconscious and his legs were badly burned. Jake, Chezlor and Alya rushed into the room, each breathing hard as they had run as fast as they could when they discovered Flipper was back.

"What happened?" Jake demanded.

"How bad did he beat FireKing?" Chezlor inquired.

"Is he okay?" Alya wondered.

Fox turned. "He put up a good fight—better than I expected." Fox stepped aside so they could see Flipper. "He's passed out from exhaustion, or pain, or both. His legs are burned and paralyzed, but I expect him to survive. We'll have to wait and see." Jake and Chezlor looked stunned. Tears ran from Alya's eyes.

Nicole came into the room. "I have bandages, ointments and medicine. We'll get him cleaned and doctored up."

Sierra entered with a bowl of warm water and some clean rags. She set it beside Nicole and stepped back. Nicole started cleaning Flipper's wounds.

Alya walked over to Flipper and picked up one of the rags. "Here, let me help."

General Jaxxen stepped into the room and saw the look of shock on the boys' faces. "Actually, Flipper fought bravely for a kid, but he lost because he was afraid. He is not going to be any help to us in our battle. There is no room in war for fear. For now, I want everyone out of here. Let Nicole," he paused, "and Alya nurse him and let Flipper get his rest. We will meet first thing in the morning to discuss our next plan of action. Everyone go get some rest, it's late."

***

Early the next morning Fox, Sierra, and Nicole were together with General Jaxxen in his office.

"How is Flipper this morning?" General Jaxxen inquired.

"He's still sleeping," Nicole replied. "He hasn't had more than a sip of water all night. I am afraid he will be quite dehydrated when he wakes. Alya helped me change his bandages this morning. She is with him now, in case he wakes up. His legs are bad. It's likely he will never walk again."

"I'm sorry for that," General Jaxxen said, "but right now we have much bigger issues to deal with. A couple of our spies escaped before the Lizards had the capital completely under control. They were transported to the hospital in Katar. One of the spies, Jostel, woke briefly and was able to give us some useful information. As of an hour ago, they are both unconscious, but the doctors are optimistic they will survive. Whether they can provide any further details that may help in our fight remains to be seen. Right now, they are our only lead." He paused, letting this sink in. "Jostel told us that the Lizards have developed a force field that can engulf the city. We brought in more troops and have the city completely surrounded, but I am afraid that Jostel's information was correct. To this point, none of our attempts to penetrate their force field have been successful."

"Of course, it's only a matter of time before the Lizards bring in more troops and attempt to expand beyond the capital," Fox added.

"Was Jostel able to tell us how they are generating the force field?" Nicole asked.

"No. Unfortunately, we have no leads on how to get past it. Not only is it blocking our people from entering or exiting the city, but it is also blocking signals of all types. All communication has been cut off from the capital, and anyone who has been brave enough to try to teleport out has ended up adrift.

"What about our underground tunnels leading into the city?" Sierra asked.

"General Rostein and his men tried the tunnels to no avail. The force field is like a bubble. It encircles the capital, including underground. We haven't been able to penetrate it from any direction."

There were a few moments of silence as everyone contemplated the bleak report.

"If things weren't bad enough," General Jaxxen continued, "Jostel said that the Lizards had inside knowledge of our locations and procedures."

"So there is definitely a mole," Fox said thoughtfully.

"Yes, and somehow we need to find the mole or we may be fighting a losing battle."

"Maybe we can use Flipper after all," Sierra said.

"What are you talking about?" General Jaxxen asked.

"What if we used him as bait?" Sierra said thoughtfully. "We could leak a message that we know how to take down the force field and that Flipper is the key. Whoever the mole is will share this with the Lizards and they will try to eliminate Flipper. We can set a trap and capture them. It may also help us discern who the mole is."

"Where do you suggest we set the trap?" General Jaxxen was skeptical.

"We can't risk transporting Flipper right now," Nicole said. The hospital in Katar is too busy treating the injured from our battle with the Lizards to help transport Flipper properly. Besides, he is in too much of a fragile state to be moved."

"We can't set the trap here," Fox said. "It would require us to give up our location."

"I suspect whoever the mole is already knows our location," General Jaxxen said.

"This sounds risky..." Fox started.

"I think we should do it," Nicole cut in.

Fox, Sierra and General Jaxxen all turned towards Nicole with looks of surprise.

"I still believe the computer was right in sending us Flipper," she said adamantly. "But what it didn't tell us was how Flipper was to be used to defeat the Lizards. Maybe he doesn't need to fight. Maybe his presence is enough to give us the opportunity to gain invaluable and potentially devastating information."

"I am not as optimistic as Nicole, especially about the computer," Fox said. "But I don't remember the last time Sierra and Nicole agreed on a plan. That's enough for me. I think we should give it a try."

General Jaxxen thought for a moment. "Okay, but not a word of this to Jake, Chezlor, and Alya. They don't need to know what is going on. I will have them secured. Then I will send for more troops to help fortify our shelter and help set the trap."

CHAPTER 9

The blare of Flipper's scream caused Alya to leap from her chair. She grabbed his hand. "It's okay, Flipper. It's okay."

"Allison?"

"No, it's Alya."

"Allison, my legs hurt so bad!" Flipper cried. "Do something. Please!"

Nicole ran into the room, to the opposite side of the bed. "Flipper, it's Nicole. Alya and I are going to take good care of you."

"Are you going to make my legs feel better?" Flipper asked.

"We're going to try," Nicole assured him.

Jake and Chezlor ran into the room. Nicole turned to them and said, "We need a glass of water. Make it two." They turned and left.

"Flipper," Nicole said, "we are going to give you some medicine that will help with your pain. Alya, help me sit him up."

Alya and Nicole got on either side of Flipper, reached their arms underneath his shoulders and lifted his upper body forward.

Jake and Chezlor returned to the room, each with a glass of water.

"Jake, you and Chezlor hold up Flipper," Nicole instructed. "Alya, give Flipper a drink of water. I will get the medicine ready."

Jake and Chezlor set their glasses down and supported Flipper. Nicole left the room while Alya held a glass to Flipper's lips so he could take a drink. When Nicole returned the first glass was empty. "Great! He desperately needs to drink a lot of water."

"Nicole?"

"Yes, Flipper?"

"My legs still hurt!"

"Okay," Nicole said. "I have some medicine that will ease the pain, or at the very least help you sleep." She gave him a shot in the arm. He drank almost another whole glass of water before he decided he didn't want any more. Jake and Chezlor gently laid him back down.

"Flipper, how are you feeling?" Nicole asked.

Flipper was talking slower. "That stuff works really fast. The pain is going away some, and I'm feeling sleepy."

"Let's let Flipper get some rest now," Nicole said. "We should still keep someone in here with him in case he needs help."

"I'll stay with him," Alya volunteered.

"Hang in there Flipper," Jake said as he gently squeezed Flipper's shoulder.

"You'll be fine soon," Chezlor said. "Then we can get back to defeating the Snaders."

"If you need anything just tell Alya. She will take good care of you," Nicole said.

"Okay, thanks," Flipper managed to mumble.

After they left, Alya moved the chair next to Flipper's bed and sat down. She felt so sorry for him. He was in such pain and there wasn't anything they could do for him except to medicate him so that he could sleep through it. Her eyes teared up. She felt Flipper looking at her. She wanted to be strong for him but was struggling to keep her emotions contained.

"Alya." Flipper waited for her to look at him. "Thank you for taking care of me."

Alya smiled, then started to cry. "It was so unfair—them making you fight FireKing like that."

"My dad always says that life isn't fair."

"But now you're injured and in pain. It's just not right."

Flipper began to reflect. "It's my own fault I'm injured. I had FireKing beat. He was injured. I was on his neck with the sword ready to kill him. I just had to slice him and I would have won and my legs would still be fine."

Alya blew her nose. "What happened?"

Flipper looked away, ashamed. "I got scared. Instead of cutting FireKing's throat, I dropped the sword. Instead of teleporting away to safety, I froze. Instead of killing FireKing, I got my legs burnt and almost died. Instead of winning, I lost."

"You couldn't help that. Everybody's afraid of something," Alya said.

"Maybe…. But if I could have kept fighting even though I was afraid, I would be a hero now—a success instead of a failure."

Alya scolded him. "Flipper, you are not a failure!"

"Yeah, you're right," he conceded. "My dad always tells me that there is nothing to be ashamed of when I fail. It's a sign that I am trying, that I'm not afraid to fail, and that it's an opportunity to learn."

"Your dad sounds pretty smart," Alya said.

"He says he's not that smart, he's just experienced. And that I can either listen to him and learn from his mistakes, or start over and learn them all on my own."

Alya laughed.

Flipper seemed to finally give in to the medicine. He closed his eyes and Alya watched him drift back to sleep.

***

Sierra and Fox were in the medical room with Nicole. She just finished changing the bandages on Flipper's legs. He had eaten a little, which Nicole and Alya were thankful for after their many attempts to get him to eat. He was now asleep again. General Jaxxen walked in. "Jake, Chezlor, and Alya are secured and all of the men are in place. We have made it look like there is very little security, but this is probably the most secure room on the planet. We will get the mole."

"Flipper has fresh bandages and we have all the supplies in here we should need for the next several hours," Nicole informed him.

"Fox will be stationed right outside this door," General Jaxxen said. "When we leave, I want you to lock the door until we have captured the perpetrator."

"Yes, Sir," Sierra and Nicole agreed in unison.

"We have the facility secured so no one will be able to teleport in," General Jaxxen said as he and Fox left the room. Sierra closed and locked the door, and they sat and waited.

***

A couple of hours later, Nicole and Sierra had hardly said a word to each other.

"What if the computer was correct?" Nicole asked, breaking the silence. "What if Flipper is to still play a vital role in defeating the Snaders? More than just this trap, I mean?"

"Nicole, let it go."

"But there's no logical reason the computer could be wrong."

"Just because you can't explain it, doesn't mean it isn't true," Sierra said. "Flipper should be dead, and would be had it not been for Fox. It's obvious he isn't cut out for this and can't defeat an entire hostile species. If it wasn't for the computer, he would still be at home uninjured."

"But the computer..." Nicole started to protest.

"Stop with the computer! It was wrong—accept it."

Flipper twitched and started to moan.

"Flipper, this is Nicole. How do you feel?"

Flipper didn't open his eyes, just continued to moan.

"I think he's talking in his sleep," Nicole said. "I'm going to give him a shot to ease the pain. It seems the last one may be wearing off."

Fox spent most of the time pacing around the commons room, waiting for someone to come and try to take Flipper. He often had assignments that required him to be stationary for long periods of time, but most of these were outdoors. Sitting inside with nothing to do caused him to be anxious. He thought a lot about the computer program that had predicted Flipper would help them defeat the Snaders. Obviously it was wrong, but why? The only one who had access to the results was Nicole. What if the computer had actually selected his cousin, Allison? That certainly made more sense to Fox after observing them both for a day. Nicole could have easily switched the results so they took the wrong person. If that was true, that would make Nicole the mole. As hard as it was for Fox to believe it, she was as likely a candidate as anyone. General Jaxxen trusted her, but she had only been with him for a few years. Sure they had checked her background thoroughly, but a traitor would be good at covering up the red flags that would indicate they were a risk. Fox felt a sudden sense of panic. Nicole was in there with Flipper. But she couldn't do anything—she had no way out. He smelt something and quickly turned around to face the secured medical room. Smoke seeped out from underneath the gray, secure door. He banged on it but didn't get an answer. He powerfully kicked the door open and saw Sierra and Nicole unconscious on the floor. He rushed to the bed, covering his face, trying not to inhale the smoke. The only thing he could do was get Sierra and Nicole out of the room.

Flipper was gone.

CHAPTER 10

A quarter moon shone as Saturday turned into Sunday; all but a few had deserted the main streets of Roswell. Josh stood at Kentucky Avenue and College Boulevard, the southwest corner of the New Mexico Military Institute campus. He straightened his bow tie, not because it needed straightening but because he sometimes reverted to nervous ticks. Allison was late. He had no trouble sneaking out after his parents went to sleep. In fact, his parents had been asleep for two hours before he climbed out of his bedroom window. His parents were always in bed by ten, even on the weekend. Allison's parents stayed up late. He hoped she was waiting for them to go to bed and hadn't been caught trying to get away. That would seriously hinder their plans for the evening, not to mention that his parents would certainly get a call from Allison's parents. That was a conversation he did not want to have with his dad.

"Josh, is that you?"

He breathed a sigh of relief at Allison's voice.

In his best, but still horrible British accent, Josh said, "Don't call me Josh. Tonight, I'm The Doctor." He reached into his pocket and pulled out two items. He held one in each hand. "This is my sonic screwdriver and this is my psychic paper."

Allison laughed. "You are so silly."

Josh absentmindedly straightened his bow tie. "You won't be laughing when these help us out of a tight jam."

They quickly walked to the museum. It was a chilly evening and Allison wore a light jacket over her sweatshirt. Josh had a jacket over his shirt, both complementing the bow tie.

The wind was from the south and carried the pungent smell of the dairy farms. It was dark but the street lights gave them more light than they needed. They were alone on the streets except for an occasional car passing by. At this time on a Saturday night, all five cars passed with a loud thumping from their more than necessary powerful subwoofers. They spent a few minutes looking around the outside of the museum, but quickly made their way to the storm door.

"Are you sensing anything?"

Allison looked around, like the feeling might suddenly appear from behind something. "No, I don't feel the presence like I did this afternoon."

Josh looked at the dented yet solid door. "Are you thinking what I'm thinking?"

"We need to get in and see what's down there."

"Exactly!" Josh pulled on the handle but the door didn't budge. He pulled out his screwdriver. "It's locked, but leave it to me."

"How is that going to help us?"

"I don't pretend to know how it works. I just know that it can do all sorts of amazing and impossible things."

He got on his knees and went to work on the two hinges of the door. He struggled, but got the screws out. He pulled the door up but only got it to rise about a foot. Allison crawled through the opening.

"See, I told you the sonic screwdriver would come in handy," Josh beamed.

Allison pushed the door from underneath but Josh couldn't squeeze through.

"What are we going to do now?" he asked, confounded.

Allison turned on her flashlight and shined it around her. "Josh, give me your sonic screwdriver. I'll use it to open the door."

"Excuse me?"

"I'm sorry. Doctor, give me your sonic screwdriver and I'll use it to open the door for you."

Josh reached his arm under the door and handed her the screwdriver. "How are you going to open the door?"

"I don't know, Doctor. I just know that it can do all sorts of amazing and impossible things."

Josh shook his head and stifled a laugh. He didn't want Allison to know her irreverence for the power of the sonic screwdriver made him laugh.

Allison opened the door and Josh was stunned. "How did you do that?"

Allison laughed, "The door was unlocked silly."

"Good grief," he said as grabbed his screwdriver and returned it to his pocket.

Allison took the lead as they walked down some stairs. She stopped before entering the short hallway.

"I feel the presence again. It's not strong, but I feel it."

"Maybe we should turn back."

"No, we have to see what's down here. This is our only lead to Flipper."

After twenty feet, the hallway turned left and led them into a large room—just large enough to fit the spaceship that was in it.

Josh stood still with his mouth open. Allison ran over and touched it. "Wow! A real spaceship. I knew it!"

Josh continued to gape. He couldn't believe what he was seeing. Although he wasn't ready to admit it was a spaceship, he had never seen anything like it and, with his dad being an officer in the Air

Force, he had seen most of the aircraft the Air Force used. The spaceship wasn't round like he had seen in pictures and movies. It was rectangular, except the nose, which was rounded, much like an airplane. The front was all glass and allowed them to see into the cockpit, which contained five chairs and a digital control panel that was strangely lit up. The outside of the spaceship was dark, but Josh didn't think it was black. Maybe a dark gray, he thought. It wasn't big, probably not longer than his house.

"Josh, look! The door's open. Let's go take a peek inside."

"I-I-I… I'm not sure that's a good idea," Josh stuttered.

"Come on, you big chicken."

He reluctantly followed Allison up the ramp and into the spaceship. The cockpit was to their immediate left. It was bigger than the airplane cockpits Josh had seen—about the size of his parent's master bathroom. There were two chairs in the back, one in the middle and two up front, with several screens surrounding each chair.

Allison sat down in one of the front chairs and said with awe, "Real aliens flew this."

Josh felt uncomfortable. "I'm going to go look around the outside of the spaceship."

"Okay." Allison started playing with the buttons and gadgets on the control panel.

Outside, Josh took his time to look around the room. The walls were solidly built with cinder blocks. It felt a lot like an underground bomb shelter. There was no other way out of the room except the way they had come in.

Josh was still skeptical about aliens. The spaceship definitely didn't look like anything Josh had ever seen before, but that didn't mean it came from another planet. It could have been an experimental plane the military had created. Maybe it didn't test well, which is why he had never seen it. He heard a noise and quickly turned around.

In the middle of the back wall, a door had opened—one that hadn't been open a minute ago. He ran up the stairs of the spaceship, right into Allison.

He was near panic. "Allison, the wall opened! Someone is going to find us!"

"No they aren't. I was the one who opened it."

"What? How? Why?..."

She giggled. "I'm not sure. I was messing around with the switches and one of them opened the door. I was coming down to go see what's behind the wall."

Josh sighed heavily. "What a relief! I thought someone on the other side of the wall opened it and was about to catch us."

As they reached the door, they could feel a coolness seeping out. Allison turned on her flashlight and shone it inside. The tunnel they were peering into was roundish, about ten feet wide. The walls, ceiling and ground were all dirt. They stepped in for a better look. Suddenly, the door behind them shut. They turned back but it was useless. There was no way for them to open the door from inside the tunnel.

Allison pulled her cell phone from her pocket. "No signal."

Josh's phone didn't work either. They looked toward the path ahead of them.

"Where do you suppose it leads?" Josh asked.

Allison shone the light down the tunnel. "I guess we're going to find out."

CHAPTER 11

Sierra and Nicole were stirring as General Jaxxen returned to the commons area.

"What happened?"

Nicole wiped her eyes. "I don't know. The last thing I remember, I was preparing a shot for Flipper. I-I guess I passed out."

Sierra was slower coming around than Nicole. She squinted at the light as her eyes adjusted. "What happened?"

General Jaxxen responded. "It looks like you and Nicole were sabotaged. It appears someone teleported in and gassed the room to knock you out. Then they took Flipper and teleported out. Did you see anyone?"

"No," Sierra said. "I don't remember seeing or hearing anything. Flipper was moaning and I was trying to make out what he was saying. The next thing I know I'm lying here on the couch."

Jake, Chezlor and Alya entered the room. They were followed by one of the General's men who had been standing guard just outside the shelter. The man faced General Jaxxen and stood to attention. "Sir, we received a report that a Snader spaceship just left the capital. It is heading in the direction of Rex. We believe Flipper is aboard that ship, although it couldn't be confirmed."

Jake, Chezlor and Alya looked shocked.

"Thank you. Dismissed," General Jaxxen ordered.

Jake spoke, stunned. "Those Lizards broke in here and took Flipper?"

"Somehow they were able to get past our traps and get around the teleporting blocks we had set up. This should not have been able to happen," General Jaxxen said angrily.

"How are we going to get him back?" Jake asked.

General Jaxxen paused and looked at the others before he responded. "We aren't going after Flipper."

"What?!" Jake yelled. "We have to go get him!"

"Son, we have a serious war going on that is threatening the lives of all the people on this planet. We cannot send resources away from Vetrix chasing after one boy who isn't even one of us."

"But it's your fault he's in trouble. You kidnapped him from Earth and then you let him get kidnapped by the Lizards. You have to do something!"

"If we go after Flipper, we risk the Lizards taking control of Vetrix. If they do that, their next target will be Earth. We can't risk billions of lives for only one," General Jaxxen argued.

"But we owe it to Flipper," Jake's voice continued to rise.

General Jaxxen took a deep breath. "I'm sorry. It was a mistake to go down this path. We have wasted a lot of time chasing after this false hope."

"But Flipper is still alive. We don't know that he isn't still the key to defeat the Lizards," Jake shouted.

"Yes we do, Son. He wasn't who we hoped he was. The computer was wrong and we have to accept it."

"But…" Jake started.

"This discussion is over," General Jaxxen said shortly. "Team, into my office. We need to discuss our next action plan."

Jake stormed out of the room.

CHAPTER 12

Jake entered the commons area without purpose and slower than normal. Chezlor and Alya were sitting on the couch in awkward silence. They stood when they saw him.

"I'm so sorry, Jake," Alya said. "I know this is hard for you."

"My dad never listens to anything I have to say."

"Maybe he would if you rescued Flipper," Chezlor said.

"Yeah, like that could ever happen."

"I've been thinking—why couldn't it?"

"My dad wouldn't even let us go watch Flipper fight FireKing. He would never let us try to rescue him." Jake plopped himself on the couch without making eye contact.

"I didn't say we should ask."

"What are you talking about?"

"Let's go get Flipper."

"How would we do that?" Alya asked.

"There's an aircraft just outside this shelter. We can take it to Rex," Chezlor said excitedly.

Jake raised his eyebrows. "You're serious?"

"I'm always serious." Chezlor's innocent smile gave away his sarcastic intent.

"But we don't know how to fly," Jake said.

"No we don't—but Nicole does."

"How are we going to talk Nicole into stealing an aircraft and flying us to Rex to save Flipper?" Jake was sitting forward eagerly and looking at Chezlor.

"I'm glad you asked. I have an idea." Chezlor sat down beside Jake and explained his plan.

When he finished Jake smiled. "That devious mind you use to play pranks may finally come in useful."

***

Chezlor ran up to Nicole, panting heavily. "Nicole, come quick! Jake is on his way out to the aircraft. He's determined to go save Flipper!"

"We need to go find General Jaxxen," Nicole said.

"No!" Chezlor said as he grabbed her arm. "We don't have time. Hurry!"

Chezlor began pulling Nicole outside and she quickly followed. "Alya is trying to talk him out of it, but I don't think she can change his mind."

Chezlor and Nicole ran to the aircraft, up the stairs and into the cockpit. Nicole found Jake strapped into the pilot's seat. Alya was in a seat behind him. The aircraft was running.

Nicole tried to keep her voice calm. "Jake, what are you doing?"

"Flipper is our responsibility. Someone has to go after him and since no one else is, I'm going."

"Do you know how to fly this thing?" Nicole asked.

Chezlor came into the cockpit area. "The door is shut and secure."

"No, I can't fly this, but you can."

"Oh, no," Nicole said. "Your dad... General Jaxxen gave very clear orders that he wasn't going after Flipper."

"But he never said we couldn't," Alya argued.

"You know what he meant."

"Do you believe the computer?" Chezlor asked Nicole.

Nicole turned to look at Chezlor who was standing behind her. "What?"

Chezlor spoke slowly. "Do you believe your computer program was accurate in selecting Flipper?"

"Yes, of course I do."

"So do I! That's why we have to go after Flipper. We have to help him defeat the Snaders."

Nicole started to say something, then paused. Chezlor took that as a sign she could be persuaded. "Nicole, I believe the computer was right about Flipper. He *is* going to save the universe from the Snaders. I don't know how, but I believe he is. If we go after him, we have a chance of being a part of saving our planet and others like it. If we don't go after him, then I believe he will still defeat the Snaders—we just won't get to be a part of it."

He paused, glanced at Jake and Alya, then back to Nicole. He was fired up and spoke with passion. "If you really believe the computer it's time to prove it. Otherwise, saying you believe means nothing—it's just a bunch of empty words. Do you want to sit back and watch history unfold, or do you want to be a part of making it happen?"

"Chezlor… Jake… Alya…" Nicole said, looking each of them in the eye. "You have a lot of nerve trying to pull a stunt like this."

Chezlor's heart sank. He had thought he could persuade her but that tone of voice was the same his mom had used when she was still around. It meant that she wasn't going to argue with him any longer. But then Nicole did something his mom had never done.

"Jake, move over to the co-pilot's seat. Chezlor and Nicole—get buckled in."

"Yes, ma'am," all three said with excitement.

Nicole climbed into the pilot's seat and strapped herself in. "Even if Flipper does defeat the Snaders, there's no guarantee we will survive just because we help him."

"Like Dad says, 'some fights are worth sacrificing for'," Jake quoted. "We're ready to die fighting for what is right."

Nicole looked at them. "You realize what you're asking me to sacrifice, even if we're successful?"

Chezlor didn't know what to say to that. He remained quiet as did Jake and Alya.

Nicole looked straight ahead, reflecting, almost to herself. "You realize if we disobey General Jaxxen things will never be the same for any of us."

"I'm okay with that," Jake piped in.

"Me too," Nicole mumbled to herself. "I'm the expendable one."

"What?" Chezlor asked.

She shook her head. "It doesn't matter."

Nicole took a deep breath and just before she took off, she turned to the children and said, "I won't be surprised if you three change history someday. That is, if you survive today."

CHAPTER 13

"Hello! Is anybody there? Explain yourself at once!"

Nicole reached down and turned off the radio. "I can't concentrate on flying with the General's voice yelling at me."

"We'll get enough of that when we return," Jake remarked.

"Yes, we will," Nicole agreed. "If I'm lucky I'll just get kicked out of the military. But, realistically, they will lock me up and I'll never see daylight again."

"Don't worry," Chezlor said. "When we help Flipper defeat the Snaders they won't have any choice but to reward you. There's no way they could lock up a hero."

"You really believe we are going to succeed?" Nicole asked.

"I have no doubt," Chezlor said with absolute confidence.

"If you are so sure we are going to pull this off, what's your plan?"

"When the Snaders' ship reaches Rex it will probably land in their main military base," Jake butted in.

"We can't fly directly towards there because the Snaders are likely to shoot us down," Alya interrupted.

"In order to land safely, we will need to land a few miles from their base," Chezlor said.

"How do you plan to get Flipper from there?" Nicole asked.

Chezlor cleared his throat and almost mumbled, "Well, the Snaders will see us coming and will send troops out to capture us when we land.

They will take us and our spaceship back to their base. From there we will have to figure out a way to escape, find Flipper, rescue him, steal our spaceship back, and fly out of there without getting shot."

Nicole looked back at Chezlor. "You know, I would feel better if your plan had a few more details and a little less interaction with the Snaders."

Jake nodded. "So would we."

CHAPTER 14

Flipper lay on a bed in what looked like a hospital room. His legs were still in extreme pain. He knew he was on a spaceship but he didn't know where he was heading or why he had been taken… again. The previous day was a thick fog in his mind. He had a strap around his waist and one around his shoulders that secured him to the bed. His arms were snug against his body and he couldn't move them. He furiously jerked his body and tried to pull his arms free, but it was no use—he was stuck.

A tall, red being whom Flipper assumed was a Snader came into the room wearing a lab coat and a mask over his mouth. One of the being's ears was pointed, there were several large bumps on its forehead, and those eyes—they were dark and ominous. Flipper decided the being was a man, partly due to the tall, stout build and in part because he didn't want to think that a female was that ugly. Then again, this was the first Snader Flipper had met. Perhaps he was one of the better looking ones.

The man glanced at Flipper but didn't say a word. He went to one of the two trays in the room containing equipment. The man had his back to him so Flipper could not see what he was doing.

"Are you a doctor?" Flipper asked. "My legs are killing me and I could really use something to make them feel better."

The man didn't respond.

"While you're at it, I've had this mole on my neck since birth. I was thinking maybe you could just go ahead and take it off? You know, if it isn't too much extra trouble."

The man continued to work without speaking.

"You know, I can't move my legs, so there's no reason to strap me down to keep me from escaping."

There was still no response. Flipper fell silent, then asked, "What's your name?"

The man spoke without turning. "My name is Dr. Needles. The straps aren't there to keep you from escaping."

"Then what are they for?"

Flipper heard a buzzing noise. Dr. Needles turned around, holding in one hand a long device with a circular end. "The straps are to keep you from moving."

Dr. Needles held up a rock about the size of a cantaloupe with his other hand. He took the rock and cut it clean in half. Although a mask covered his mouth, his cheeks and eyes told Flipper the frightening doctor was smiling.

"I don't think you're a real doctor," Flipper challenged. "Can I see your medical license?"

Dr. Needles set the half of a rock down and came toward him with the saw.

"No! You can't do this! You know what? Forget about the mole. I'm kind of attached to it anyway. Stop!" Flipper shouted.

Dr. Needles stood above him while Flipper was frantically but hopelessly squirming his upper body. Dr. Needles raised the saw towards Flipper's head. Flipper screamed frantically. "NO!!! HELP! NO!!!!!"

Dr. Needles grabbed Flipper's hair. Flipper rolled his eyes up trying to see the doctor's hand. Flipper closed his eyes and screamed, "AAAWWWWW!!"

Dr. Needles took a handful of Flipper's hair, cut it off and turned the saw off. It took Flipper a minute to realize the saw was off and his head was still attached. He stopped screaming but panted heavily and was still quite frightened. He watched Dr. Needles closely, anticipating the buzzing sound starting again. Dr. Needles took the hair and put it into a plastic container. He wrote on the container and set it on the tray. Then he picked up a needle and returned to Flipper.

Flipper reached panic stage again. "I didn't mean it when I said you were ugly."

"You never said I was ugly."

"Oh, well, I mean, if I ever thought that, which of course I didn't, but just IF I did, well, I wouldn't have meant it."

"You talk a lot," Dr. Needles said.

"I'm a little nervous. And I talk a lot when I'm nervous."

"There's no reason to be nervous. Have I hurt you yet?"

"Not yet, but what's the needle for?"

Dr. Needles chuckled. "This is going to turn you into a Snader. You will have bright red skin just like me."

Flipper started to scream again as Dr. Needles stuck the needle into his arm. He hooked the needle up to a tube and Flipper could see his blood flowing out of his arm, through the tube and into a bag.

Flipper started to cry. "What are you doing?"

"I have to remove all of your blood. Then I will replace it with Snader blood that has special chemicals in it to complete the transformation."

When the bag was nearly full, Dr. Needles clipped the tube and the blood stopped flowing. "Don't move your arm yet." He unhooked both straps from Flipper, freeing his arms. He placed a cloth with firm pressure on Flipper's arm where the needle entered and pulled the needle out. "Hold this cloth on your arm with your other hand. Keep good pressure on it and raise your arm in the air." Flipper did as he was told.

Another Snader entered the room. If Flipper had thought that all Snaders were ugly, this one proved him wrong. She was very pretty and had a friendly smile. The lady looked at Flipper and certainly noticed his red-rimmed eyes from crying. "Dr. Needles, have you been torturing another patient?"

The man laughed. "You should have seen his face when I cut off his hair! It was priceless."

Dr. Needles' laugh was deep, much like his voice. It caught Flipper off guard. He had expected a sinister laugh, but it sounded almost jolly. Flipper was mad. He tried to sit up in bed like he was going to get up and kick the doctor's rear. Reality hit him hard when he couldn't move his legs. He began to feel lightheaded and fell prone. The lady rushed over to him and took his arm. "Now, now. You just had some blood removed so you need to take it easy for a while. Lots of rest and liquids. I'll go get you something to drink as soon as I bandage your arm."

For the first time since Dr. Needles had entered the room, Flipper started to relax. "My name is Brianna," the lady said, as she wrapped a bandage around his arm.

"My name's Blake, but everyone calls me Flipper."

"You have become quite popular lately," she said.

"I'm going to drop Flipper's samples at the lab. I'll bring him back something to drink," Dr. Needles said on his way out of the room.

Flipper looked up at Brianna. "Why did you guys take me? What am I doing here?"

"I don't know exactly. I'm sure our captain will be in shortly to talk to you."

Brianna was so nice that Flipper forgot she was the enemy. Or was she? Maybe he just thought the Snaders were bad because the Gudes told him they were. What if it was the other way around?

"Why did Dr. Needles take my hair and blood?" Flipper asked.

"We're going to run some tests to see what we can learn about you."

Dr. Needles re-entered the room and handed a glass of water to Flipper.

With great difficulty and help from Brianna, Flipper sat up and took the glass. He gulped it down. "Thanks."

"Now, I need to do one more test," Dr. Needles said.

"Is your name really Dr. Needles?"

He chuckled. "Yes. Yes it is."

Brianna had been at the equipment tray and now had two needles in her hand. "Here you go, Doctor."

"Flipper, I'm going to give you a shot in each leg. It will increase the pain for just a minute, but then the pain will go away," Dr. Needles explained.

"Okay, I guess. It's not like I can stop you."

Dr. Needles and Brianna both smiled, thinking Flipper was being funny, although he was completely serious.

Dr. Needles gave him a shot in his left leg, then walked around the bed and gave him a shot in his right leg. Both shots stung but Flipper was determined not to scream any more. He held his breath until the pain went away and with it all the feeling in his legs.

"I can't feel my legs," Flipper started to get worked up again.

"It's okay, it's only temporary," Brianna said.

"Now, I'm going to scrape off some of the skin from your leg. You won't feel a thing," Dr. Needles said.

"What for?" Flipper asked.

"We're going to run tests on your skin like we are with your hair and blood. We hope to learn more about you and your species," Dr. Needles said.

"What do you mean more? How do you know anything about us?" Flipper asked.

"We have had people on your planet for a very long time," Dr. Needles replied.

Flipper felt drowsy, so he lay back down. "How? Where? Who do you have on Earth?"

"Those are enough questions for now," Brianna said as she stroked his hair, much like his mother often did. "You need your rest. When you wake up we will be on Rex."

Flipper closed his eyes and drifted off to sleep.

CHAPTER 15

Josh sniffed and wondered what he would be willing to trade for a tissue to blow his nose. He would give his bike or even the television in his room. He sniffed again and decided he would agree to go to school on Saturdays if someone would give him a tissue. His nose had run the majority of the time (and it had to be several hours by now) that he and Allison had walked along the drastically sloping downhill tunnel. His jacket wasn't enough to keep him warm and his hands were numb. He saw Allison shiver and blow on her hands and knew she was just as cold as he was. For the past hour or so, the tunnel had been getting smaller, making Josh and Allison nervous. Finally, they came to a dead end.

Josh was beat. "Great. Now what do we do?"

"I don't think this flashlight is going to last much longer. Can your sonic screwdriver shine light for us?"

"It does everything but that."

Allison rolled her eyes. "I don't think we can make it back before the flashlight dies."

"It wouldn't do any good anyway," Josh moaned. "It's a dead end that direction too."

"Wait, I see something." Allison squatted and shone her flashlight into a small opening near the ground. "I think there's enough room for us to crawl through if we go one at a time."

"I'm not really excited about small confined spaces."

"We have to keep going,." Allison insisted.

Josh stared at the narrow opening. He didn't like either of his options.

"Fine, I'll go first." Allison lay down on the ground and started to squirm head-first through the opening.

Josh watched as her feet gradually disappeared into the hole. "What do you see?"

"Nothing except dirt. Whooooaa! Joooooooosh!" Allison's scream quickly faded away.

Josh stuck his head in the hole but Allison was gone. "Allison? Are you okay?" There was no response so he yelled louder, "Allison? Where are you?" He crawled into the hole and said out loud, "That's not fair, you took the flashlight!"

He couldn't see a thing. He crawled a few feet and felt the path in front of him drop dramatically downward. He yelled once more for Allison but again there was no answer. He counted to three and pushed himself down, sliding down the slope at a horrifying speed. Even the slides at the water park don't go this fast, he thought to himself. He tried to drag his feet behind him to slow down but was unsuccessful. He slid for a couple of minutes before he was spat out onto a flat surface. He coughed as he gasped for breath. His face was covered with mud.

"Josh, are you okay?"

He spat what he could out of his mouth. "Yeah, I'm fine."

He stood up and did his best to wipe the mud off his face. He opened his eyes and was stunned. They didn't need a flashlight any longer. The room was lit up from the glow of another aircraft. It was at least four times the size of the one they had seen a few hours ago. Josh figured it was about twice the size of the airplane he had flown in last summer when his family went to New York. This aircraft looked older and sturdier than the other one, although a similar shape, like a rectangle with rounded edges.

"It's gorgeous," Allison sighed.

"Look at the legs," Josh pointed out as he walked underneath the aircraft.

"What about them?"

"They don't have wheels on them. That means it would have to land straight down." Josh demonstrated the aircraft landing on the ground with his hands. "It must be able to hover—defy gravity."

Allison pointed towards the other side of the aircraft. "Look! I bet we can get in over there."

She ran and Josh reluctantly followed. "Didn't I already mention today that I don't have any desire to go inside an aircraft?"

"Aircraft?" Allison sounded shocked. "It's a spaceship."

"I still haven't bought into the whole alien thing," Josh pointed out.

Allison huffed then returned to her excitement. "We have to check it out!"

"What if someone's in there?"

"We'll be super quiet."

Josh took a deep breath. "Has anyone ever told you that you are stubborn?"

"Almost every day," she beamed with pride and almost sprinted up the stairs. Once inside, she turned right and froze. Josh caught up with her and they slowly walked down the corridor, Allison sliding her hand along the bright red, snake-like figure that ran from one end of the hallway to the other. Set against the clear black backdrop on the wall the eerie creature looked both beautiful and vile.

At first, the wall looked long and solid but as Josh examined more closely he could see occasional creases, like there were doors. The other side of the hall also had a black backdrop with tiny dots that at first Josh thought were stars. As they looked closer, it was clear they weren't stars but tiny red spiders—hundreds of them. It was the glow from the tiny spiders and the long thick snake that gave light to the passageway. At the end of the hallway, appearing a bit out of place, was a closed, dimly lit white door. Allison put her ear to the door. "I don't hear anything," she whispered.

There wasn't a doorknob. Josh tried to slide then push the door open without success. Beside the door was a dark pad that blended in with the wall. Allison placed her hand on the pad and to both of their surprise the door opened. Josh cautiously looked for signs of life as he slowly entered the room. "It's all clear."

The control room was as big as their classroom at school. There were several padded red chairs around the room. The top half of the far wall, which was the front of the spaceship, looked like a blank movie screen. The bottom half contained hundreds of dimly lit digital buttons and gadgets. The left wall was filled with screens. To their right were three cots, end to end. On the back wall to the right was a table with two chairs underneath it. On the back wall, to the left, was a mirror that took up the whole wall. In fact, it looked like the mirror was the wall. There were no lights on the ceiling. The ceiling was the light. It was lit up, but dim. They agreed that the strangest part was the wonderful smell. It made them think of summer, although neither of them could place exactly what it was. The cockpit was clean. No signs of dust or cobwebs or other things you would expect to see in an old, abandoned spaceship. The best part was the warmth. They were cold, dirty and tired. Josh lay down on one of the cots and closed his eyes. He was so exhausted that he immediately began to drift off to sleep. Allison sat in a chair and closed her eyes. She imagined what it would be like to be soaring through the sky, passing by planets and exploring new galaxies. She imagined Flipper out there, somewhere, in one of those galaxies. Her thoughts quickly faded to dreams.

Chapter 16

It was a bright sunshiny day in Roswell. Allison was on a swing in the playground at her school. She watched Flipper kick a soccer ball around the open play area. There was no one else around. She screamed with delight and ran towards him, shouting ,"Flipper, you're okay!"

"Of course I'm okay."

She gave him a huge hug. Flipper stood still, not sure what to make of the sudden show of affection. "What are you doing?"

Allison wasn't ready to let go of him. "I can't believe you're here. How did you get away from the purple aliens?"

Flipper broke her hug and stepped back. "What purple aliens? What are you talking about?"

"You were kidnapped by a purple alien on Halloween."

"Allison, it's spring."

"It's not spring, it's November."

"It's spring. I leave for the World Cup tomorrow. I need to get my practice in."

"You're going to the watch the World Cup in person?" Allison asked, surprised.

"No, silly. I'm playing in it." Flipper tossed the ball up in the air, kicked it, and then chased after it.

Allison sat down. She was confused and needed to think. It felt like spring; there was a warm sun beating down and a strong, gusting wind.

She was trying to remember how she got to the school. "What was I doing before this?" she asked herself. The last thing she remembered was Josh and her being lost underground. They had found a spaceship and gone inside. She had been looking around the cockpit, had sat down in the Captain's chair and fallen asleep. Did that mean she was dreaming right now? Yes, she must be!

She jumped up and ran over to Flipper. "What is the last thing you remember doing before coming to the school?"

He bounced the soccer ball in the air using his legs, knees and head as he spoke. "I remember speaking to the crowd a couple of weeks ago when they put up the statue of me for being the first kid to make a World Cup team."

Allison was amazed. Flipper had always been a pretty good soccer player, but now he was keeping the ball in the air and making it look easy. "What? What statue?" she asked.

"The one in front of the school. Don't you remember? I'm sure you were there."

She ran to the front of the school and gasped. There was a statue of Flipper with a soccer ball all right. It was made of gold and must have been twenty feet tall. Just as she was about to run back around the school, the name on the front of the building caught her eye. Flipper Middle School. What was going on? When she returned to the back of the school, she froze. There were hundreds of people circled around the field watching Flipper practice. He had two balls bouncing in the air and neither one was hitting the ground. She chuckled. "This couldn't get any more ridiculous."

She made her way through the crowd, which started booing when she knocked the balls away from Flipper.

"What are you doing?" Flipper demanded.

"Don't you think this is all a bit strange?" Allison challenged.

"What?"

"The fact that you are on the World Cup team. That our school has put up a statue and renamed itself after you. That five minutes ago you were practicing alone but now hundreds of people have shown up out of nowhere to watch you. That the last thing you remember is from two weeks ago."

"Are you jealous?"

"No! I just don't think this is reality."

"If this isn't real, then what is?" Flipper asked.

"You were kidnapped by a purple alien who I saw in my dream. Josh and I are currently trying to find you but are trapped miles underground in a spaceship." After saying it out loud, Allison had to admit his reality wasn't any more bizarre than hers.

"Flipper, it's time to get in the limousine and go to dinner," said a lady with dark hair and a very thick English accent.

"Okay, Martha. Thanks for the reminder."

Allison's eyes nearly popped out of her head. "What is Martha Jones from Doctor Who doing here?"

"Don't you remember?

Allison folder her arms and shifted her weight. "Humor me."

"Well, it turns out they are really big soccer fans in England. When I was doing the interviews with Sports Center, after making the World Cup team, I talked about how much I liked the show Doctor Who. The producers of the show saw the interview and spread the word with the current and former cast members. Martha called me and volunteered to be my agent."

"You do know that Martha isn't her real name?" Allison said condescendingly.

"I know, but I asked them if I could call them all by their names from the show. It's fun and they enjoy it, although it gets confusing when more than one of the Doctors is around."

"And now you're going out to eat with Martha?"

"And Rose Tyler, Amy Pond and Doctors ten and eleven. And a few of the other cast members. You should join us."

Allison loved *Doctor Who*! She wanted to meet all of the characters. But she knew, or was pretty sure, this was all a dream. "Flipper, listen real close. I think we're dreaming. This feels like my dream with the purple alien, which turned out to be real. I think that when you wake up you'll remember that you were kidnapped by a purple alien. If that happens, please remember that Josh and I are looking for you and will find you."

Flipper turned to Martha. "Martha, you do remember that my cousin gets into *Doctor Who* a little bit too much, don't you?"

Martha chuckled. "Yes. How can I forget Christmas Eve when she made us all watch every *Doctor Who* Christmas Eve episode?"

Allison had no idea what Martha was talking about, but it sounded like her idea of a wonderful time. Allison heard the electronic theme music from the show. Martha reached into her pocket and pulled out a cell phone. "Hello? Yes… No… Okay…Okay… Cheers. Bye."

Martha turned to Flipper. "That was your Mum. She said to remember to be home by nine. You have a big day tomorrow—pack and prepare for your World Cup trip."

"Aunt Dee has to call Martha to talk to you?" Allison asked in disgust.

Flipper and Martha laughed. "No. She just calls me because we are really good friends. Besides, Flipper usually doesn't carry his phone with him."

Her Aunt Dee and Martha Jones from Doctor Who were friends? Allison was starting to wonder what her life was like here in Flipper's dream world.

Suddenly, Flipper disappeared, followed by everything else around her. Allison stood in complete darkness. Slowly, the darkness faded away and everything went black.

CHAPTER 17

Allison slowly opened her eyes and tried to make out her surroundings. She wasn't in her bedroom or her living room. She had no idea where she was and couldn't decide where she was supposed to be. Home? Roswell? Traveling to the World Cup with Flipper and his soccer team? She looked around and saw Josh asleep on a cot and her memory began to return. She was on an alien spaceship, underground. Her dream with Flipper had seemed so real. It was like she had transported to another time and place. Her situation fully dawned on her when she heard a loud noise from not far away. She froze, afraid to breathe. The noise was extremely loud. She glanced at Josh and couldn't believe he continued to sleep through it.

She quietly stood up and crept over to him. "Josh, Josh. Wake up," she whispered fiercely, shaking his shoulder.

Josh slowly opened his eyes and Allison put her finger over her lips so he wouldn't make any noise. She pointed toward the back of the spaceship. He nodded his understanding. The temporary silence vanished when they heard footsteps coming their way. Josh pointed and they quickly scrambled under the cots, each pulling a blanket far enough down to hide them underneath. The footsteps came right to the door of the cockpit. They buried their heads and heard a door open. They waited in silent dread, hoping the hanging blankets wouldn't be noticed. There was movement from the room next door.

Then they heard a door close and the footsteps walk away. A loud bang preceded an even louder sharp, steady grinding. They crawled out from underneath the cots and went to the door. Allison opened the door silently and peeked out.

"What's going on?" Josh whispered.

She shut the door noiselessly. "There's a man out there. He's closing the door to the spaceship. We are about to be trapped inside."

Josh shook his head adamantly. "I don't want to be trapped in here."

"I doubt there is another way out."

"Maybe we can sneak out," a hint of panic crept into his voice.

"Listen to that door!? There's no way we're getting out of here without that red alien knowing it and if..."

"A red alien?!"

Allison slammed her hand over Josh's mouth and gave him a fierce look. When he nodded that he understood, she slowly removed her hand.

"So now we have red and purple aliens?" Josh whispered vehemently.

"Yeah, I guess so."

"What are we going to do?"

"I don't know. If we can't find another way out I guess we have to hide until he leaves."

The grinding noise finally stopped and Josh and Allison again hid underneath the cots. They listened as the footsteps grew near and once again stopped just outside of the door to the flight deck. Another door opened and they breathed a sigh of relief when it turned out not to be the door to the flight deck. They heard movement from the room next to them, so they laid beneath the cots as quietly as they could.

***

At least an hour passed before the faint noises from the adjourning room stopped. Josh still lay under the cot. With the wall on one side and the blanket hanging over the edges of the cot, he felt like he was enduring mind torture in a coffin. One moment claustrophobia told him to get out of there, while the next moment his fear of whoever was in the next room told him to stay put. Sure, Allison said it was a red alien, but he hadn't seen it for himself. He refused to believe he was in a spaceship with an alien creature from outer space. His mind was in a constant battle with itself. He couldn't take it any longer. He quickly rolled out from under the cot, ecstatic at his newfound freedom.

Allison joined him as they stood and stretched.

"Josh, do you know what amazes me the most about this?"

"What?"

"How did this spaceship get here?"

Josh scrunched his forehead and tilted his head. "Are you kidding me?"

His looks never phased Allison. "What I mean is, this large spaceship is probably miles underground. It's in one piece, undamaged, and there's no hole in the ground above that it could have come down in. How did it get in here?"

"You saw Flipper get kidnapped by a purple alien and now we're standing in our second spaceship today, miles underground, trapped by a red alien in a spaceship that has come from who knows what planet and from who knows how far away and who knows how long ago, and the most amazing thing to you is that the spaceship is in good condition?"

"Well, when you put it that way it does make me sound a little crazy." Allison smiled meekly.

Josh bent over and touched his toes. "I'm starting to think you might be."

"I have always believed aliens existed, so most of what has happened the last few days doesn't surprise me. But how did they get a spaceship this far underground without damaging it?"

Josh shook his head. Allison never stopped amazing him.

They sat for a few moments in silence when Allison suddenly became excited and said a little too loudly, "Josh, that's it!"

"Shh!" he reprimanded.

She put her hand over her own mouth.

"What's it?" he responded.

"This spaceship. If the red alien got it down here, he should be able to get it out. Maybe that's how we can go save Flipper."

"Your plan is to talk a red alien into flying us around to look for a purple alien, using a spaceship that is currently miles underground?"

"There you go again, Josh, saying it so it makes me sound all crazy."

Josh put his head in his hands and looked at the ground. Everything happening sounded unbelievable to him. He wasn't sure he could tell the difference between normal and crazy anymore. "How do you plan to talk a red alien into helping us?"

"I don't know yet. But this guy is all alone, maybe he's bored down here and needs some adventure in his life," Allison surmised.

Josh lay down on the cot. "Maybe… But I don't think he would be too excited if we woke him up. Besides, he may not be happy we're here at all. There's no telling what he might do. Let's at least sleep on it before asking "

Allison lay down on the other cot. "I agree. How long did we nap?"

"Not very long—maybe an hour," Josh guessed. "Besides, we were up all night."

They lay quietly for a few minutes before Josh said, "Allison, you know what?"

"What?"

"I'm starting to believe you about the aliens."

CHAPTER 18

When Flipper woke up he was still in bed, but in a completely different room. This room looked like a room used for surgery. There were several machines in the room and a bright light shining down on his legs, which were freshly bandaged. He lay thinking about the strange dream he had had. Being the first kid on the United States World Cup Soccer team, his school being named after him, and being good friends with the Doctor Who cast. It had all seemed so real. Then Allison had shown up while he was practicing. That wasn't strange, she had been in other parts of his dream before that. She had spent the Christmas holidays with him and their families and part of the cast from Doctor Who. She had been at the unveiling of his statue and the name changing of the school. But, when she showed up at his practice she had seemed different.

What was it about her that seemed different? Flipper wondered. He couldn't put his finger on it, but it was like she didn't remember the other events in his dream.

"That was weird, it was my dream." Flipper said this out loud. "And it was like she knew about the Gudes. She said she and Josh were looking for me."

Flipper remembered a Doctor Who episode where they went back and forth between two dreams and had to decide which was the dream and which was reality. He hoped reality was him being on the U.S. World Cup Soccer team and he was dreaming he had been kidnapped by aliens. But he suspected that wasn't the case.

He gave a big sigh. "Dreams are really bizarre sometimes!" He then remembered how he had juggled two soccer balls in the air at the same time with his legs and head. How cool would it be to do that?! Wait… His legs. He could feel them… and they didn't hurt!

Brianna entered the room. "Oh, good, you're awake! How are you feeling?"

"Okay, I guess. I can feel my legs a little but they don't hurt," Flipper said as he slowly sat up.

"We operated on them," Brianna said.

"What? You can't do that—my parents didn't sign a form!"

"Relax," Brianna said with a smile. "We fixed them."

"You fixed my legs? How? I was told I would probably never walk again."

"Our technology is superior to yours on Earth and also much of the Gudes' technology. We took your skin off, repaired the damage to your nerves and muscles, and then covered your legs with a thin layer of skin developed in our lab. It's fused in with your original skin at your waist. Your body will automatically begin growing new skin. By this time tomorrow, your legs will be as good as new."

"Why would you do that? Don't you know that I was selected to defeat you?"

"Yes, we've heard that silly rumor." Behind him, an older gentleman had appeared in the doorway. He was wearing a thick, dark shirt—similar to a turtleneck—that covered most of his long neck, baggy pants the same color tucked into what looked like boots without any sort of laces or straps.

"Who are you?" Flipper asked, catching sight of him.

102

"Oh, excuse me! My name is Captain Kreeker." He walked around the bed so that Flipper could look at him without straining his head backwards.

"If you don't believe I was chosen to defeat you, then why did you take me?"

"We took you because some of the Gudes do believe it. We wanted to see how much they believe in you and why," the Captain said.

"How are you going to do that?"

Captain Kreeker smiled. "If they truly believe you are meant to help them fight, then they will try to rescue you. If they try to rescue you, well, let's just say we are ready for them."

Flipper hung his head. "There's no way General Jaxxen is going to send anyone to rescue me."

"I don't know about that. We are keeping our eyes on an aircraft that left Vetrix shortly after the flight your were on did. It's heading this way. We think it could be a rescue squad."

Flipper didn't believe anyone was coming for him. "Why are you fighting with the Gudes anyway?"

"It's a long story. I'll be glad to talk to you about it when you are recovered. But for now, I'll get out of here so Brianna can finish checking on your progress."

Captain Kreeker left and Brianna walked over to Flipper. "I need to change your bandages, then you can get some more rest."

"Thank you," Flipper said. "By the way, please tell Dr. Needles that I said thank you."

Brianna smiled. "I will."

Chapter 19

Flipper got out of bed and jumped up and down. He couldn't believe that yesterday his legs had been in pain and were useless and today they looked and felt like normal. He jumped up and down again in disbelief. After a moment, he realized there was something on his neck. It was a bandage. He pulled it off, feeling smooth skin. His mole was gone. He hadn't realized that Dr. Needles had even heard his flippant request. He would have to remember to thank him. Flipper picked up a reflex hammer and began flipping it in his hands. He paced around the room and thought about all that had happened to him over the last few days. He didn't know what to think. What he believed today was a lot different from what he had believed a few days ago. For starters, he had not believed in aliens! But that had certainly changed.

He despised the Gudes for kidnapping him. The Gudes had said the Snaders were evil and trying to take over the universe. Assuming they were telling the truth about the Snaders, how could the Gudes believe he could help save the universe? Besides, the Snaders had repaired his legs. The Gudes were going to lock him up to keep him out of the way. They had made him risk his life to fight a dragon! The more he thought about it, the more he didn't care about their squabble. He just wanted to go home.

Dr. Needles came into the room and interrupted his thoughts. "It looks like those new legs are working."

"They are amazing! I can't believe it—I really thought I might never walk again. Thank you, Dr. Needles!"

Dr. Needles smiled. "You are welcome!"

"And I noticed you even removed the mole on the back of my neck. Thank you!"

"I thought you would appreciate that." Dr. Needles smiled and set his electronic chart on the counter. "What are you doing with the reflex hammer?"

Flipper looked down at his hands, realizing he was still flipping the hammer. He stopped. "I was flipping it. It helps me think."

Dr. Needles raised his bushy eyebrows. "Really?"

"Yeah, I've been doing it for as long as I can remember. That's where I got my nickname—Flipper. My dad started calling me that when I was really young and it kind of stuck. My favorite thing to flip is a plastic railing from my train set. But I will flip anything that is available—books, pencils, toys—even a reflex hammer." Flipper smiled and held up the tool. "Flipping helps me concentrate," he continued. "I come up with some of my best ideas while I flip. Some people call flipping a bad habit. My parents call it an obsession. I call it inspiration." The last part he said with dramatic flare.

Dr. Needles smiled again as he took a seat. "Flipper, I have two things I want to go over with you. First, I want to take a look at those legs and run a few confirmation tests. Why don't you hop up on the table over here and let me take a look."

Flipper did as he was asked.

Dr. Needles cleared his throat. "Um, I am going to need that reflex hammer."

Flipper grinned sheepishly and handed it over.

Dr. Needles tested his legs' reflexes, strength, balance and speed. He had Flipper hop, jump, walk, run and spin. He poked and prodded, and even tickled his feet.

"I would say everything looks satisfactory with your legs. Your skin has regenerated as expected and you have full use of your muscles and nerves. We'll just want to keep an eye on them the next few days to make sure no side effects develop, but that would be really rare."

"Great!" Flipper said.

Dr. Needles sat back down. "Now, the second thing I wanted to talk to you about…" He trailed off. Dr. Needles picked up the device he had set down when he entered the room. Flipper thought it looked like a cell phone. The doctor touched the screen a few times before speaking. "We ran dozens of tests using the hair, blood and skin samples I took from you. In fact, while you were asleep and recovering, we took more samples and ran more tests because we couldn't believe what we saw. But the tests were consistent. I know that the results are accurate, I am just having a hard time understanding, or even believing them."

Flipper was confused. "What are you talking about, Doctor?"

Dr. Needles gave a big sigh. "You have Snader blood in you."

CHAPTER 20

"What do you mean? That I am part Snader?" Flipper asked, almost shouting.

Dr. Needles tried to explain. "The tests show that you still have a fairly strong amount of Snader blood in you, which means that one of your relatives had to have been a Snader. I would say probably a grandparent or great-grandparent."

Flipper thought about his grandparents. His mom's parents, Grandma and Grandpa Scales, were both still alive. He didn't think either one of them could be a Snader. Their family had lived in Roswell for generations. Could one of their parents have been a Snader? He didn't know. His grandparents on his dad's side had passed away before he was born. He didn't know much about them.

"How sure are you that your tests are correct?" Flipper asked. "There's no one in my family with red skin that I know of."

"The results are conclusive. There's no doubt you have a Snader as an ancestor. I just can't determine the exact number of generations. As far as the red skin goes, I'm not sure exactly what to tell you. I know you humans have people with different skin colors, unlike our race. A Snader and a human, a white or light brown human in your case, would probably have a child with mixed skin color, though it is possible their skin could come out stronger one way or the other. What I am saying is, it is quite possible that the child born to the

Snader and human parents could look a lot like a normal human. Maybe enough so that no one would ever notice there was anything different about him or her."

"You know what, Doctor?"

Dr. Needles raised his eyebrows.

"My life keeps getting weirder and weirder." Flipper hung his head and shook it.

"I'm sorry. I know it's a lot to take in all at once." This same doctor who had relished frightening Flipper two days previously, now sounded genuinely sympathetic.

"This could only happen in real life," Flipper said.

"What do you mean?"

Flipper looked back up at Dr. Needles. "I was kidnapped by purple aliens and told I was the key to saving the universe. I fought a dragon and nearly died. Finally, I was kidnapped by red aliens, had my paralyzed legs healed and was then told I was related to them. What I mean is, if I wrote all this in a story, no one would read it because it is too far-fetched."

CHAPTER 21

As they neared Rex, Nicole steered away from the main military base. She turned on the electronic map and asked Jake to find a large, open space a short distance from the base to land. Nicole's mind raced. She had served all her commanding officers, including General Jaxxen, with complete dedication and obedience, but here she was, responsible for stealing a spaceship with three children. Sure, Chezlor had made a strong and impassioned argument, but that's not why she had agreed to help them rescue Flipper. Deep down, she believed Flipper could help the Gudes. She knew that computer program inside and out. She had examined the results with skepticism but couldn't find a flaw in them or with the program. The kids hadn't talked her into going with them—they had presented her with an opportunity to do what she had already wanted to do. No matter. She was now on a path that had only one direction. She wouldn't be allowed to serve with the Gudes any longer, but she was going to do whatever she could to get Flipper in a position to help them.

Jake studied the map. "It looks like there is an open field north of the base. That should put us just a few miles away."

"We should be ready to land in a few minutes. We may not be landing on a flat surface so it could be bumpy," Nicole said.

"Probably not as bumpy as the rest of our plan." Everyone looked at Chezlor. He gave them a sheepish grin that said he knew it was a bad joke.

Nicole caught sight of something on the rear view screen. She quickly veered her aircraft to the right and accelerated.

Everyone screamed.

"What's going on?" Alya hollered.

"We have a spaceship coming towards us." Nicole quickly pointed to the screen. "They have a larger aircraft than we do. I'm going to try to out-maneuver them, so make sure your seatbelts are on tightly." She made another sharp turn to the right, then a few seconds later turned sharply back to the left.

Just like that, the doubts flooded into her mind. Was she going to get them all killed before they even had a chance to rescue Flipper? She tried to concentrate on flying.

The spaceship had been closing in, but Nicole's maneuvering was helping her put some distance between them. She cranked the ship to the right and held it there as she descended. Nicole continued to pull away. The Snaders continued following her but they didn't dip as low as she did. They were now flying only a few hundred feet above the ground. The terrain was mountainous and she was hoping to use the peaks to help them lose the Snaders' aircraft. She kept hearing things from the kids like, "Whoa!", or "OOhh!", or "Yikes", or "I think we should just go ahead and slam into one of the cliffs so we can just get this over with because my heart can't take it any longer." The last one she only heard once.

It only took Nicole a couple of minutes to lose sight of the Snaders' aircraft thanks to her aggressive flying. She remained close to the ground for a couple of minutes before she took their spaceship higher, to a safer flying altitude. She had such a tight grasp on the control sticks that it took her a few seconds to relax her grip. She flew around for a few minutes looking for the other aircraft. When there was no sign of it, she had Jake relocate the open field on their map. They once again set course for it.

"Hey, guys," Alya said hesitantly. "Did you notice they didn't shoot at us?"

"You're right! That is strange," Jake said.

"What does it mean?" Chezlor asked.

"I don't think they were following us to shoot us down," Nicole responded. "They probably wanted to escort us. That's why they backed off the chase when I went low and the flying became dangerous."

"It would have been nice if they had just told us," Chezlor retorted.

"Oh, oops!" Nicole reached forward and turned a knob. "I turned the radio off earlier and never turned it back on. They might have been trying to get in touch."

"Why would they want to escort us instead of just killing us?" Alya asked.

Nicole shook her head. "I don't know."

***

"When do you think I'll be able to go home?" Flipper asked Captain Kreeker.

Captain Kreeker, Dr. Needles and Brianna were in Flipper's hospital room. "We will have a spaceship leaving for Earth very soon."

"Can't you just teleport me back?" Flipper asked.

"No, we don't have access to teleporting technology," the Captain said. "That's one of the reasons we're having such a hard time fighting the Gudes. We've learned how to scramble their teleporting abilities, but we haven't been able to duplicate them."

"Oh, I figured it was something all aliens could do." Flipper sounded disappointed.

The Captain smiled. "In the meantime, we have something you could do that would be very useful for us."

"What is it?" Flipper asked.

"It would be risky on your part, but I wouldn't ask you if I didn't think we could keep you safe. We have someone on the inside of the Gude military who has been working with us for some time now. This person has provided us with valuable information. In fact, we would not have control of their capital if it wasn't for this person. We would like you to work with us."

"But why do you need me if you already have someone?"

"Some of the Gudes believe you have been chosen to lead them in defeating us. We'd like to use that against them. Have them follow you right into a trap."

Flipper hung his head. "I lost my fight against a dragon. They don't believe I can still help them defeat you guys."

"You're wrong. Right now, there is a spaceship heading this way to rescue you. Someone still believes."

Flipper was skeptical. "Who's coming? I doubt the spaceship's for me."

"One of General Jaxxen's advisors, Major Styler. She left Vetrix with three children on board."

Flipper wasn't sure why they would be coming for him—if that's even what was happening. He was still trying to sort things out in his head. "If you are trying to protect yourselves from the Gudes, why are you the ones taking over their capital?"

"A very good question. The Gudes are bent on destruction. We've tried to live at peace with them in the past, but they won't stop trying to take over our planet. We're trying to send them a message to leave us alone by taking their capital and destroying their military."

"Okay, I am really confused about who the bad and good guys are here. And it sounds to me like the Snaders and Gudes have been fighting for a long time. Why does it matter to me? I don't care who wins and who loses. I just want to go home. I don't want to help either of you."

"I understand the way you feel. But keep in mind that today, the Gudes are fighting with us. Tomorrow, they may attack Earth. They have proven that they can come and go as they please on Earth, like when they kidnapped you."

Flipper thought that was a very good point. "The Gudes said you were the ones who wanted to attack Earth next. I know you have spies there."

"Of course both things are true," the Captain admitted. "We have agents on Earth to keep watch over it. We want to know immediately if the Gudes try to interfere with the humans. And of course the Gudes made us sound like we wanted to take over the universe. They were trying to convince you to help them. You have to decide if you're going to trust who kidnapped you from your home and got your legs paralyzed or who healed your legs."

The Snaders had certainly been better hosts than the Gudes. "If I decide to help you, what's your plan?"

"We are going to capture the Gudes who are coming to rescue you. We'll let Nicole and two of the children escape with you to return to Vetrix. It will look like you rescued them—make you a hero. When you return to Vetrix many more of the Gudes will believe you are meant to lead them to victory because you were able to orchestrate an escape from Rex. You need to pretend to believe you were chosen to defeat the Snaders and convince the Gudes to follow you into an attack on the capital. You will work closely with our insider to plan this out. Of course, what you'll really be leading them into is a trap. We'll be ready for them and should be able to capture them without any casualties. This should defeat them militarily and also kill their morale. From there, we can find out if they are planning to attack Earth and stop them. Flipper, you can help save Rex as well as Earth."

"Did you say you are only letting two of the children escape?" Flipper asked.

"Yes. I'm afraid we need to keep one of them—Jake. If this plan doesn't work we'll need him as leverage against General Jaxxen. Additionally, our keeping Jake as hostage will increase General Jaxxen's anger and make him more likely to follow you into the capital."

"I don't think the others are going to leave Jake behind."

The Captain looked at Dr. Needles and Brianna, then back to Flipper. "We thought about that. We are going to convince them that we killed Jake."

Flipper jumped down off the bed. "No, you can't hurt him! He's just a kid!"

The Captain shook his head and tried to calm Flipper. "We aren't going to hurt him; I promise. We're just going to tell Nicole and the kids that so they'll leave with you without trying to rescue him. Remember, we may need him later if our plan with you doesn't work. But, if everything goes as planned, we will return him as part of a peace treaty."

"Okay, but I like Jake. I don't want anything to happen to him."

"You have my word that Jake will be safe. I'll give you some time to decide."

Flipper turned to Dr. Needles, who had been quietly sitting alongside him, listening to Captain Kreeker and Flipper talk. "Can I borrow that reflex hammer again please? I need to think."

***

Nicole circled the open field, looking for the best area to land. An unfamiliar voice came over the radio. "Major Styler, are you out there? What is your location?"

They all looked at each other. Nicole pressed a button so she could respond. "How do you know who I am?"

"That is inconsequential," the voice said. "What is important is that we know you have three children on board with you, one of whom is your General's son. We know you're here because you think you can rescue the Earth child."

"Who is this?" Nicole asked.

"This is Lieutenant Stanford with the Snader Defense Fleet. I am flying the ship you eluded a few minutes ago. We have been trying to contact you regarding your presence here and our intentions. Our orders are to not shoot you down, but to bring you in. I would like you to follow me to our military base."

"And if we don't follow you?"

"We have a fleet of ships ready to attack. We have permission to shoot you down only if you refuse to cooperate."

"Okay. We will head towards your military base from the west. I will look for your escort before approaching."

Nicole muted the microphone and looked back at Chezlor, "Is this what you had in mind?"

Chezlor gave a nervous chuckle and said sarcastically, "Yeah, they're falling right into my trap."

The radar started beeping as it picked up a spaceship approaching them from the south. Nicole slowed down and waited for the Snader spaceship to fly in front of them so she could follow.

"This is Lieutenant Stanford approaching from the south. Follow me at a distance between one to two kilometers. When we arrive, land your spaceship fifty meters in front of mine."

Nicole flew in behind Lieutenant Stanford's spaceship and followed him toward the Snader military base. Within a minute, three other spaceships had come towards them. One of the spaceships flew beside them, one above, while the other stayed behind them.

"I get the feeling they don't trust us," Jake said drily.

A few minutes later they came upon the Snader military base. It looked like a large city. There were buildings everywhere, several of which towered hundreds of meters in the air. They flew over the buildings for a couple of minutes before a field lined with spaceships came into view.

"Wow, look at all of those spaceships!" Chezlor gawked.

"There must be thousands of them," Alya leaned forward to see better.

They flew past the spaceships and towards a lone flat building. Beyond it there were a couple of dozen spaceships parked in a large circle. There were two pilots in each spaceship and several more armed Snaders standing outside the planes, inside the circle.

Lieutenant Stanford landed his plane inside the circle, surrounded by Snader military. Nicole glided past and landed their ship in front of him, as instructed. The other three spaceships peeled off and were quickly out of sight. Immediately after landing, the armed Snader soldiers ran towards their spaceship and surrounded it.

"Here's your welcoming party, guys," Nicole gulped.

They unbuckled and walked to the back of the ship. Nicole pressed in the code. The door opened and the stairs lowered. She looked back at the three children. She could see the fear in their faces, but there was nothing that could be done about that now. "I'll go first. Stay behind me and let me do the talking. And, good luck."

Nicole walked down the steps followed by Jake, Alya and Chezlor. The Snaders had their weapons aimed at them, so Nicole raised her hands to show she was unarmed. Jake followed her lead, then Chezlor and Alya also raised their arms. When Nicole stepped onto the ground, three Snaders ran up to her. One kept his gun pointed at Nicole's head, while the other two searched each of them for weapons. Once the Snaders were satisfied the visitors were unarmed, they backed off, leaving the four to stand alone surrounded by soldiers.

The circle parted in front of them and a tall, husky man walked through. Once he had passed, the men reformed their circle. He walked towards the foursome and stopped about ten feet in front of them. "My name is Sergeant Lyndon, commander of the Snader Defensive Military Base. Which one of you is Jake Jaxxen?"

Jake looked at Nicole and then back to Sergeant Lyndon. "I am."

"Harvey! Wilson!" Sergeant Lyndon shouted.

Two men from the circle stepped forward and said in unison, "Yes, Sir!"

Without taking his eyes off Jake, the Sergeant said, "Take Mr. Jaxxen to the Commander's office."

"Yes, Sir!"

Nicole whispered quickly to Jake, "It's okay. We'll find you. I promise."

The two soldiers approached Jake. One of them ordered Jake to follow him. He started walking and Jake fell in behind. The second soldier walked behind Jake. After they had departed the circle, Sergeant Lyndon turned back to Nicole, Chezlor and Alya.

"Why have you come to Rex?" he asked.

Chezlor spoke with volume and confidence. "We came to rescue Flipper, but now we are going to rescue Flipper and Jake."

Nicole turned sharply to Chezlor and snapped under her breath, "I told you to let me do the talking."

"I thought he was looking at me."

Alya scolded him. "Why would you tell him what we plan to do?"

"Why else would we be here? They know why we came."

"If they know why we came then why would they ask?" Alya argued.

"I don't know. Why don't you ask him?" Chezlor pointed at Sergeant Lyndon.

Sergeant Lyndon laughed. "The fact that you think you could come to Rex and rescue someone is humorous. Since you're being up front, what is this great plan of yours to rescue your friend?"

Chezlor looked at Nicole then over to Alya. Neither of them made a sound. This time Chezlor spoke quietly, "We don't have a plan."

This brought more laughter, not only from Sergeant Lyndon but also from some of the soldiers surrounding them. When the laughter died down Sergeant Lyndon spoke with gritted teeth to the two soldiers on either side of him, "Men, take these three to their new living quarters."

Chapter 22

Allison stood in the middle of nowhere with the warm sun setting in the distance. Other than scattered trees and a small, indiscernible item in the distance, all she saw was red dirt in every direction. She thought it odd that there were trees but no other signs of life or water.

She walked nearly a mile and the disturbing sense she had felt around the purple alien returned and steadily grew. As she neared what had been the spec in the distance, it gradually took shape as a spaceship. She was careful to use the trees as much as she could to keep from being seen from the spaceship. With the trees being sporadic she could only hope she wasn't being watched. She only saw one person as she approached—he was purple, which explained her feelings. When she got close enough to have a clear view, she couldn't believe it! The purple man looked exactly like the same man she had seen kidnap Flipper! He was working on the outside of the spaceship. He looked in her direction and Allison quickly ducked behind a tree. She waited a moment then took another quick look. The purple alien walked up the stairs and inside the spaceship. Something caught her eye—the alien's gun had been left leaning against the stairs. Before she had time to consider the risks, she bolted towards the spaceship, grabbed the gun and hid beneath the steps. A few minutes later the man returned down the steps. Allison jumped out and pointed the gun at him. "Where is Flipper?" she demanded.

The man jerked around and looked shocked, then seemed to recognize her. "You're the girl that could see me. Let's see… Allison, right?"

"And you're the one who kidnapped my cousin. What's your name?"

"Fox."

"Okay, Fox. Where is he?" Allison demanded.

"Well, he, um, he's not here," stammered Fox.

"Tell me where he is right now or I'll shoot." Allison didn't know if she could actually shoot him, but she tried to convince them both she would.

Fox tried not to, but he chuckled.

Allison was not amused. "What's so funny?"

"Why don't you put the gun down and I'll answer your questions."

"You would like that, wouldn't you?"

"You can't fire it."

"I think I can. And you gave me a good reason when you kidnapped Flipper."

"Yes, I agree. And I understand why you want to shoot me. What I mean is, the gun won't fire for you."

Allison glared at him. "Why? Is there some kind of off switch or safety or something?"

This time Fox couldn't help himself. He laughed. Allison pulled the trigger. She pulled it over and over again, but nothing happened. Fox realized he was making her mad by laughing, so he tried to ease the tension. "I'm sorry, Allison. I shouldn't laugh. It's just that the gun is programmed only to be fired by the person wearing this uniform I have on." When Allison gave him a strange look he added, "It's an advanced technology that isn't available on Earth."

Allison reared back and threw the gun. Fox ducked, relieved when the gun flew in a different direction, smashing against the side of the spaceship.

"I understand you're angry and I owe you some answers. I'll be glad to trade questions with you as I have some myself. I'll answer first. You asked where Flipper is. Unfortunately, before we were able to return him to Earth, he was kidnapped by the Snaders. He's on their planet, Rex. Now, it's my turn. When I was on the earth how were you able to see me?"

"What do you mean he was kidnapped? Again? And who are the Snaders?"

Fox used his tough military voice. "Wait, it was my turn. When I was following you the other day on Earth, how were you able to see me?"

"Why wouldn't I be able to see you? You're not invisible."

"I just told you our technology is beyond yours on Earth. I have the ability to make myself unseen by humans. I've been to Earth many times and have never been seen before. But, somehow you're different. I just don't know how."

"Actually, I didn't see you during the day. That night I had a dream and relived the day. In my dream I could see you," explained Allison. "Do you remember seeing me when I saw you in my dream?"

"I don't know about your dream, but I know you looked at me in the classroom, when you were walking home from school, and while you were walking around that evening. Later that night, when I was holding Blake, you could see me. You shouldn't have been able to see me," Fox shook his head, still astonished. "And how are you here? How did you get here? Are you able to control your dreams?"

Allison also wanted answers to those questions, but she remained determined. "Wait a minute, it's my turn. What do you mean Flipper was kidnapped? How come you're here and not on your way to get him? Are you planning to return Flipper? And when?"

Fox wasn't sure how much he should tell her. "We have a team on their way to rescue him. As soon as we can travel safely, we'll return him. Now, how did you get here?"

"I don't know. The last thing I remember was talking to my friend Josh in the spaceship just before I fell asleep, and then I woke up here. How did you just disappear from Flipper's living room?"

"I'm able to teleport. All Gudes can. I simply thought about where I wanted to be and went there. So, you're asleep and dreaming?"

"I guess so. How come you don't just teleport, get Flipper, then teleport him back to Earth?"

"The Snaders have intercepts that cause us to go adrift if we teleport, so it's too dangerous. You have seen me twice in your dreams. Have you had any other dreams like this?"

"Yes, I had a dream last night. I was with Flipper, but he wasn't himself. He was a world famous soccer player. Really weird, but it seemed as real as this does. Where are we now?"

"This is the planet Vetrix. What spaceship are you asleep on?"

"I don't know. Some spaceship Josh and I discovered underground. Are you dreaming?" Allison asked.

"No. Have you ever met anyone else from another planet?"

"No, but there's a red alien on the spaceship. Who are the Snaders?"

"They're our enemies and a serious threat to the universe. Has anyone in your family ever met someone from another planet?"

"No, not that I know of. Why did you kidnap Flipper?"

"We thought he could help us. Does the Snader know you're on the spaceship?"

"No. Is Flipper okay?" Allison asked.

"Well…" Fox didn't want to answer this one but knew she would find out soon enough. "He kind of got his legs burned and paralyzed when he fought a dragon. He can't walk, his life is in danger on Rex, and he's a bit upset with us for kidnapping him and then refusing to take him back to Earth. But, he still had his sense of humor. You're in danger too. The Snaders—you need to…." Fox's voice faded away.

And so did Allison's dream.

CHAPTER 23

The loud, grinding noise of the spaceship door opening woke Allison with a jolt. She yawned and stretched, but couldn't shake the feeling that she was still extremely tired.

"How did you sleep?" she asked Josh as he hopped up and down a few times on his tiptoes.

"Horribly. I had a nightmare that aliens kidnapped Flipper and we were trapped underground in an alien spaceship. So glad it was just a dream." He gave Allison a half smile.

She smiled back. "It amazes me that you can keep your sense of humor, no matter what is going on around you."

He opened his mouth wide in mock surprise. "Are you trying to tell me that it wasn't a dream?"

Allison just shook her head at him. "How long do you suppose we slept?

"I'd say all night," he said with energy. "I feel great!"

"I feel like I hardly slept. I had a really strange dream. I met the purple alien who kidnapped Flipper."

"What I would do if I could get my hands on him."

"Yeah, I tried to shoot him but the gun didn't work."

"Well, I hope he shows up in my dream next."

"He said that Flipper was badly injured and had been kidnapped by another group of aliens who took him to another planet." Allison's voice broke.

"Allison, it was just a dream."

"I don't know. It was so real. And he knew that I had seen him the day Flipper was kidnapped."

"Of course he did! That was during your dream too. It's all in your head."

"I wish I could believe that. I really do." She shifted her thoughts away from the dream. "What if the red alien won't help us? We could be trapped down here forever."

Josh shrugged his shoulders. "As it stands now, we're lost underground with no way out, so we don't have much to lose by asking."

"That's a simple way to look at it," Allison smiled.

"And accurate," Josh added.

"Well then, let's go get this over with."

As they walked down the aisle towards the door, Josh said quietly, "I hope this guy has something to eat. I'm starving."

Once outside the spaceship, Josh called timidly, "Hello? Is anybody there?"

There was no answer, so he spoke a little louder, "Hello?"

When there was still was no answer, he shouted, "Hello? Is anyone here?"

When they had arrived the previous day, their attention had been on the spaceship. Now, they took time to look around the room that housed it. The hole in the stone wall they had slid through looked out of place. It was a perfect square and appeared man-made rather than natural, like the rest of the room. The room reminded Allison of the caves she and her parents had visited in the Ozarks.

"Do you see anywhere he could have gone?" Josh asked.

"I don't see any openings other than the one we came through."

"I'm not going to try to climb back into that thing," Josh sneered.

"I doubt he could have crawled up it. It was steep. Let's see if we can find another opening," Allison suggested.

After unsuccessfully searching the rock wall for an exit they decided to give up and explore the inside of the spaceship instead.

"Let's start with the Snader's room," Allison suggested.

"What's a Snader?" Josh asked.

"Oh, uh, that's what the purple alien called the red alien." When Josh looked at her askance, she clarified, "In my dream."

"Well, it's just a dream, but it's as good as anything else we could call it."

They got to the Snader's room door and Josh knocked. "Just in case," he winked.

He placed his hand on the pad but the door didn't open. He tried again, but still nothing. He stepped over to the door of the cockpit and placed his hand on that pad. That door didn't open either. He looked at Allison and shrugged his shoulders. She put her hand on the pad to the cockpit door and it opened. She touched it again and the door closed.

"How did you do that?"

"I don't know. I just touched it."

Josh tried again but still the door didn't open. Allison placed her hand on the pad to the Snader's door and it opened immediately. She gave Josh a smug smile. "I guess it takes a girl's touch."

Josh rolled his eyes. "Whatever."

The room was simple: A bed in one corner and a desk in another. On the floor were two stacks of books and a pile of clothes.

"Not much to look at in here," Josh stated the obvious.

Allison was at the desk flipping through a book. "I think this stuff looks interesting!"

"I'm going to go look around the rest of the ship. He's got to have some food around here."

"Good luck," Allison said without looking up.

***

She was still reading when Josh returned an hour later.

He set a cup of water on the desk. "I found a kitchen in the back of the ship. There's a large supply of water and these yellowish plant things that don't taste too bad."

Allison looked up. "Oh my! Where did you find that outfit?"

Josh was dressed in white. The shirt had a v-neck with the collar turned up. The bottom of the pants were wide. He tried to do his best imitation of Elvis Presley. In the deepest voice he could muster he said, "Thank you. Thank you very much."

Allison cracked up.

"There is a room in the back with all sorts of clothes in it."

"It would feel wonderful to change out of these filthy clothes." She gulped down her water and followed Josh back to the kitchen. She drank more water and tried some of the yellowish plants. They weren't great, especially with their rough and string-like texture, but she was in no position to be picky. After eating, Josh showed Allison the room full of clothes. There were clothes hanging all along the back wall. Against another wall clothes were neatly folded in piles almost as high as they stood. Against a third wall there was a mountain of unfolded clothes. They pulled out casual clothes of all different sizes. The clothes were old but in good shape. From what Josh had seen in old movies and photographs the clothes could have all come from America. There were all sizes too—from tiny infant clothing to XXXL sizes. The fourth wall contained a section of costumes. They each found a jacket, a sweatshirt and a pair of jeans in their size. Allison asked, "Where do you suppose all of these clothes came from?"

"I don't know," Josh said. "Who knows how long this Snader has been down here or what he's been up to?"

"I do."

"You do what?"

"I know how long they have been down here and what they are up to."

Josh took a deep breath. "What do you mean by they?"

"I found a journal the Snader's been writing. There are a lot more of them down here—somewhere. They have been living underground since 1947. They hate humans and any other form of life that isn't Snader."

"Holy cow! What are we going to do?"

"I don't know, but I don't think Dyson is going to want to help us."

"Dyson?"

"Yes. His name is Dyson. I think the next time he leaves we should watch where he goes and follow him to see what he does. Maybe he will lead us to the other Snaders."

"Oh, great, more aliens," Josh said sarcastically.

"And by the way, that is their real name—Snaders, just like Fox said in my dream."

"Now that's really bizarre!" Josh exclaimed.

They spent the next hour exploring the rest of the spaceship. They found a room that was dusty, dirty and full of cobwebs and decided it would be the best room to hide in. Allison cleaned it enough for them to stay in while Josh straightened the kitchen and wardrobe room back to how he had found it.

"Allison, look what I found buried in the clothes." He handed her a small computer-looking device. "What do you think it is?"

She found the power button. "Whatever it is, it has power. Let's go to the cockpit so I can see if I can figure out what it does."

While Allison worked on the device Josh lay on the cot, daydreaming about cheeseburgers and video games. Eventually he decided thinking about food was too torturous so he got up. All the screens on the cockpit wall had images on them; each a different angle of the spaceship or a different angle of the outside from the spaceship.

"Wow! How did you do that?"

"It took a pretty technical mind to figure out. I'm not sure you would understand," Allison said, not looking up from the device.

Josh was insulted. He knew he wasn't the brightest, especially compared to Allison. She was smart and always did well in school, and she knew a lot about computers. Josh struggled to get decent grades, but he didn't think he was as stupid as Allison had just made him feel. "Tell me what you did, I bet I'll understand."

She shook her head and continued to fiddle with the device. "I don't know, Josh. It took me quite a while to figure it out."

Josh was suddenly cross. "Allison, just because you are super smart doesn't mean you have to make me feel dumb! I'm not stupid! You aren't the only one who's clever."

Allison realized she had pushed Josh too far. He was good at dishing it out, but he had a hard time taking a ribbing. She couldn't help laughing. "And you aren't the only one who can be a smart aleck!" She walked over to the wall and pressed a button. The screens went blank. She pushed it again and the screens came back on. "I just pressed this button."

"Okay," Josh chuckled. "That was a pretty good one!"

"I'm trying to get this… hold on… there!" She showed the device to Josh and he could see himself on the screen.

"Wow! You are good!" he said appraisingly.

"This is some sort of transmitter. By touching the screen we can change the angles of the camera or change which camera shows on the screen."

She flipped through some different camera views. She stopped when the room they had decided to stay in showed up. "I think we better go cover up the lens to that camera in case Dyson also has a transmitter. We don't want him to see us."

"I saw some duct tape in one of the closets," Josh said.

"Duct tape?!"

"Sure, it's like the Force from Star Wars."

"How is duct tape like the Force?"

"It has a light side and a dark side, and it holds the universe together." Josh smiled.

"Good grief!" Allison moaned.

Josh ran to get the duct tape and Allison went back to their room. When he returned, Allison stood with the transmitter looking up into a corner. "The camera's so tiny I can't see it, but the picture is coming from right up there."

Josh moved the cot to the corner and stood on it. He tore off some duct tape and carefully placed it on the wall so that it covered the area Allison pointed at.

"That's perfect," she said. "Now I just have a black screen on the transmitter."

Josh hopped down and Allison let out a huge yawn.

"You should take a nap," Josh said as he returned the cot to its original position.

"I would love to go to sleep, but I'm afraid I'll have another dream," Allison admitted. "I keep thinking about something Fox said. Maybe I can control my dreams."

"You might as well try. You can't stay awake forever."

"I know," Allison admitted reluctantly.

"You dreamt about Flipper before. Why don't you try to dream about him again?" Josh suggested.

"Yeah," Allison felt a sense of hope. "Fox said he was on the Snaders' planet, um, I can't remember the name."

"That shouldn't matter. Try thinking about the Snaders and their planet as you go to sleep," Josh encouraged her.

Allison remained sitting, reluctant to lie down.

"I'll stay in here with you," Josh said as he lay down on the floor. "I wouldn't mind a short nap myself."

Allison laid down. "Thanks, Josh."

She thought about Snaders and tried to picture their planet. Within minutes she was asleep.

CHAPTER 24

Dr. Needles had just finished his examination of Flipper's legs when Captain Kreeker came into the room. He looked at Dr. Needles and asked, "How is our brave patient doing?"

"Great! His legs are strong and show no signs of rejecting the procedure. I give him a one hundred percent bill of health."

"That's good news," the Captain said. He turned to Flipper. "Have you made a decision regarding our proposal?"

Flipper hesitated because he wished he didn't have to make a decision. "Yeah, I'll do it, as long as you promise that you won't harm Jake."

"You have my word," the Captain said. "The Gudes have arrived and been taken into custody. Jake is alone in a secure location. The other three are in a room together in the area we call the dungeon. They're each chained to the wall. Tonight at midnight I am going to bring you the keys to unlock them."

"Wait," Flipper interrupted, "Nicole, Chezlor and Alya are chained up in a dungeon?"

"Yes, why?" the Captain asked.

"I guess I pictured aliens having a more high-tech way of locking people up rather than in chains and in a dungeon."

Dr. Needles chuckled but the Captain didn't look amused. He glanced at Dr. Needles and handed Flipper a piece of paper. "Here is a map of our facility. The dungeon is here." He pointed. "I have drawn a path for you to take to get to the dungeon. To escape, follow these arrows from the dungeon; they will take you underground towards their ship. If you come up here, you will be within a hundred yards of where their ship is parked."

Flipper studied the map until he felt comfortable with the directions. "Is anyone going to try to stop us?"

"As long as Jake remains in his cell and there is no attempt to rescue him, then no one is going to stop you."

Flipper nodded his understanding.

"Good," the Captain said. "Study your map and get some rest. I will see you at midnight."

***

Jake was alone in a cold, dark room. It was pitch black and he couldn't see his hands in front of his face. His arms and legs were chained to the wall. There was a little slack in the chains but not enough to allow him to sit. He had been standing for hours and felt exhausted. He wanted to sleep and he wanted to cry, but at the moment he wasn't able to do either. The door slowly opened and the light from outside pierced the darkness and Jake's eyes. He slammed his eyes closed and turned his head.

Two tall, burly men in black uniforms wearing brimmed caps escorted between them a third man dressed in a dull yellow pullover shirt and dark pants. The whole ceiling was a light and lit the room and Jake's eyes slowly adjusted. Jake recognized the two men who had escorted him into his dark prison cell. They each held a tall container and stopped as the man in the middle continued until he was within a few feet of Jake.

"I'm Captain Kreeker, in charge of this facility," the man said with an arrogant tone. "The results of your mind read are in."

Before they had locked him up, the two soldiers had escorted Jake to a lab where they had strapped him to a chair, given him a couple of shots, and hooked wires up to his head. He had had no idea what they were doing. Mind reading? Was that even possible?

"Mind read?" Jake asked dubiously.

"Yes." Captain Kreeker put his hands behind his back and began pacing as he spoke. "Our scientists have developed a machine that can read minds. To be honest, it is still a work in progress. At present we are able to draw small bits of information from a mind, but eventually we hope to get to the point where we can penetrate a mind and glean any information we want."

The thought chilled Jake, but it scared him more wondering why Captain Kreeker was telling him this.

"We weren't able to get the information we hoped from your mind." The Captain's words put Jake temporarily at ease. "However, we did find one bit of information that we think is going to be, well, if not useful...at least fun."

Captain Kreeker smiled and stepped back between the guards. "Go ahead, Lucky," he said without taking his eyes off Jake. This guy was giving Jake the creeps.

One of the guards stepped towards Jake. "Let me see your hand, boy." He grabbed Jake's hand, turned it upside down and balanced his container on the back of it. He laughed, "I wouldn't move your hand if I were you."

The second Snader took his other hand and did the same thing. The containers were about a foot tall, open at the top, and filled with some kind of liquid. Jake didn't recognize the metallic material they were made of.

"These cups contain a special explosive chemical," Captain Kreeker said, almost cheerfully. "If it tips over and spills on you it will burn right through your skin and bones. If the cup falls onto the ground from this height, well, let's just say that there probably won't be enough of you left to identify."

The two guards laughed as the lights went out and the door closed behind the three of them. Jake was alone again in the dark cold room; he felt very tired. But now he had bigger problems. He was about to die. The question was: How? Was he going to burn and disintegrate or explode?

"Curse you, Chezlor," he mumbled furiously. His worst nightmare had come true. "I knew one of your pranks would get me some day. I just didn't know how."

***

As midnight approached, Flipper felt refreshed and awake. He had tried unsuccessfully to nap, but his adrenaline was strong and he felt more alert than ever. He was going over the map one last time before Captain Kreeker arrived with the key. Since the Captain had given him the map, he had gone over it so many times that he knew the layout by heart, but he was nervous and looking at the map distracted him from staring at the clock.

A couple of minutes before midnight, the Captain came into his room. "Are you ready, Flipper?"

"Yes. I have the map memorized," Flipper said folding it and putting it in his pocket.

"Good. Here are two keys. One will allow you access to the dungeon. The other will unlock all the chains on the Gudes. Remember, tell them you overheard someone say some kids from Vetrix were captured, so you found a map while snooping around and stole the keys from a guard who wasn't looking."

Flipper looked at the Captain and nodded his head.

"It's time for you to be the hero, Flipper. After all, the computer selected you," the Captain said in a somewhat sarcastic tone.

"Thank you for letting us go," Flipper said and shook his hand. He took a deep breath and started for the dungeon.

Chapter 25

The room was cold but Jake's tense body was covered with sweat. He tired of listening to the myriad of voices running through his head so he started talking out loud. "Chezlor, I wish this was one of your pranks. I could spill these, you would have a good laugh, and we would have a big mess to clean up. Oh my! The Snaders attacked right after your last prank and we didn't clean up after I spilled that red juice. That's going to stain permanently!"

He clenched his jaw. He knew that if he didn't pull it together, he would drop one of the jars. He decided he didn't care. He might as well get it over with and stop prolonging his agony. The moment he was ready to quit was the moment he had an idea. He might die trying but that was better than quitting. He knew that's what his dad would want. He slowly brought his left hand towards his head, careful to keep his right hand steady. He carefully brought the jar to his mouth. He couldn't see the jar nor tell how full it was, which made his next move extremely risky. He carefully found the edge of the jar with his lips, opened his mouth and gradually slid the jar into his mouth. When he thought he had enough of the jar in his mouth he bit down tightly. He held it in his teeth just long enough to turn his hand over and get a good solid grip of the jar. For the first time since he had been taken away from the others, Jake felt hopeful. He knew he needed to stay focused and calm. He brought his right hand up towards his mouth, concentrating hard. He repeated the maneuver and soon had both jars grasped firmly in his hands. He breathed a sigh of relief. He wasn't sure what he was going to do next. The chains were too short for him to set the jars down on the ground but at least he could hold out for a while longer. He tried to think of a way to use the explosives to get the keys from a guard so that he might escape. No guard would come near him when they saw he had the jars in his hands. Assuming the guards were carrying the keys, it wouldn't do him any good to throw a jar at one to kill them as the keys would be too far away for him to reach.

Suddenly it hit him. "Wait! The Captain said the chemical would eat clear through my bones. I wonder if it would eat through these chains?"

Jake stretched his left hand away from him and pulled the chain taut. He pressed his legs up against the wall to avoid any drips. There was a lot that could go wrong with this plan, but he decided it was his best option. He reached his right hand across his body until he could feel the chain that was attached to his left hand and slowly tilted the jar until he heard a fizzle. The chain broke and he gave a big sigh. With his left hand free, he carefully reached down and set the jar up against the wall, as far away from him as he could stretch. He took the other jar and repeated the process to free his right hand. He did the same for both legs and, within a few minutes, he was free from the wall. He still had the chains around his wrists and ankles, but he was no longer bound. Jake felt his way along the wall until he could feel the door. His adrenaline was high, which he needed for what he had to do next.

He poured a little bit from the jar into the crack between the door and the wall. He heard a fizzle and after a few seconds, the door released. He quietly pulled it open.

The guard standing just to the right of the doorway turned in surprise. Jake quickly poured some of the chemical onto his foot. The guard dropped to the ground and screamed in pain.

"Give me the keys," Jake demanded.

"Never, you purple freak!" The guard lunged and swung his arm, striking Jake's legs. It was all Jake could do to keep his balance and not drop the deadly container. As he stumbled backwards, the chemical spilled on top of the guard's head. The guard fell inert, silent.

Jake turned away. He couldn't stand the sight of what remained of the guard's head. He carefully took the guard's gun and put it in his pocket. He found keys and unlocked the chains from his hands and ankles. He knew that one day he would be in the military and would be expected to kill in the line of duty. His dad and his brother both had but he hadn't expected his first kill to be so soon. Although, if he were honest, he knew when they decided to come to Rex that they might have to kill some Snaders to escape with Flipper safely. He had thought they would be doing it together. Yet, here he was and he had done it alone. He wasn't even sure how he felt about it. He hadn't meant—hadn't tried—to kill him. It had been the guard's own doing. He pulled himself from his thoughts, he didn't have time to dwell on it. He needed to get going. He hadn't been blindfolded when they had brought him to his cell, so he had a reasonably good idea how to get out of the building. His first concern was finding Chezlor, Alya and Nicole, but he had no clue as to their whereabouts. He found the stairway and went up. When he got to the top he paused. He needed to catch his breath before he faced more guards. He only allowed himself half a minute to rest. He knew if he paused too long his fatigued body and mind would remind him of how afraid he should be. He had enough going against him. He couldn't allow his thoughts to cripple him. He stood to the side and cracked open the door that led into the hallway. He waited and listened but didn't hear anything.

Tense and anxious, he peeked into the hall, expecting to see several guards, but saw none. He walked noiselessly down the hall, not sure what to do next. He felt his best chance to find his friends was to find a guard and make him talk. He assumed his friends would each be in a different room, as he had been. They may have already been killed by the chemical or by some other method.

"Stop thinking about that," Jake reprimanded himself. "I have to stay positive!"

Jake suddenly stopped to listen. He heard footsteps close by. He hurried to the nearest door and opened it. He breathed a sigh of relief when he found no one inside. He stepped in and closed the door quickly. He pulled out the gun and waited for the guard to pass by so he could come up behind him.

Jake heard the guard walk into the hall and stop. He held his breath and tried not to make a sound. What could only have been about a minute seemed much longer. Finally, the guard began walking again. As soon as Jake thought the guard had passed far enough to be out of reach, he opened the door, stepped out and pointed his gun at the receding figure's back.

"Don't move. I have…." Jake stopped mid-sentence. He was speechless.

The person in front of him put his hands in the air and slowly turned around, confirming Jake's initial impression.

"Flipper!" Jake yelled louder than he should have.

"Jake!" Flipper shouted with equal excitement.

CHAPTER 26

Allison woke in a dark, smoky room. She recognized the smell—cigars. Her dad's uncle Phil smoked cigars, even though her mom refused to let him come in the house smelling like them. The room was warm and, at first, felt welcome to her tired, cold body. It was only a matter of seconds before the warmth began to be uncomfortably hot. A screen emanated light across the room. It was only twenty feet away, but the thick smoke kept Allison from seeing the picture on the screen. She looked behind her and felt the wall. It was hard and moist, much like the walls in the cave. She guessed she was still underground and had failed to control her dream and find the Snaders' planet. She saw the top and back of a bald red head sitting in front of the screen. Her breathing went immediately into hyperdrive as panic surged through her entire body. She was afraid her presence would be detected and desperately tried to calm herself. It didn't matter.

"I know you're here, child." The gruff voice coughed. Allison was able to see the redness of the man's skin through the fog when he stood and turned towards her. He was shorter than Allison and was about as wide around as she was short. He walked towards her, slowly coming into view. She gasped and backed up until her body slammed against the solid wall. She turned her head and locked her eyes shut. The closed eyes didn't help her fear. She could still smell, hear and sense the man approaching. What scared her the most was the image burned in her mind. Although she didn't open her eyes to confirm what she thought she had seen, later she swore the man had had eight legs.

A bead of sweat dropped from her nose and she could feel more sweat moving down her temples but was too frightened to wipe it away.

The man stopped a few inches from her, took a big puff of smoke and blew it in her face. Allison began to cough uncontrollably and, feeling light-headed, she slowly and painfully lost consciousness.

***

Allison's eyes remained tightly closed from fear. She could still smell the cigar; could feel the smoke in her lungs. But, something was different. She was lying on her back. The coolness chilled her sweating body. At last, the hope of the abominable creature being gone overtook her fear of seeing him again and she cautiously opened her eyes. She recognized the soft white ceiling above her and breathed a sigh of relief. She tilted her head to the side and saw Josh lying on the floor, eyes wide open and staring straight up at the ceiling.

She wondered about the strange expression on his face, but not for long. She heard the sound of footsteps approaching until they passed their room. They heard movement in the kitchen next door. Allison picked up the transmitter and searched for the camera feed from the kitchen. She found it and she and Josh watched as Dyson sat down to eat. They tried not to move, afraid that Dyson might hear them. He was in the kitchen for about twenty minutes eating some of the yellowish plant and a black, crumbly substance. Finally, he got up and walked back to his room.

Josh broke the silence, whispering. "Was that dirt he was eating?"

"Yes. They eat dirt. I read a lot about their lifestyle when I was in Dyson's room. The dirt has a lot of nutrients," Allison explained. "How long was I asleep?"

"Only a few minutes," Josh said. "Did you have any luck? Did you find Flipper?"

Allison shook her head. "It was horrible—as bad as any nightmare. I was in a room with some red creature who smoked and had eight legs. He was awful looking."

"Was he a Snader then?" Josh asked.

"I don't know," Allison conceded quietly. "He didn't say anything and I wasn't there long, thankfully."

"Dyson's going outside," Josh whispered excitedly and grabbed his jacket.

Allison switched camera views on the transmitter and they watched as Dyson climbed up the wall behind the spaceship. He climbed to about twenty feet high and disappeared into the wall.

"What in the world?" Josh asked, his mouth opening in surprise.

"There must be a hole in the wall up there," Allison said. "But I can't see it on this small screen.

"I'll be right back."

Josh hurried out of the room while Allison set the transmitter on the cot and put on her jacket. She went into the hallway and waited for Josh. A couple of minutes later, he came out of the clothes room wearing all black with a cape and a black mask across his eyes with tall pointy ears.

Josh walked up to Allison and in a gruff voice said, "I'm Batman."

Allison laughed. "Come on Batman, before Dyson gets away."

They ran outside and found the spot where Dyson had climbed up.

"Do you think we can climb up there?" Allison asked.

"Sure!" Josh reached up and grabbed hold of a rock. "This will be like climbing the rock wall at the rec center." He found a ledge for his foot and lifted himself off the ground. It only took him a minute to find the opening that Dyson had crawled through.

"What do you see?" Allison asked.

"Nothing. It's just black in there," Josh said.

He crawled into the hole and disappeared from Allison's sight. She waited anxiously until his head popped out of the hole.

"I know which way he went. Come on up." Josh waved for her to climb.

Allison climbed. She had a much harder time than Josh and lost her footing a couple of times on the way up. On her third try she made it high enough for Josh to reach her.

"Give me your hand."

Allison reached up and took hold of his hand. He grabbed her tightly and pulled as she pushed with her legs. The opening had plenty of room for them to fit in and to crawl, but not enough to turn around. Josh crawled backwards and Allison followed him going forwards. They only had to crawl for about thirty yards. The tunnel opened up into another room, this one about the size of their room on the spaceship. The only floor in the room was a ledge about four feet wide. In front of them hung a rope looped around a pulley. The rope was moving up one side and down the other. It appeared that Dyson was descending.

Josh looked over the edge. "I can't see down more than a hundred yards or so. A minute ago I could see the top of the elevator. Dyson is lowering himself. He must be going a long way down."

"Over a mile." Josh gave Allison a surprised look, so she explained, "I read it in Dyson's room."

"I guess if we want to follow him we'll have to wait until he gets all the way down and then pull the elevator back up," Josh said.

They sat and waited until the ropes stopped moving. They waited a few more minutes, in hopes that Dyson would move away from, and out of sight of, the elevator.

Josh reached out to grab the rope. "Let's hope no one sees the elevator moving or we're going to be in big trouble."

Strangely, pulling the elevator up turned out to be easy. Josh mentioned it and Allison explained how Dyson had developed a complex set of pulleys to make his traveling up and down simple. They took turns pulling the rope until the elevator reached the top, then stepped onto it and began their descent.

After a few minutes of lowering them down, Josh said, "You know, I would have thought that aliens, with their advanced technology, could have built an automated elevator."

Allison chuckled. "According to Dyson, elevators are not a priority to them."

As they neared the bottom, Josh slowed their descent and carefully came to a stop. They were in an empty, enclosed room, which was three times the size of the room at the top of the elevator. Fortunately, there were no Snaders in sight. The only light in the room came from a narrow tunnel, the only other exit besides the elevator. They walked about fifty feet through the narrow tunnel and carefully crept to the small opening at the end and peeked out. The room they peered into was humongous! It was so big they couldn't see the other side. It was almost like looking at an underground city but there weren't any buildings. Instead, there were dozens and dozens of different sized spaceships, both on the floor and up on the ledges. The middle section must have been a hundred yards wide. On both sides were slopes that led to another level area that stretched on as far as they could see. The room was as light as being outside in the bright sun.

"Wow! Look at all of those spaceships!" Josh gawked.

"They have two hundred and ninety-eight spaceships down here," Allison said.

Josh looked at her in astonishment. "Are you kidding me? You didn't tell me that!"

"I told you there were other Snaders living down here." Allison said defensively.

"Yeah, but I didn't picture anything like this." Josh continued to stare in amazement. "Did you read how they got them all down here?"

"The Roswell Incident. Back in 1947 there were four Snaders that survived the crash. Shortly after being captured by our military, they escaped, went underground and settled here. They began stealing spaceships from around the world that different governments had acquired over the years. Some of the spaceships were theirs, some came from other aliens. Over half of the spaceships they stole had been stored in Area 51 in Nevada.

"They had an opening that ran straight up from here, which they used for access, until the Air Force paved some additional runways on their base. Since then, they have lived down here multiplying."

"I didn't come across any of that when I did research for my presentation at school," Josh said.

Allison laughed. "I'm sure the government made sure no one knew aliens had escaped and stolen their stolen spaceships back."

"I don't think the government knows about this place," Josh said.

"Neither do I," Allison agreed.

CHAPTER 27

Thousands of Snaders moved and worked and played completely oblivious to the two human kids lurking just out of their vision on the other side of a dark doorway, watching.

"Look," Josh whispered pointing to their left.

Allison looked and saw two Snaders carrying someone. "That's a purple alien!"

"So there are purple aliens down here too?"

Allison shook her head. "No, according to what I read in Dyson's room, they're all Snaders down here."

"I wonder how they got a purple alien?" Josh asked thoughtfully.

"Let's follow them and see what we can find out."

She didn't wait for Josh to respond. She ran to a large boulder, which she used to shield herself from sight of the Snader colony. Josh was right behind her. They watched closely as the two red aliens carried the purple alien through an opening in the rocky wall and out of sight.

"Do you see anyone nearby?" Allison asked.

Josh glanced around "No, no one's looking."

"Let's go."

They stayed low as they made their way to the same opening the Snaders had gone through.

"Make sure no one is following us."

She peered inside the opening. "It's clear."

They stepped into the opening, out of sight, and felt momentarily safe.

"Did anyone see us?" she asked.

"I don't think so."

"Good."

They continued forward, on high alert, as the brightness from the underground city quickly dimmed. The path turned to the right after thirty feet and they came to a set of stairs. As they neared the bottom of the steps, Allison stopped so quickly that Josh walked into her, causing them both to tumble down the last few steps.

Josh was irritated. "Why did you stop?"

Allison pointed into the darkness behind him. He rolled over and looked at the purple figures that had caused her to hold her breath.

He whispered, "What do you think?"

It took all her strength to answer him. "I-I don't know."

Josh slowly stood. When nothing bad happened, Allison got the courage to stand up, but she hid behind Josh. The figures didn't move or speak. Josh took a couple of steps towards them to get a closer look. Allison wasn't so sure that was a good idea, so she stayed right where she was. He took a couple more steps. Allison was ready to run back up the stairs.

He approached until he was right beside one of the figures. Finally, he looked back and waved his hand for her to come. "Look at these."

She cautiously walked towards Josh and cringed when she saw him poking the figure.

"These aren't aliens," he said. "They're robots. This is a robot of a purple alien." He inspected each of the robots. "There are several purple and human robots."

Now that Allison wasn't so tense with fear, she scanned the area and saw that Josh was right. In fact, most of the robots were in piles, missing limbs.

"I wonder what these are for?" Josh questioned.

Suddenly, they heard a loud, excited scream. They both jumped and looked in the direction of the sound. They cautiously walked in the direction of the scream, until they came to an opening into an arena. There were bleachers all the way around, and in the center was a flat area with humans and purple aliens standing scattered around. Around the arena was a short wall with cracks that allowed Josh and Allison to hide behind and still see the activity happening inside the arena. One Snader, tall and muscular, squatted in a fighting position. Allison thought he looked like he could be a linebacker playing football. Unlike Dyson, who had red hair to match his red body, this Snader had dark black hair. His receding hair reminded Allison of her dad's hair.

A loud horn sounded and the Snader took off at a run. He dove feet first towards the first purple alien he came to. He knocked the robot down, landing feet first on the robot's chest. He didn't slow as he continued running towards a human robot. Just as the Snader got to the human, the human did a round kick at the Snader's head. The Snader slid on his knees, just under the kick, and snapped the robot's leg in half. As he approached the next purple alien robot, two other robots joined to surround the Snader. The robots each had a laser gun. One fired at the Snader, but he dove towards it, below the laser shot. The shot missed him but hit one of the other robots, blowing it to pieces. The Snader came out of his roll and grabbed the robot that had fired at him around the neck. Another robot ran toward them. The Snader pulled the robot backwards and swung him around. He let go and both robots collided, sending sparks flying and starting a fire. The Snader continued around the arena until he had destroyed all of the robots; the last were only a few feet from where Josh and Allison were hiding. The Snader leaned over and put his hands on his knees. He was breathing hard, but his face showed contented pleasure.

"That was awesome Red Fox!"

Josh and Allison looked to their left and saw two more Snader men running across the arena towards Red Fox. One was really fat. He was probably twice the size of the Snader he was running beside, whom they recognized as Dyson. His tall, lanky body was a contrast to the other two.

The first robot Red Fox had knocked down attempted to get up. Dyson flipped a switch on the robot's back and it stopped moving. "Do you always have to destroy the robots? They can't be repaired overnight, you know."

Red Fox chuckled. "Relax, Dyson. That's what this training facility is for. We need to be prepared for the day we get to destroy real Gudes and humans."

"That must be what the purple aliens are called—Gudes," Allison whispered to Josh.

"I know," Dyson said. "But you can beat them without destroying them."

"What fun would that be?" Red Fox and the big guy chuckled. "Besides, Fungus and I help build and repair these robots as much as you do."

Josh and Allison looked at each other. "Fungus?" Allison mouthed.

"Do you think we will ever be able to talk the others into leaving this place?" Fungus' voice was squeaky—a lot different from what Allison had expected.

"I know we will," Red Fox snarled. "We just need to figure out how to motivate them."

"None of us has ever been in a real fight, except the Original Four. And that was over sixty years ago," Dyson countered.

"That's why everyone," Red Fox glared at Dyson when he said 'everyone', "needs to come down here and do their training. We will rise to fight again!"

Allison thought that fighting brought too much pleasure to Red Fox.

"I know," Dyson said, not sounding like he agreed with Red Fox. "I still think we should send out a scout team. No one has been above ground in sixty-six years. We don't know exactly what we will face if we get up there."

"When we get up there," Fungus corrected him. "Don't worry about the humans. They were so far behind our technology sixty years ago that we could stay down here for another hundred years and still have the advantage over them. All our technology works fine. They won't have a chance against us. Besides, when we attack we will have the element of surprise."

Fungus seemed like a dangerous combination—big and smart.

"Help me carry this robot back to the shop, little brother," Red Fox commanded Dyson.

Red Fox grabbed the robot's shoulders and Dyson picked up the legs. Fungus picked up the robot next to them and carried it easily by himself.

After they had left the arena, Allison looked at Josh. "Did you hear that?"

"Yeah, that guy's name is Fungus. Who names their kid Fungus?" Josh was serious.

"No," Allison said. "They want to attack Earth. We have to warn somebody that they are down here."

"First, we have to figure out how to get out of here."

"Maybe Dyson has something in his room that talks about how to get to the surface," Allison suggested.

"That's a good idea," Josh agreed. "We should get back to the spaceship anyway. We have to beat Dyson back or we could end up locked out of the spaceship for the night. I don't want to hang down here any more than I have to."

CHAPTER 28

"What are you doing?" Flipper asked Jake. "Did you escape?"

"Yeah. How about you?"

"It's a long story. How did you get out?"

"They tried to kill me but it didn't work."

"What?! They tried to kill you?"

"Yes, they put these jars of chemicals on the backs of my hands and waited for me to spill or drop them." Jake held the jar up so Flipper could see it. "The chemical burns right through you, and I mean all of you." He paused and his voice became somber. "Trust me, it does."

Flipper was angry. "They said they weren't going to hurt you."

"Who said they weren't going to hurt me?"

"Captain Kreeker told me they wanted to keep you as insurance to make sure I did what they wanted and so they would have leverage against your dad."

"What do they want you to do?"

Flipper realized he said more than he should. He was even more confused about what to do. "I don't know. They are going to let me escape with the others as long as I help them later." He hated to lie to Jake, but the Snaders had treated them a lot better than the Gudes. They had treated him as one of their own, which he was. He felt an odd bond with Jake, but the Gudes had not been good to him.

"You were going to leave me here?" Jake's tone reflected his surprise.

"I'm sorry, but it was a chance to get the others safely home. Besides, they told me the Gudes were the ones that were fighting against them and trying to take over Earth."

"And you believe them?" Jake was astonished.

"Why wouldn't I?" Flipper snapped. "The Snaders healed my legs and promised to take me home. Your dad had me kidnapped and made me fight a dragon where I got my legs paralyzed."

Jake's whole body tensed and Flipper could tell he struck a nerve. "I don't blame my dad for bringing you to Vetrix. I read the computer's assessment and, well, I can't explain it but I had a strong feeling you could help us. That's why we stole a spaceship and came to rescue you."

Why did everything have to be so confusing? Jake was right; they had risked their lives to come help him. "You're right, Jake. I do appreciate it. Let's go get the others and get out of here."

Flipper started to walk away but Jake stopped him. "You go get the others. I'll turn myself in so you guys can escape safely."

"No! I don't know who's right or wrong, the Gudes or the Snaders. I don't trust either side. You've been a good friend and I was wrong to agree to leave without you."

Jake smiled. "You have a plan to get us out of here?"

"Yes. I have the keys to unlock Nicole, Chezlor and Alya from the dungeon. I have a map to get us from the dungeon to the spaceship so we can fly out of here. They are letting us go as long as we don't try to rescue you, but when they find out you have escaped they are going to come after us. We better hurry."

Flipper displayed the keys from his pocket then quickly unlocked the chains still around Jake's wrists and ankles.

Just as they were about to run Jake grabbed Flipper's arm. "I have an idea. You go unlock Nicole, Chezlor and Alya and I'll be right back." He ran in the opposite direction.

"Where are you going?" Flipper shouted after him.

"To make it look like I died!"

***

Jake went as quickly as he could back down the hall and up the stairs. He returned to the room he had been chained up in and set the jar down. Jake dragged what was left of the guard's body into the room and left it in the spot where he had been chained. He picked up both jars and stepped out of the room. He tossed one of the jars towards the dead guard and ran.

The room exploded.

***

Flipper followed his memory to the dungeon room where Nicole, Alya and Chezlor were. He unlocked the door, opened it and looked in.

"Flipper!" Nicole and Alya screamed.

They were each chained to the wall and weren't able to sit. Flipper could tell they were tired. In fact, he thought it looked like they had all been crying. He suddenly felt bad for all the special treatment and rest he had received over the last couple of days.

"Did you escape?" Alya asked excitedly.

"Kind of… It's a long story," Flipper tried to avert the question as he ran to Alya and started unlocking her chains.

"It's so good to see you," Nicole beamed.

Once Alya was free she gave Flipper a big hug, making him blush. "Thank you."

He hurried over to Nicole to unlock her. "Flipper, what happened to your legs? You couldn't move them a few days ago. I thought you might never walk again."

"The Snaders fixed them. My legs are as good as new." Flipper jumped up and down, reminded of the excitement he had felt at having the use of his legs returned.

"Why would they do that?" Nicole wondered aloud.

Flipper hesitated. "I'm not talking about you because you came to get me, but the Snaders have been a lot nicer to me than the Gudes have. I still don't know which side I should help. I wish I wasn't involved." The silence felt awkward. "We need to get out of here before I change my mind."

"Thank you," Nicole said as Flipper finished freeing her.

Flipper noticed that Chezlor hadn't said anything. He went over to him and could tell he was upset. Flipper started unlocking his chains. "Are you okay, Chezlor?"

Chezlor didn't reply.

"He's having a really hard time; we all have been, since we heard about Jake," Nicole was somber.

"What did you hear about Jake?" Flipper asked.

"Oh, I assumed you knew." Nicole paused, choking on her words. "They killed Jake."

Flipper had finished unlocking Chezlor's legs and stood up. He had forgotten about Captain Kreeker's story and felt horrible for not mentioning that Jake was fine when he first entered the room. "No, they didn't."

"They didn't what?" Alya asked.

"They didn't kill…"

"Jake!" Chezlor ran to Jake, who was standing in the doorway, and gave him a big hug.

Jake held his arm out, away from Chezlor, being careful not to spill or drop the deadly chemical inside the jar. "Easy, Chezlor! This jar will explode if I drop it."

Nicole and Alya each gave him a gentle hug. Jake looked at the three of them crying, then looked at Flipper and, with a puzzled expression, mouthed, "What's going on?"

Flipper put his hand over his mouth to stifle his laugh.

"Okay, that's more than enough affection for one day," Jake said, clearly uncomfortable.

Alya pulled back and looked at him. "We thought you were dead."

"I am now."

"What?" Chezlor asked, confused.

Jake smiled triumphantly. "The Snaders tried to kill me, but I escaped and made it look like they blew me up." He looked at Chezlor. "And I have you to thank for it."

"What did I do now?" Chezlor asked.

"I'll tell you all about it later, but right now we need to get out of here."

"I have a map to get us from here to our spaceship, but we need to hurry." Flipper was in the hall motioning for them to follow. "If they figure out Jake isn't dead they are going to come after us."

"Won't they come after us anyway?" Alya asked.

Flipper looked at Jake. "They were going to let us go if we didn't try to rescue Jake. When they find out he's with us, they aren't going to be willing participants in our escape."

"Then lead the way." Chezlor motioned his arm for Flipper to guide them.

As they started, Jake pulled the gun out of his pocket and handed it to Nicole. "Here, we may need this."

Nicole took the gun. "Where did you get this?"

"I took it off a guard."

She raised her eyebrows and gave Jake an impressed look.

CHAPTER 29

They were halfway to the spaceship when alarms began blaring from every corner of the hallway.

"Now we're in trouble," Jake said. "My trick must not have fooled them."

"Let's run," Flipper yelled, and they all ran as fast as they could.

They didn't get far before Nicole stopped, the rest behind her following suit. They could see in the distance ahead, two men heading towards them.

There was a door to their right, so Nicole tried it. When it opened she said, "Quick, everyone in here."

They all darted into the room and Nicole shut the door. They waited quietly, listening as the men neared, but stopped short of their door. They heard the men knock on a door down the hall, kick the door open and fire several shots. The pattern repeated door after door as the men got closer to their hiding spot.

"They'll find us in just a few minutes. What are we going to do?" Alya asked.

"I have an idea," Jake said. "Everyone get back."

The group carefully made their way through complete darkness to the wall farthest from the door. Jake put his ear to the door and listened. Every few seconds the sound of a door being kicked in and shots being fired rang louder. Jake knew he needed to be patient and get his timing perfect. If he miscalculated their distance and they got too close, the men would kill them all. When he thought they were the ideal distance away, he anxiously waited for them to kick open the door. The moment he heard them shoot, he opened his door, stepped into the hallway and tossed the jar at them. The men turned towards Jake and aimed their weapons. The jar exploded before they could fire. Jake dove back into the room, narrowly avoiding the brunt of the blast.

***

Chezlor, Alya and Flipper helped Jake off the ground and checked to see if he was okay. They quietly waited a few moments, listening for any movement from outside the room. Nicole peeked into the hallway. When the smoke cleared, she stepped out of the room, pointing the gun in the direction of the men. There was a large hole in the floor and massive damage to the walls but no sign of them.

She shouted to the others. "It's safe, but we're going to have to find another way to the spaceship."

The others filed out of the room and saw the hole that stood between them and their freedom.

Flipper took out the map and started looking for another way to the spaceship. "It looks like we are going to have to backtrack. Follow me."

He ran down the hallway with Nicole right behind him, gun in hand. The others followed behind her. They came to some stairs and made their way up. They were six levels below ground so they had to climb a lot of steps. When they got to the top of the stairs, they tried to walk quickly down the hallway without making noise.

Flipper suddenly stopped and looked back. "I hear someone coming." They ducked into the closest room.

Tense and tired, they shut the door and waited. The room was small and there were too many of them with too few places to hide. As the footsteps grew louder and louder they prepared to pounce when the door opened. The door did not open and soon the footsteps began fading away. Flipper had to push away several beakers and tubes to lay the map flat on the table in the middle of the room. Nicole and Jake gathered around him to study the map.

Flipper pointed. "If we keep going this same direction, it will lead us straight to their main headquarters."

"The only other way out, according to this map, is the underground tunnel with the big hole in the middle of it," Nicole noticed.

"It looks like there is a door to the roof," Jake observed.

Nicole pondered a moment. "That might be a possibility, if we can find a way off the roof."

Suddenly, they heard a voice reverberate throughout the room. "Blake, Flipper, it's me, Dr. Needles. Brianna is with me. We are in a secret passageway behind the back wall. We are unarmed and want to help you. There is a hidden door we can open and come through, but only if you want our help."

Everyone looked around. There were no speakers in sight, yet Dr. Needles' voice seemed to come from every direction.

Nicole studied the back wall but didn't see a door. There were shelves lining half the wall, a filing cabinet in the middle, and pictures of what appeared to be the Snader anatomy on the other side. Nicole didn't like this development.

"We can't trust any of the Lizards," Chezlor said.

"I'm not willing to take a chance," Nicole confirmed.

"What do you think, Flipper?" Jake asked.

Flipper dropped his head. Nicole felt sorry for him, aware he was feeling the pressure of making such a big decision.

"I like Dr. Needles and Brianna and think I trust them. They haven't lied to me."

"Let's not forget they have the special power of persuasion," Chezlor chimed in.

Flipper looked at him, puzzled. "What does that mean?"

Nicole explained. "One of the Snaders' special abilities is that they are persuasive. They are able to make others do and believe things they normally wouldn't be inclined to. It's not quite mind control but is very similar. It's a dangerous weapon they know how to use well."

"So you're afraid they could convince us to turn ourselves in?" Flipper asked.

"Or that they've already convinced you they are nice and trustworthy and they aren't," Chezlor added.

"I..I'm..." Flipper grappled with what to say but resolved to remain quiet.

"If we don't agree to let them in, they may let the others know where we are," Jake said.

"But there isn't any way to know if we can trust them," Alya lamented.

"There may be," Jake said. "I'll go see if they have weapons."

"You can't go in there by yourself!" Alya protested.

"We have no other way of knowing their intentions," Jake argued. "If I come back that means they are unarmed. If I don't… Well, open fire."

Jake looked at Nicole and she could tell he was awaiting her approval. Like it or not, she was the adult, so they would look to her to make the hard decisions. What would she tell General Jaxxen if she let his son walk into a trap? Nicole was used to giving her opinion about what to do in tough situations but she wasn't used to being the one who ultimately made the final decision. She had a new appreciation for the pressure General Jaxxen faced. She turned to Jake and nodded her head, then looked back at the wall and hoped Flipper was right in trusting these two Snaders.

Jake walked over to the wall. "Dr. Needles, this is Jake. Open the door. I'm coming in to make sure you and Brianna don't have weapons!"

Instantly, the filing cabinet slowly slid forward. A narrow opening was revealed but it was too dark to see into. Jake looked back at Nicole and stepped into the darkness. Time slowed. What was perhaps thirty seconds seemed like several minutes to Nicole.

Finally, they heard Jake's voice. "They're unarmed!"

***

Slowly, Dr. Needles and Brianna stepped out of the darkness with their hands in the air. Jake followed behind them and saw everyone breathe a collective sigh of relief.

Dr. Needles looked at Flipper first. "I'm glad you're okay. I'm glad you're all okay."

"Why should we trust you?" Chezlor demanded.

Dr. Needles looked at each of them and lastly at Nicole, who still held the gun towards him and Brianna.

"You don't have any reason to trust us, but we don't have much time. Captain Kreeker will be here soon."

He looked back at Flipper. "I'm sorry, but when we fixed your legs we put in a tracking device. We can track you wherever you go, anywhere in the universe. That's how I knew you were in here. And that's why Captain Kreeker will be here any minute."

"I was able to jam the signal," Brianna said, "but the captain will have someone get past the jam soon. I can do a more permanent scramble on the tracking device but I need time."

"There's something you need to know." Dr. Needles looked at Nicole. "I have something in my pocket I need to show Flipper."

"Keep one hand in the air and move very slowly," Nicole instructed.

Dr. Needles reached into his lab coat pocket and pulled out a small device. "What is that?" Nicole asked.

160

"I have Flipper's medical information on here," Dr. Needles explained. "It has everything—all our examinations, test results—everything. I want you to have it, but I need to tell you something first. We weren't completely honest with you earlier."

"What are you talking about?" Flipper asked.

With his thumb Dr. Needles pressed a few buttons on the device. "It's true that you have a Snader as an ancestor but what..."

Everyone gasped.

"What do you mean Flipper has a Snader as an ancestor?" Nicole asked Dr. Needles.

"I'm sorry," Dr. Needles said apologetically. "Of course, he hasn't had a chance to tell you yet. We ran tests on him using his hair, blood and skin. We discovered that Flipper has a Snader ancestor—probably a grandparent or a great grandparent."

"Are you serious?" Chezlor asked.

"Yes. We ran the tests multiple times and are sure of the results. I want Flipper to take this with him. Your people will be able to verify the results are accurate." Dr. Needles turned and looked at Flipper. "But there's more. The tests we ran showed you also had a Gude as an ancestor. The test showed it was the same distance as the Snader ancestor—probably a grandparent or a great grandparent. Captain Kreeker didn't want you to know this so we withheld that information from you. I'm sorry—you have a right to know."

Flipper was speechless. He tried to process Dr. Needles' words. What did it mean? Where did he come from? Who was he really? Flipper became lost in his thoughts, flipping the folded map in his hands and tuning everyone else out.

Nicole handed the gun to Jake. She looked him in the eyes, "If they try anything, shoot them both."

Nicole walked over to Dr. Needles. "Let me see that."

Dr. Needles handed Nicole the device. She fiddled with it for a few minutes while everyone watched and waited. "This looks legitimate. We won't know for sure until we get home and test it, but I think he's telling the truth."

Nicole looked at Dr. Needles. "Bruce and Ava?"

Dr. Needles nodded his head. "That's what we believe."

"Who are Bruce and Ava?" Chezlor asked curiously.

"I'll explain later," Nicole said. She turned to give the device to Flipper. That's when everyone noticed he was flipping the map and pacing.

"Flipper, are you okay?" Nicole asked.

Hearing his name snapped Flipper back into the moment. "What?"

Nicole squatted down and put her hand on his arm. "Are you okay?"

"I don't know." Flipper was grasping for what to say. He looked up at Nicole. "I guess so." He looked towards the ground. He was clearly not okay.

Nicole felt sorry for him. However, they didn't have time to dwell on it. She knew she needed to get them out of there and hoped he could hold it together. "Flipper, I know this is a lot to take in. We will help you figure it all out but right now we need to get out of here."

Flipper looked up at Nicole again. She smiled at him and he nodded. She continued to look at him. "We came because we believe the computer was correct. You are the key to protecting Vetrix and Earth. Any doubts I had before this moment are gone. We can and will get you safely out of here."

"Thanks," Flipper said, forcing a grin.

Nicole handed the device to Flipper. He looked at it for a moment and put it in his pocket. Nicole stood. "Jake, you can take the gun off of Dr. Needles and Brianna. We need to get out of here."

"I know how to get you to your ship without being seen. There are some hidden passageways that very few people know about. I can guide you through them," Dr. Needles offered.

"Let's get going," Nicole said as everyone turned toward the back wall to leave through the opening.

Suddenly, the door burst open and they heard the captain's voice. "Stop right there! Put your hands in the air where I can see them and slowly turn around."

***

Everyone froze. Captain Kreeker had a gun aimed at them and certainly more troops would follow.

Flipper felt exhausted and helpless. What else could go wrong?

Nicole, Chezlor, Alya, and Flipper put their hands in the air. He saw Jake slowly, reluctantly, lower his gun. Their eyes met as Jake shook his head in defeat. Suddenly Flipper had an idea. He rolled his eyes desperately from Jake to Dr. Needles and Brianna. They may be the only hope of getting away.

Jake abruptly spun and aimed his gun at Dr. Needles. The Captain gave a sinister grin. "Don't try anything stupid, kid."

Flipper thought he saw Jake give Dr. Needles a quick wink. "If you don't leave, I'm going to take out your doctor and nurse." Jake's threat sounded so convincing Flipper wasn't sure if he was bluffing or had gone mad. He hoped the first.

"Be smart, you have a lot more people to lose here."

"You've already tried to kill me once. Why would I believe you are going to let any of us live? If we can't escape, I might as well take as many down as I can."

There was a pause before Brianna spoke up. "Captain Kreeker, I'm so glad you're here. We tried to sneak up on them from behind, but they heard us coming."

"Dr. Needles, Brianna, I want you to slowly walk around these scum and over to me." The Captain kept his eyes on Jake. "Don't be a fool. I want you to set the gun down and sit against the wall." There was something different about his voice now. It was slow and calculated. "I want you all to sit against the wall."

Jake obeyed, as did the others. Flipper watched as they each sat down. Something was odd. What happened to their fight? He looked at Alya. Her fear was gone. She looked relaxed. They all did. That's when it hit him! This must be what they told him about the persuasive powers the Snaders have. The Captain hadn't convinced them to obey—he was controlling them!

But Flipper wasn't being controlled. He looked at Dr. Needles and Brianna, then turned to see Nicole, Alya, Chezlor, and Jake, sitting calmly against the wall. Captain Kreeker and Flipper met eyes. "Sit down with the Gudes."

Maybe he could try to convince Captain Kreeker he was still working with him. After all, it wasn't his fault Jake escaped. Maybe he could still get his ride home and away from this crazy mess. Instead he picked up the gun Jake had set on the table and aimed it at the captain. "No!"

The captain couldn't have looked more surprised if Flipper had slapped him in the face. "How...What..."

Behind Captain Kreeker, Dr. Needles smiled. "Remember, Captain, he has Snader blood in him."

"Your persuasive power doesn't work on me," Flipper boasted, "and neither will your gun."

The captain's eyes narrowed. "Which means, of course, your gun will not work on me."

Flipper had to admit that was a good point. Before he could consider his next move the captain continued. "However, my gun will work just fine on your friends."

Okay, that was an even better point. Flipper tossed the gun back onto the table like the useless item it was.

"Dr. Needles, do you have anything in here to tie these people up with?" The Captain asked.

"Yes, Sir." Dr. Needles stepped back towards a cupboard and opened it.

"Brianna, call in our location so the troops can come secure our prisoners," the Captain said as he handed his radio to her.

"Yes, Sir."

Brianna took the radio and spoke into it while looking back at Dr. Needles. "Attention! All troops! This is Brianna, Dr. Needles' nurse. I am with Dr. Needles and Captain Kreeker. The Gudes are trying to escape with the Earthling. They are underground heading south, away from their own spaceship. We assume they have someone on the inside, one of our own Snaders, to fly them out in one of our spaceships. All troops head immediately to the main hangar and make sure none of our spaceships take off."

The Captain turned sharply towards Brianna but before he could say anything, Dr. Needles inserted a needle into the back of his neck. Dr. Needles caught the Captain as he collapsed.

Brianna continued talking on the radio. "Dr. Needles is heading to the Gudes' spaceship with the Captain. They will use the Gudes' own spaceship against the intruders if they are able to take off in one of ours. Be careful, you don't know who you can trust out there."

Nicole and the kids looked stunned.

"Well played, son," Dr. Needles said to Jake as he dragged the Captain across the room and into the darkness of the wall.

Alya looked at Jake, "You knew what you were doing the whole time, didn't you?"

Chezlor added, "That was an amazing bluff!"

"That was very brave. You're going to make a great leader," Nicole added.

"Thank you. It was Flipper's idea," Jake said modestly.

"How could that have been Flipper's idea? He couldn't say anything," Chezlor challenged him.

"He looked at me and rolled his eyes towards Dr. Needles," Jake bragged as he looked at Flipper. "I don't know how, but I knew what he was thinking."

Flipper nodded his head. "I knew Dr. Needles and Brianna were our only hope of getting away from the Captain. We couldn't let him know they were helping us or we didn't stand a chance."

Chezlor looked at Brianna, "What if no one believes what you just said over the radio?"

"They will," Brianna said. "I was calling from Captain Kreeker's radio and only he has the access code to it. No one will doubt the authenticity of my message."

Dr. Needles stepped back into the room. "We bought some time to escape but we still need to hurry. Eventually, someone will figure out what is happening."

Brianna walked over to Flipper and put her hand on his shoulder. "It was a wonderful honor to meet you, Flipper. I will cherish this experience for the rest of my life. I wish you total success in your mission, which I do not doubt you will have."

Flipper got emotional. "Can't you come with us?"

Brianna shook her head. "No, I am going to stay here and scramble the controls so you can't be traced through your leg. Otherwise, you will never be safe. It's going to take me longer than you have time to wait."

"But what will happen to you?" Alya asked.

"Don't worry about that, dear."

"The Captain is going to know you helped us escape," Flipper protested.

"Yes," Brianna admitted. "No matter my fate, I don't want to flee just for the sake of saving my life when I can stay and advance the greater good. I would rather die young doing something to make a positive impact on the universe than to live a long empty life. This is my chance to invest my life and I am going to take it."

Flipper grabbed and hugged her, choking back tears, as they all were.

"Th-Thank you for everything," Flipper managed to choke out.

"You're welcome. Now you get going. My staying won't do any good if you don't escape."

Dr. Needles and Brianna looked at each other. Dr. Needles tipped his head to her. "Follow me," he said to the others, as he disappeared into the wall.

They each thanked Brianna quickly as they passed her before following Dr. Needles into the wall. When the last had gone, Flipper let go and looked up at her. "I'll never forget you."

Brianna smiled as Flipper reluctantly left her and followed everyone into the wall.

CHAPTER 30

Dr. Needles led the group through several hidden passageways and tunnels. They encountered no resistance, just as he had said.

"We need to go a little past the spaceship and then backtrack to it," Dr. Needles said. "That way, we are less likely to be spotted."

"How do you know where all of these secret tunnels go?" Flipper asked.

"My dad was in charge of building this facility," Dr. Needles explained. "I grew up playing in these tunnels while the buildings were being erected. He showed me all of them. I would sit and look at his blueprints for hours. My brother and sisters and I played a lot of hide and seek down here. I've known every inch of this place most of my life. This is it." Dr. Needles climbed up a ladder. He pressed some buttons and the ceiling above slid open. After they had all climbed up, Dr. Needles closed the floor. They were standing in what appeared to be a small utility room with a lot of computers and electronic equipment.

Dr. Needles cracked open the door and peeked outside. "Good, I don't see anyone."

They stepped outside.

"You need to get to your spaceship and take off as quickly as possible. I am going to sabotage the communication equipment and do what I can to keep anyone from following you."

"You aren't going with us either?" Flipper was flabbergasted.

Dr. Needles looked at Flipper. "I would like nothing more. You're a special young man and I believe in you. I can do you the most good by staying here to ensure your escape. Go and fight—until we meet again."

"Thank you for everything." Flipper gave Dr. Needles a big hug. "My legs and everything. Even for scaring me." Flipper pulled away and looked up at Dr. Needles. He smiled at Flipper and then ruffled Flipper's hair with his hand. Flipper started choking up again, but they didn't have time for a long or emotional farewell.

Nicole looked at Dr. Needles. "Thank you."

Dr. Needles nodded.

Nicole took charge. "Let's get off this planet!"

They ran. Chezlor was at the spaceship in a few seconds; it took the others at least a minute.

"How did you run that fast?" Flipper asked, panting.

"It's a special ability. I was born that way."

"Do all Gudes have a special ability?"

"No, just a few of us," Chezlor said.

As they started up the stairs, Nicole barked out orders. "I'll start the spaceship and prepare for take-off. Jake, sit beside me in the co-pilot's chair and help me. Chezlor, make sure the door is shut and secure. Alya, do a sweep of the spaceship and make sure everything is turned on. Flipper, find a seat and get strapped in."

They each quickly completed their task. Within a couple of minutes, they were all strapped into their seats and ready to go.

Nicole shouted, "Hang on, here we go!"

Flipper was scared and excited as the spaceship rose. As he had been asleep when the Snader left Rex after kidnapping him, this was his first conscious spaceship take off. After just a few seconds of rising straight up, Nicole pulled back and the ship leapt forward.

CHAPTER 31

Josh and Allison ate some of the yellowish plants, but neither of them tried the dirt. When they finished, Allison set the transmitter to show the outdoor cameras so they would know when Dyson returned. They went to Dyson's room and searched for information on how to get to the surface. Allison flipped through the book she had looked through earlier. Josh snooped around the room for any clue that might help them escape.

"This is just a history book. It's interesting as it talks about what they've been doing down here, but I don't see anything that will help us get home."

"I may have something here."

Josh held an electronic device in his hands and was trying to figure out how it worked. "This shows a picture of a spaceship flying out of the ground." He handed the device to Allison. "See if you can get it to show us more."

Allison took the device and handed him the transmitter to watch for Dyson. After a few moments she said, "Josh, I-I-look at this."

Josh sat down beside her on the floor. Allison set the screen between them so they could both watch. "It looks like a simulated attack."

They watched as hundreds of spaceships flew from the underground hideout, straight up through a tunnel in the ground. The first few spaceships attacked large cities close to Roswell—Albuquerque,

Dallas, Phoenix, and Denver. Spaceships kept spreading out in every direction, eventually covering the whole Earth. The simulated time for the total conquer of Earth was just over a week.

"That's scary!" Allison said.

"So these guys even have a plan," Josh said. "But in their simulation, there isn't anyone fighting back. Surely we are going to fight back?"

"Unless they know how to keep us from fighting back," Allison pondered.

"How could they do that?" Josh asked.

"I don't know, but with their technology we don't know what they are capable of."

Allison fiddled with the device for a while before she decided she wasn't going to find any more information on it. "Where did you get this? I'll put it back."

"It was lying on the floor underneath the bed," Josh said.

Allison lay down on the floor and slid the device underneath the bed. When she slid it back she felt the floor move. There wasn't enough room under the bed for her to get a good look, so she felt around with her fingers. She found a crack and used her fingers to pry. Up popped a square board. She held her breath and felt around in the hole. She felt something move but couldn't quite grasp it to pull out.

"Josh, I can feel something in here but I can't get it. Will you see if you can pull it out?"

Josh handed her the transmitter and crawled on the floor. His arms were a little longer and he grabbed the item without much trouble. He pulled it out and sat up.

"Here," he said, trading Allison for the transmitter.

She studied it. "It looks like some type of recorder."

She pushed a button and up popped Dyson's face. His face wasn't as dark red as he had looked to them earlier. His face was smooth and he looked younger than he did now, maybe not much older than they were. When he spoke, they noticed his voice wasn't as deep as it had sounded in the arena.

"I don't know what to do any more. I've grown tired of Red Fox's constant talk of fighting and conquering. We have a great life down here. Why do we need to leave? And if we did leave, why not go back to our own home planet? The Earthlings haven't done anything to us. Sure, they shot down some of our spaceships and captured our people, but we were intruding into their world. Anyone would have done the same to protect their planet.

"There are thousands of us down here and no one has ever seen a human or a Gude, yet many of us act like it's their fault we live underground in seclusion. Whatever war there was between us and the Gudes could have ended decades ago, for all we know. We haven't had contact with the world outside our colony for nearly sixty years.

"My brother, Red Fox, is the worst. All he thinks about is the day he will get to fight the humans and then the Gudes. I love my brother but I don't agree with him. I'm so glad I found this spaceship to live in so that I can get away by myself.

"The others agree with him, but most of them want to stay down here. They like it here. However, more and more of them are being persuaded by Red Fox. It probably won't be long before he talks the majority of our colony into leaving. I hope not, but he is so determined. I wish there was a way to change his mind."

Josh and Allison had been so engrossed in the video that they hadn't kept an eye on the transmitter. Josh glanced at it and saw that Dyson was walking toward the ship. He almost shouted in his panic, "Dyson's coming!"

Allison tried clumsily to turn off the recorder. "I can't get it off."

"We have to hurry!" Josh hissed.

"Cover the hole under his bed, we have to get out of here!" Allison said, flustered.

"What about the recorder?" Josh asked.

"We'll have to take it and bring it back later. We can't leave it here or he will hear it and know someone has been here."

Josh hurriedly covered the hole and they made sure everything was back the way it had been when they entered. They left Dyson's room and shut the door.

Josh watched the transmitter. "Allison, he's coming up the stairs. If we try to go back to our room he'll see us."

"In here," Allison said, opening the door to the cockpit. They hurried inside and shut the door. They ran over to the cots and crawled underneath them. The sound of the spaceship door closing drowned out the sound of Dyson talking on the recorder.

"If we don't get that turned off, Dyson is going to hear it when he goes to his room," Josh said.

"I know, I'm working on it!" Allison snapped.

She couldn't figure out how to turn off the recorder but as the door shut, she found the volume button and muted Dyson's voice. They lay underneath the cots for a long time. Allison used the transmitter to find Dyson in the kitchen. He took his time eating and drinking before he went to his room. They remained quietly beneath the cots until Dyson had been in his room for a few minutes. They cautiously crawled out and sat in two of the chairs. While Allison had been lying under the cot, she had been able to get the recorder turned off. As they sat and talked, she set the recorder and the transmitter down. They didn't need to watch Dyson when they could hear him moving around in the next room.

"Did you get it turned off?" Josh asked.

Allison nodded. "Dyson sounds so miserable."

"Are you feeling sorry for him? He's one of the enemy," Josh said.

"Maybe not. You heard him, Josh. He's not like the others. Maybe he would help us."

"I don't know. I think it's too risky to ask him," Josh said.

"Do you have a better idea for getting out of here?" she asked.

"Well, no, not yet," Josh admitted.

They sat in silence for a few minutes.

"Josh, what if we can't find Flipper? What if we never get back home?"

Josh stood and paced. "Don't talk like that."

"But we're lost—trapped miles underground. How will we ever find our way back?"

"By not giving up!" Josh sounded more confident than he felt. "I know it's lonely and scary down here, but we will get home."

"How?" Allison almost pleaded.

Josh shook his head. They were tired, homesick, and neither of them had an answer. After a long silence, they decided to sneak back to their room.

As Allison lay on the cot, Josh asked, "Are you going to try to dream again?"

"I don't know," Allison sighed. "I don't know how not to dream and I don't know how to control my dreams. I'm scared to go to sleep because I could end up anywhere, but I'm also so tired because I'm not getting any sleep."

"I wish I could help," Josh said. "And I really wish you could go to Rex to find Flipper."

"Where do you suppose they got the name Rex from?" Allison pondered.

"Maybe it means red in Snader talk," Josh joked.

They fell silent as Allison slowly drifted off to sleep.

CHAPTER 32

After Nicole and the kids fled Rex, it took them a couple of hours to relax. They kept expecting Snader spaceships to come after them. Thankfully, Dr. Needles must have been successful in preventing the Snader spacecraft from taking off after them. Flipper hadn't said a word since they left; Alya could see the concern in his eyes.

"I'm sure Dr. Needles and Brianna are going to be okay."

"No, they won't," Flipper sulked. "The Snaders seem like the type that will torture or kill them for what they did."

Nicole spoke up, "Dr. Needles is a very clever man but even if he gets caught, he is doing what he believed was the best thing for the universe. He is a hero. And so is Brianna."

Flipper choked up and didn't say any more. The cockpit fell into a somber silence for a few minutes.

"Who are Bruce and Ava?" Chezlor asked, breaking it. "You and the doctor mentioned them. They sounded mysterious."

"Bruce and Ava fought against the Snaders decades ago when the Snaders were on the rise, shortly after their rebellion against the sanctions. Many believe they are mythical because they lived in space. There weren't any planets that would allow them to settle."

"Why not?" Jake asked.

Nicole paused before continuing. "Bruce was a Snader. Ava was a Gude. No one trusted Bruce because he was a Snader. Most thought he was using his marriage with Ava as a cover to build trust and penetrate other life groups. Not even the Gudes would allow them to land on their planet. There was too much to risk."

They all listened intently to Nicole. Alya asked, "How does that relate to Flipper?"

"Bruce and Ava had a son, Robb, who fought with them," Nicole explained. "They were shot down and crashed on Earth when they were trying to defend Earth against a Snader spaceship. The crash happened near Roswell, where Flipper and his family live."

Flipper sat up straight as a light bulb went off in his head. "The Roswell Incident!"

"Yes, what you Earthlings refer to as the 'Roswell Incident'," Nicole said.

"But there was only one spaceship that crashed. My friend Josh just did a report on it."

"That's what your government told you because that's what they want you to believe."

"So there were two spaceships that crashed?" Flipper asked, confused.

"Yes," Nicole confirmed.

"Why does it matter if we think there're one or two spaceships?"

"We don't know. I suppose it's easier for your government to explain away one spaceship, rather than two. Besides, the eyewitnesses never claimed to have seen two different spaceships."

"I wonder what happened to the spaceships?"

"Your military would have taken and run tests on them, attempting to understand some of our technology."

"Did anyone survive the crash?" Chezlor asked.

"We had assumed all these years that Bruce, Ava and Robb were all killed in the crash, but if Robb survived and had a baby with a human, then that child would be part Gude, part Snader, and part human," Nicole explained.

Although what Nicole said made sense, Flipper couldn't accept it as real. "So, you are saying that my grandma or grandpa is an alien?"

"That's what it looks like. We won't know more until we have your tests analyzed, but I don't think there is any reason to doubt Dr. Needles' conclusions."

Flipper was quiet for a moment, wishing he had something to flip in his hands as he thought about having aliens as grandparents. "Why would the Snaders want to attack Earth? Are they just bullies?"

The kids chuckled. Nicole smiled. "Actually, that's part of it. The Snaders are mean, like to fight, and they don't care about anyone or anything except themselves."

"Dr. Needles and Brianna weren't mean," Flipper countered.

"No, they weren't. Occasionally a Snader will recognize the evil behavior of their kind but until today, I had never seen it."

"It seems that the only enemies the Snaders have are the ones they make by attacking others," Flipper observed.

"Hm... That's true," Nicole said, "but they don't see it that way."

"You said that being bullies was part of the reason the Snaders attacked Earth. What are the others?" Flipper asked.

"Like the Gudes, the Snaders live long lives, sometimes three to four times longer than humans. Unlike us, the Snaders reproduce very quickly. The Snaders can outgrow a smaller planet within a few hundred years. They are constantly looking for new places to inhabit.

"The Snaders have been harassing the planets of the universe for tens of thousands of years, ever since they developed the technology to travel out of their solar system. A few thousand years ago, many of the planets united to fight against them. Eventually, the Consolidation was able to defeat the Snaders and confined them to three planets.

The Snaders signed a treaty agreeing not to attack any other inhabited planet ever again.

"The Snaders held to their agreement, at least until recently. We don't know how long they have been planning their attacks, but they have been carefully taking over planets and eliminating other life forms for the last two hundred years or so."

"You said that Bruce and Ava and Robb were trying to protect Earth from the Snaders. Why would they want to help protect Earth?" Flipper asked.

"When Bruce defected from the Snaders and married Ava, they made it their life to defend and protect Earth. It's a newly inhabited planet and your technology is inferior to much of the rest of the universe. You don't have a chance on your own. Vetrix is the closest inhabited planet to yours. The Gudes have been protecting Earth since we populated it thousands of years ago.

"Wait! What?! The Gudes populated Earth?" Flipper was stunned.

"Yes," Nicole said. "Ten thousand years ago during the war, the Snaders wiped out a whole planet, Gordone. The Snaders inhabited and slowly eliminated all the natural life forms on Gordone. A group of Gordonians tried to escape from the attack but the Snaders shot their ship down. There were two survivors, the only two survivors from their planet. They were young—a boy and a girl—about your age.

"The two teenagers were very disturbed, suffering from severe trauma and shock. We worked with them for several years. They never talked about what they had experienced before their escape, but it had a tremendous effect on them. We slowly introduced them to animals and they responded well, but were never able to handle being around other people.

"Earth had been recently discovered by one of our explorers and tested to have an atmosphere similar to ours. There were no living beings on your planet at that time. It was decided that the best thing for the two survivors was to let them start over together on their own planet. They agreed, so we wiped their memory and set them up on Earth in a nice luscious garden."

"You wiped their memory?" Flipper was stunned. "How come?"

"It was at their request," Nicole explained. "They didn't want to remember anything from their past. We could have started them out any way they wanted, but they wanted it simple. They refused to have any technology—thought it had caused too much destruction in their lives. We understood and allowed them to relocate, if they would agree to let us protect them. They agreed, but they didn't want to know about it. They wanted their world to be alien and technology free. The Gudes agreed to do everything we could to protect Earth without humans ever knowing of our existence."

"Wow! They don't teach us any of this in our history classes."

Nicole laughed. "You're the first human to hear the true story of how Earth began."

Flipper let that sink in for a moment. "What were their names?"

"Brogs and Sind," Nicole said.

"Oh, that isn't what I expected you to say."

"Those were their original names. When they came to Earth they changed their names to Adam and Eve."

CHAPTER 33

"You can't do that," Alya whispered.

Chezlor tried not to laugh. "Just watch, it'll be so funny."

"You're so mean. I can't watch." She stormed back to the cockpit where Nicole and Jake sat.

Flipper had been exhausted, so Jake and Alya had taken him to one of the bedrooms on the spaceship. He had been asleep for nearly ten hours and they were nearing Vetrix.

Chezlor finished applying the hot sauce he found in the kitchen to Flipper's lips and rejoined the others in the cockpit.

A few minutes later, Flipper woke up screaming. "My lips are on fire! Help! They burn so bad!"

Alya couldn't stand it. She hurried back to Flipper and grabbed his hand. "Follow me."

She took him to the kitchen in the back of the ship. She got him a glass of water and he drank the whole thing. While he drank, she took a clean rag and wet it with cold water. When he finished drinking, she handed Flipper the rag and he held it on his lips.

"Are you okay?" Alya asked, concerned.

"Yeah, I think so."

"Here, let me rinse that out for you."

Flipper handed her the rag and she rinsed it off, then soaked it again with cold water and handed it back.

Flipper touched the rag to his lips. "Ouch! Ouch! Ouch!"

Alya grabbed Flipper's hand. Flipper squeezed her hand tightly, but she didn't pull away.

"I'm so sorry," Alya said.

"It's okay. It's not your fault," Flipper said. "I wonder what happened to my lips?"

Alya chuckled.

"What?"

Alya did her best to keep from laughing. "Chezlor put hot sauce on your lips."

They both laughed, until they realized at the same time that they were still holding hands. They quickly let go.

After a moment Flipper said, "Well that was awkward."

"I thought it was nice," Alya said and walked away.

Chapter 34

"It's about to be the moment of truth," Nicole announced.

They landed in the same spot they had left. Nicole called in their approach so the Gudes would know the spaceship returning from Rex was coming in on friendly terms.

"I can't believe General Jaxxen sent you guys to come get me," Flipper said.

"Well, he didn't exactly send us," Jake stammered.

"What do you mean?"

"We kind of tricked Nicole into helping us steal the spaceship to come rescue you," Alya confessed.

"Wow, you guys are really great! Thanks!" Flipper said.

Once the landing was complete, they saw General Jaxxen, Fox and Sierra walking towards the spaceship. General Jaxxen did not look happy.

"I'll go first," Nicole said. "This was my responsibility." No one argued with her.

As the door opened and the stairs lowered, several troops stood with weapons drawn, prepared for whatever or whoever might emerge from the spaceship. Once the stairs were down, several men ran up them. A soldier in front asked Nicole, "Are you alone?"

"Yes," she answered.

The other men filed past them and scattered throughout the spaceship.

"We need to make sure the ship is clear of any Snaders or items they may have planted," the soldier informed them. "You will be debriefed shortly. You may exit now."

"Thank you, Lieutenant," Nicole said.

They walked down the stairs where General Jaxxen waited with Fox and Sierra standing behind him.

Nicole stopped in front of General Jaxxen and stood at attention. "Sir, if I could…" she began.

General Jaxxen cut her off. "What you have done is irresponsible and inexcusable. What would possess you to think it was a good idea to run off to Rex with three children? You were one of my most trusted advisors and confidants but you betrayed me and your people! You will be lucky if you don't spend the rest of your life locked up!"

"But dad, it wasn't her fault!" Jake exclaimed.

"Quiet, Jake!" General Jaxxen pointed a silencing finger at his son. "I will deal with you in a moment." General Jaxxen turned to his right and addressed one of the soldiers. "Escort Major Style to the interrogation room and have two men stand guard."

As two soldiers marched off with Nicole, General Jaxxen turned his attention to the children. He looked straight at Jake and spoke with the same authority and anger he had used with Nicole.

"What were you thinking, running off like that? Fighting these Lizards isn't some game—it's war! You're lucky to still be alive. You should all be locked up like Nicole is going to be. You're just kids and don't know what you're doing. Jake, you have let me down. I expected you to be a great soldier someday, not a disappointment."

"Dad, you don't understand…" Jake tried to say.

"No excuses, son. I do understand. You, Chezlor and Alya get back down to the compound. I want you secured and safe. I'll be down later to deal with you." General Jaxxen turned again. "Soldier, make sure the three kids make it safely to the compound. Make sure they go straight there. And make sure they stay there!"

"Yes, Sir!" the soldier said, then led the three kids away.

Flipper was the last one left. He thought General Jaxxen was being completely unfair but knew the General wasn't going to listen to what he had to say. He looked down at the ground, knowing it was his turn to be yelled at.

General Jaxxen looked at Flipper and calmed a bit. "Young man, I'm afraid we owe you an apology. We brought you here out of desperation because of a computer program that was manipulated. Sierra discovered that Nicole corrupted the program so that we would waste our time chasing a false prediction. Sierra has also shown us that Nicole is the mole. We were careless to let you get kidnapped by the Lizards. I'm grateful you have survived and are returned to us. I'm going to have Fox debrief you. We need to know everything you saw or heard while on Rex. You may be able to provide us with some information that could be useful in our war with the Lizards. When Fox is finished interviewing you, he has instructions to return you to your home. We've caused you enough trouble and we need to return our focus to the war."

Flipper looked up. He glanced at Fox and Sierra, then back at General Jaxxen. "With all due respect, Sir, I think you are looking at all the wrong things."

This seemed to catch General Jaxxen off guard. His eyebrows raised. "Excuse me?"

"The last time you saw me I was burnt, almost dead, and paralyzed for life. Now look at me." Flipper spread his arms and looked down at his legs. "You haven't even noticed that I've been healed and am walking fine. Nicole, Jake, Chezlor and Alya were brave enough to risk their lives to come save me. I bet very few of your men would

184

have been willing to try an impossible mission like they did. There is no way they should have been able to return alive, let alone rescue me in the process. Yet they did.

"Your son, Jake, risked his own life, outsmarted the Snaders more than once, and made some hard decisions that helped us escape. He isn't going to be a great soldier someday—he already is a great soldier.

"Nicole knew exactly what the consequences were going to be, but she also knew she was responsible for me being here in the first place. She wanted to do what she could to make that right. Nicole is faithful, loyal and smart. She should be promoted, not locked up. Sierra is the one you should arrest."

Sierra gasped.

General Jaxxen was taken aback. He glanced at Sierra and back to Flipper. "Sierra? What in the world for?"

"Because she's the one who kidnapped me."

CHAPTER 35

Jake paced. "They've been in there for over two hours."

Jake, Chezlor and Alya waited anxiously in the commons. General Jaxxen had said that no one was to interrupt him and had then taken Flipper into his office. They heard Sierra had been arrested. They tried to get Fox to tell them what was happening but he claimed not to know any more than they did.

"I hope he's not being too hard on Flipper," Alya said sympathetically.

"I think you kind of like him," Chezlor said teasingly.

"I-I-" Alya started, then just turned and looked away.

Two hours turned into three. Three hours turned into four. Jake, Chezlor and Alya didn't leave the commons area. They wanted to know immediately when General Jaxxen and Flipper finished talking. They had to know what was going on.

Finally, Flipper emerged from General Jaxxen's office. Jake, Chezlor and Alya hurried over to him.

"How are you doing?"

"What's going on?"

"Are you okay?"

"Was he hard on you?"

"Guys, I'm fine!" Flipper said trying to stop the barrage of questions. "But thanks for caring."

"How did you survive four hours alone with my dad in his office?" Jake asked.

"Actually, General Jaxxen is a very reasonable man. I enjoyed our discussion."

All three of them looked at Flipper and were speechless.

General Jaxxen came out of his office and they all looked at him, waiting to see his reaction. He paused for a few moments before addressing them. "Jake. Chezlor. Alya. What you did was very dangerous. You put Nicole's life at risk and could have destroyed an expensive aircraft or escalated an ongoing war. Well, you probably did escalate the war, but we'll address that in a minute.

"What you did was also incredibly brave and selfless. You risked your lives to save Flipper, even though you didn't know him and weren't responsible for him. Although it was irresponsible of you to attempt this mission, especially without permission and backup, I know you went after Flipper because you understood his protection was the Gudes'—was my, responsibility.

"Flipper has told me everything that happened. I have to start by saying that I am extremely proud of you. If I had more soldiers like you, this war would be going in a different direction."

Jake, Chezlor and Alya gave a collective sigh of relief. They smiled as their fear and anxiety turned into pride.

General Jaxxen continued. "I'm afraid I have underestimated your courage, abilities and ideas. My focus has been on the war and I have neglected you. I apologize."

General Jaxxen lowered his head and paused. When he looked up, he looked straight at Jake. "Jake, I've ignored you and made you feel unimportant and unworthy. I'm sorry, son, and hope you can forgive me."

Jake felt the tears welling up in his eyes, but he fought hard to hold them back. Alya, on the other hand, didn't fight hers.

"Your mom was always the one better with emotions. After she was gone, the only way I knew how to relate to you was as a Commanding Officer. I've treated you more like a soldier than a son. In fact, I haven't respected you as a soldier and from what Flipper has told me, you are a very fine soldier. I am proud of you, Jake."

Jake's determination melted. Tears ran down his face.

"Jake, you were a natural leader on this mission. You made hard decisions, risked your life for the others, and never gave up. In fact, you each acted with courage, determination and wisdom. You will receive medals for your bravery." General Jaxxen's eyes were moist. "Jake?"

"Yes, Sir?" Jake said in a small voice.

"Come stand before me."

Jake walked to his dad and stood upright in front of him, looking him in the eyes. General Jaxxen gazed back into his son's eyes. The moment was one they would never forget—that none of them would ever forget. General Jaxxen grabbed his son and they hugged.

***

"I can't believe Sierra was the one who kidnapped you," Alya said.

"What happened?" Chezlor asked.

Flipper explained. "I woke up and saw Sierra toss something on the floor behind Nicole. Nicole was facing away and didn't see Sierra toss it. I saw smoke come up and Nicole pass out. I tried to say something, but didn't have the strength. I was scared, so I closed my eyes and pretended to still be asleep. Sierra picked me up and the next thing I knew we were in another room.

"I heard Sierra talking to someone, so I kept my eyes closed and listened. I heard the other person say that The Freezer was in the capital. They had some bugs to work out but soon would be able to freeze all Gudes in place so they could be easily slaughtered. The Freezer would be fully functional in a few days.

Sierra said she needed to get back to make it look like she and Nicole were both attacked. I fell back to sleep shortly after that and don't remember anything else until I woke up on the spaceship with Dr. Needles."

"Do you know any other Gudes who might be involved in helping Sierra?" Jake asked.

Flipper shook his head. "No."

"I wonder what Dad's going to do?. There could still be more Gude soldiers spying for the Snaders."

Flipper hesitated. "I think your dad has a plan."

"What is it?"

"I'm sorry. He asked me not to say anything. He wants to talk to you about it—all of you."

They looked up as General Jaxxen entered the commons area with Fox and Nicole.

"Nicole!" Alya, Chezlor, and Jake shouted and ran to hug her.

"Oh, my!" Nicole exclaimed. "It's so good to see each of you too!" She gave them each a hug then walked over to Flipper. "I understand you're the reason I'm free."

Flipper grinned and nodded his head shyly.

"Thank you. I am deeply grateful."

Flipper was uncomfortable; afraid she was going to hug him. It isn't that he minded hugs, but they made him uncomfortable when he didn't know the person well. He made an exception.

General Jaxxen cleared his throat. "Now, if everyone would have a seat."

Nicole and the kids all found seats. Fox stood behind the kids. General Jaxxen leaned on a table and put his left foot up on a chair.

"What do we know?" General Jaxxen began. "We know that the Lizards have a machine called The Freezer that will cause physical paralysis to all living creatures that aren't Lizards. We know they'll have it ready soon. We don't know how long the paralysis will last, but it won't take long for our complete destruction if we can't move to defend ourselves.

"We know that Sierra was a spy for the Lizards, but we don't know which other Gudes might be traitors. I only had a few people I felt I could trust before, and now I have even fewer. I know I can trust those in this room. Outside of that…" General Jaxxen hung and shook his head.

Chezlor spoke up. "We'll do anything you need, Sir."

General Jaxxen looked at him and continued. "Flipper helped me put together a plan, and I have consulted with Fox and Nicole. It's a good plan. I don't like it, but under the circumstances, our options are limited. This is a desperate time and we can't hold anything back. We don't have the luxury of losing another battle. Like I said, I don't like the plan because it involves you children. I worry about putting you in harm's way, but I know I can trust you and that you are capable of succeeding."

General Jaxxen looked at each one of the kids before continuing. "There are a couple more things we know. The Lizards have a force field that is keeping our troops out of Timbuktu and protecting The Freezer. We believe our satellites have been able to ascertain the location of The Freezer and the location of the machine generating the force field. However, we have no way of getting that information to the few troops we have inside Timbuktu. The force field blocks all our communication devices and all forms of life that attempt to pass through it that are not Lizards."

"Flipper is part Lizard! I mean Snader! He may be able to pass through the force field!" Jake exclaimed.

"Very good deduction. Yes, he may. And that is our hope, though we don't know for sure," General Jaxxen replied. "Our other challenge is that even if Flipper is able to pass through the force field, we don't know if there is anyone on the inside we can trust."

"What's the plan then, Sir?" Chezlor asked.

"The only way for us to get our troops into Timbuktu is for Flipper to get through the force field and shut off the generator."

Everyone looked at Flipper and told him they believed he could do it.

General Jaxxen continued. "In order to cause a distraction so Flipper can sneak in on the other side of the capital, we are going to advance our troops from this side in a futile attempt to break through the force field. This will put our troops in place so we can attack the moment Flipper disables the force field.

"We believe the generator is on top of our headquarters, which the Lizards have complete control of. Once inside the capital, Flipper will have to make his way to the generator at our headquarters and shut it off."

"What if he can't get through the force field?" Jake asked.

General Jaxxen looked at Flipper, then to Jake. "If Flipper cannot get through the force field, or if he cannot get the force field shut off, then, well, we will have to retreat."

"What do you need us to do, Sir?" Chezlor looked at Flipper. "After Flipper *succeeds* in shutting down the force field."

Flipper appreciated the vote of confidence.

"I will lead our troops into the city and attack, to initiate the battle and to cause further distraction. However, our top priority is to destroy The Freezer. If the Lizards are able to get it running then they could wipe out all the Gudes on Vetrix in a matter of a few days."

General Jaxxen went from casual to serious. "Jake, Chezlor, Alya and Nicole, I need the four of you to find The Freezer and destroy it. You are the only ones I can trust not to be working undercover with the Lizards.

"Fox will attack with some troops near where Flipper enters the force field. He is in charge of getting Flipper out of there safely. Once he has Flipper to safety, he will return to help the four of you escape.

"Once we have The Freezer destroyed and all of you safely out of the capital, we will unleash a full attack in an attempt to drive the Lizards out. We won't stop until every Lizard is off of Vetrix. This is our best shot to change the momentum of the war.

"We have a few hours to prepare. Take some time to relax. We will meet back here shortly before dark to coordinate and finalize our plans."

Chapter 36

As everyone gathered in the commons area, the atmosphere was relaxed. All were rested, nourished, and were ready for the challenge ahead.

General Jaxxen and Fox were the last two to enter the room. As they sat, the rest of the crew quieted down and gave the general their attention.

He handed them each a map. "Flipper, we can't let you carry any type of electronic device into the capital. We're certain the Lizards would detect it. The same goes for the rest of you. We don't want to risk the Lizards knowing your location. We will use paper maps instead."

General Jaxxen went over the map and plan with Flipper. "This is where Malcolm lives. He is the only one in Timbuktu I can trust to do exactly as I expect. Give him this sealed letter from me and he will set you up so you can get into our headquarters. From there, you need to shut down the generator in order to release the force field."

"Yes, Sir." Flipper felt like a soldier.

He went over a few more details with Flipper, then turned his attention to Nicole, Jake, Chezlor and Alya. They discussed the plan to locate The Freezer. Once they felt comfortable with their assignments, General Jaxxen addressed them one last time.

"I know you all can do this. It took us a while, and we still don't fully understand it, but somehow Flipper is the key to defeating the

Lizards. There's no guarantee Flipper or any of us will survive this mission, but we know for sure that any sacrifices we make will help save the universe. Now let's go out there and kick some Lizards' tail!"

***

The one thing Flipper had no control over was the thing he worried about most. If he couldn't pass through the force field then all the planning had been a waste of time. He didn't like the feeling that the whole mission was dependent on him being able to pass through it. He was afraid he was going to let everyone down. He kept telling himself that he had no control over whether he could pass through the force field or not, but his emotions were having a hard time believing his head. He was consumed with his fear of failure. He was a hundred feet outside of Timbuktu, hiding behind a large boulder. It was very dark and he was dressed all in black. Alya had covered his face and hands with black polish so the darkness would camouflage him. He carried a backpack with potentially needed supplies. Flipper looked around and didn't see anyone. "Of course, why would the Snaders need to guard the city when they have a force field surrounding it!" He reminded himself.

He ran from the boulder to the edge of town, where he could see a faint glow. He slowly reached out his hand and touched the force field. There was no sound, but the place he touched glowed a little brighter. He continued to press his hand forward slowly and it easily passed through. Flipper was encouraged, so he stepped forward. His leg entered the force field followed by the rest of his body. He took another step and was completely through. He was standing inside of the capital.

Good grief! he said to himself. I spent the last three hours worrying myself to death and that was easy.

He looked around but the immediate area was devoid of people. He didn't know if the Snaders weren't concerned about guarding the perimeter, if it was because of the time of night, or if the general and his troops advancing on the city was causing a distraction, but there was no sign of activity. Flipper carefully ran a few blocks, staying close to trees and bushes to remain hidden in case someone appeared. He found the address General Jaxxen had given him—404 Scarlet. General Jaxxen had told Flipper this was the only person inside the city he could count on to help Flipper get into the Gudes' headquarters. Flipper knocked on the door and waited anxiously. He had to knock a second time before the door opened. When it did, he found himself staring at the end of a long gun. The guy holding it towards him wasn't any taller than Flipper, but looked much older. He also looked like he hadn't cleaned himself up in quite a while. His light-purple hair was shaggy, his white beard was long and ratted, and the stench was almost unbearable.

"Who are you?" the man demanded in a gruff voice.

Flipper froze, taking several moments for his words to come out. "I'm on a mission for General Jaxxen. Are you Malcolm?"

"I'm Malcolm, but no way I'm believin' General Jaxxen sent a kid on a mission for him. Where you from? You ain't no Gude."

"I have a note in my pocket from the General."

Malcolm looked at him a minute before responding. "Go head, very slowly."

Flipper slowly reached into his pocket and pulled out a sealed envelope. He handed it to Malcolm, who forcefully snatched it away.

"Face down on the ground," Malcolm commanded.

"What?"

"Lay face down on the ground. I don't trust you not to do something while I'm reading."

Malcolm didn't seem like a patient man, so Flipper obeyed. After inaudibly mumbling to himself as he read, Malcolm laughed out loud, which startled Flipper.

Finally, Malcolm said, "Get up!"

Flipper stood and asked, "So, are you going to help me?"

"Of course." Malcolm gave Flipper a wry smile, which made him uncomfortable. "Right this way."

Malcolm walked behind Flipper, giving him directions as they walked through his house. They went three levels underneath the ground. Malcolm kept his gun pointed at Flipper the whole time.

"In that room," Malcolm said, pointing the gun toward an open door.

Flipper stepped into a small, secure room.

"General Jaxxen said you would help me out," Flipper protested.

"It looks like the General pulled a good one on you." Malcolm laughed. He tossed the letter toward Flipper before he shut and locked the door.

Flipper picked up the letter and read:

Malcolm,

Flipper has been working as a double agent. That's how he was able to get past the force field and into the city. He claims to be helping us, but I learned recently his loyalties are with the Lizards. Secure him until I can deal with him personally. I am sending him to you because I don't know who I can trust inside the capital.

Sincerely,

General Jaxxen

Chapter 37

Allison stood in the middle of a dining room. It was plain. No pictures on the walls, no decorations. The only furniture was a table whose top was level with her chin. There were no chairs.

Her first thought was, How would anyone eat at this table?" Allison's second thought was, Where am I, and what am I doing here?

She heard a noise from another room—footsteps coming towards her. A man with bright red skin like Dyson, entered the dining room, startled at the sight of Allison and dropped his plate of food.

"I've been dreading this day. Now my worst fear has come true. You've come during dinner."

"What are you talking about?" asked Allison.

The man dropped to his knees to scoop the food off the floor and back onto his plate. "I knew the Gudes would send someone for me. I expected an actual Gude though. You look like you are one of those Earthlings. Do you work for the Gudes?"

When the man stood up, Allison noticed how tall he was. He was at least a foot and a half taller than her and she thought he might be old with his gray hair and wrinkled face, although she wasn't sure because her experience with red aliens was somewhat limited.

"No, I don't work for the Gudes! I don't work for anyone. I'm a kid."

The man fidgeted nervously. "You have to be working for the Gudes. They are the only ones with the ability to teleport." He turned and started walking away. "You don't mind if I finish eating first, do you?"

Allison watched him leave the room. Out of curiosity, she followed. The old man filled another plate with food, for which the only descriptive word she could come up with was 'slop'.

"I would offer to feed you but I just have enough for myself. If you hadn't startled me, I wouldn't have dropped my plate and there would be enough for me to share."

"I'm sorry." Allison wasn't really sorry, but she felt obliged to apologize.

"You should announce yourself when you arrive."

"I didn't know where I was."

The man looked at her askance. "You don't just appear somewhere without knowing where you are going."

"But that's exactly what I did."

The man took his plate to the table. He stood as he ate. "Why would the Gudes send you without telling you where you were going?"

"The Gudes didn't send me."

"Then who are you working for?"

"I told you I don't have a job."

"Then who sent you?"

"I don't know. I don't think anyone sent me."

"Then why are you here?"

"I don't know."

"Child, you really aren't making any sense."

The conversation was exhausting Allison.

The man continued eating. "Do you like carrots?"

"Sure."

"They're good for you, but never eat too many. I ate a whole bag once. It went right through my system. I really wish I had been at home. I was visiting some friends—quite embarrassing."

Allison was glad she wasn't eating.

"Maybe your body would react differently. I really don't know much about the human digestive system."

After a brief pause, the man continued. "Would you rather eat salami or die?"

Allison just looked at him. It took her a few moments to realize he was quite serious.

"You don't talk much. Or don't you like food?" the man asked.

"I like food very much."

"If you could only eat one food for the rest of your life, what would it be?"

"I don't know. Pizza, I suppose."

"I think I would rather die," said the man.

"You would rather die?"

"Yes. I can't stand salami."

Allison assumed she was dreaming again and she was more than ready to wake up.

The man took his plate into the kitchen. "Okay, I'm ready to go."

"Go where?"

"With you."

"To where?" asked Allison.

"To wherever you are taking me."

"I'm not taking you anywhere."

"Then why are you here?"

"I don't know. I just fell asleep and woke up here."

The man's face suddenly took on a look of shock and horror. "You're a Dreamer?!"

"Of course, everyone dreams."

"Yes, but not everyone is a Dreamer."

"What's the difference?"

"You don't know?"

"No."

The man looked down for a moment and Allison didn't know if he was going to tell her. "Dreams are our subconscious making things up, sometimes remembering past experiences. But a Dreamer has real experiences while asleep. Dreamers are capable of interacting with anyone, anywhere in the universe. You can control your dreams."

"How does a Dreamer control their dreams?" Allison was suddenly interested in the conversation.

"I don't know. It's not an ability the Snaders have. Only the Gudes are capable of being a Dreamer. I've never heard of an Earthling with the ability. I don't believe they do. But here you are, so, I just don't know. Have you had other dream experiences similar to this?"

"Yes!" Allison exclaimed. She told the old Snader all about her dream the night Flipper was kidnapped, her dream of Flipper playing soccer, her dream with Fox on Vetrix, and her dream in the smoke-filled room.

The Snader listened intently. Allison found it nice to be able to talk in detail about her dreams, especially with someone who believed her.

"Is there a way I can wake myself up?" asked Allison

"Oh, sure," said the man. "Dreamers can control where they go, what they want to do, and even if they can be seen by others or not. Once you learn to control your dreams, you can do a lot of things."

"So how do I do it?"

"How would I know? I told you, only Gudes are Dreamers."

"But, you just…" Allison started, but then decided it just wasn't worth it, so she went a different direction. "You said you expected someone to show up some time. What did you mean?"

"I used to chase dreamers—trying to protect the Snaders from their intrusions. I trained most of our current dreamer chasers. I'm on the Gudes' top ten most wanted list. I've been in hiding for years, but knew that one day the Gudes would catch up with me."

"What do you mean that you chased dreamers?"

"Whenever a Snader had a visit from a Dreamer, or thought they did, they would contact our organization. We would do interviews, gather data, investigate undercover. Sometimes we were able to predict when a Dreamer might show up again. Other times, if we could figure out who the Dreamer was, we would hunt them down and eliminate them. It was very difficult and highly unsuccessful work, since a Dreamer could be acting from anywhere, although most of the time they came from Vetrix. We had our ways of getting to them, but it wasn't safe, easy or cheap."

Allison was starting to get very nervous. "What's your name?"

"They call me Red," said the man.

Allison couldn't help but giggle. "They call you Red? Really? You're pulling my leg."

Until now the man had seemed calm and unthreatening. Now, he began to raise his voice. "No, that's my name. What's so funny about my name?"

"N-No, nothing. I mean, it's just that you're red and your name is Red."

"Girl, I'm old and tired. Can we just get this over with? Let me grab my jacket and I'll be ready to go with you."

"But, I'm not…" Allison started to say.

Red walked through the kitchen into another room, but kept talking. "Would you mind helping me carry my things? I have a number of documents I'm sure the Gudes will want to see."

Allison followed. "Red, I'm not here to take you anywhere. I just went to sleep and accidentally woke up here. I would like nothing better than to wake up and be at home."

"The documents are just right over here," said Red, ignoring Allison.

She stepped into a room that was about the size of her bedroom at home. There was nothing in the room except Red. He pressed a button on a device he held and electric beams surged along the walls, the floor, and the ceiling.

Allison tensed, feeling fear in every inch of her body. "What are you doing?"

"I told you—I hunt Dreamers. Dreamers are extremely hard to capture in their dreams, because when they wake up, they simply disappear. You can't even knock them out because they just wake up where they went to sleep. They are much easier to kill. However, you fascinate me and I need to know how you became a Dreamer. These currents were specially designed to keep Dreamers from returning from their dreams. I'm going to study you."

"I told you, I don't know anything about being a Dreamer. I don't know anything about the Snaders and the Gudes. I just want to go home," pleaded Allison.

"Yours is a case I have never seen before. The information I can gain from you is too valuable to let you go."

"What will happen to my body back on Earth?" Allison asked. "Your body is still there, for the moment. Once you fall asleep here, your body will join you and you will remain my prisoner."

"You just said that if you knock someone out they wake up in their original body, didn't you?" Allison was desperately looking for a loophole to escape the whole Dreamer predicament she was in.

"Yes, if your dream body is knocked out you wake up in your real body." Red seemed to pause for effect. "But if your dream body goes to sleep then your real body joins your dream body."

"That doesn't make any sense!" shouted Allison.

"You'll get no argument from me," said Red. "But know it's true. I've seen it too many times."

"But you are in here with me," said Allison. "How will you get out?"

"The currents keep in everyone except Snaders. We can move through them without a problem," said Red.

"How long are you going to keep me here?"

"As long as I need," said Red as he walked through the current and out of the room.

Allison slumped to the floor, confused and scared. She screamed for a minute, before the tears overtook her. As she thought about her mom and dad, her Aunt Dee and Uncle Dennis, about Flipper and Josh, she cried.

CHAPTER 38

Allison bolted upright, frightened and breathing hard. It took her eyes a minute to adjust. Where was she?

She was still on the Snaders' spaceship, trapped underground. She couldn't believe the flood of joy that surged through her when she discovered she was trapped beneath the earth. Maybe it was just a dream after all, she thought, although she didn't believe it. Something very real was happening in her dreams.

Josh was sitting on the floor with his back against the wall. He was eating some yellowish plants. Allison looked at the door and it was wide open. She grabbed the transmitter and started flipping through the different camera views.

"Good morning, sleepy head," he said.

"Where's Dyson?" Allison asked, flustered.

"Which Dyson?"

"How many Dysons do you know?" she asked.

"Um… Just one," Josh said.

"Then why did you ask which Dyson?"

"I didn't know if you were talking about the Dyson I knew."

There were times when Allison couldn't tell if Josh was being serious or funny. This was one of those times.

He smiled and stood up. "Dyson left over an hour ago. You were sleeping so deeply, I didn't want to wake you. I figured if you can sleep through that door opening, then you must be really tired."

"I'm a Dreamer!"

"I dream too, but that door would still have woken me up," Josh said.

Allison stood, excited. "No, I mean how I can travel places in my dreams. I'm really there and they call it being a Dreamer?"

"Did you find Flipper?"

"Well, no," Allison tempered her excitement. "But I had another dream last night. This time I went and saw a Snader."

"Like Dyson?" Josh interrupted.

"Yes! And he explained Dreamers to me."

She told Josh all about her dream with Red, what he had told her about being a Dreamer, and how he trapped her in his room.

"So how did you get out?" Josh asked.

"I don't know," she confessed. "Like all the other dreams, I just woke up."

"Oh, I almost forgot!" Josh handed her a plate of yellowish plants and a glass of water. "I brought some breakfast for us to eat."

"Aaaahhh, that's so sweet! Thank you!"

Josh's cheeks brightened. Allison enjoyed making him uncomfortable.

As Allison ate her yellowish plants, she said, "What I would give for a big stack of pancakes, with bacon and orange juice."

"Maybe we can have that stack of pancakes soon."

"What do you mean?"

Josh reached over and picked up some papers. "I found these on the kitchen table this morning."

"What are they?"

"I think this could be our ticket out of here today."

There was excitement in Allison's voice, "How?"

"There is a machine the Snaders use to dig through the ground. They used it to build the arena, as well as some other areas down here. These are complete instructions on how to run the machine. I think we should use the machine to dig our way to the surface."

"How would we take it without getting caught?"

Josh pointed to the hand-written instructions. Some of the papers had writing on them, some had drawings, and some had both. "If this map is accurate, then the machine is located in a secluded area away from where the Snaders live. It doesn't make a lot of noise, so it is unlikely anyone would hear us leave."

Allison studied the papers for a few minutes as she finished eating. "Josh, I think this could work! You're a genius!"

She had only been awake for a few minutes and she had left Josh speechless twice already.

"Does it mention anywhere how fast the machine goes?" Allison asked.

"Not exactly." He pointed to the third page. "There's a note here that says they think the machine could dig to the surface within a few hours."

Allison finished her breakfast in bed. "Well, let's get our stuff together, pack some of this delicious yellowish plant, and prepare for our trip back to the surface."

***

Josh and Allison tried to leave the spaceship just as they had found it. The only items they took with them were the instructions to the machine and Dyson's journal, so they could show the police what was going on underneath Roswell. They knew Dyson would miss the items so it was either escape or get caught.

"What are you wearing?" Allison asked Josh as they left the spaceship.

In addition to the dirty, smelly clothes he had worn when they arrived, Josh wore a cape and a top hat, and was carrying a wand. "Since we are making our escape, I thought I would dress up as Houdini."

"I don't think Houdini wore a magician's outfit," Allison said.

"Well, I'm limited on my choice of clothing down here. It was the best I could come up with."

Several minutes later, they stepped off the elevator and peeked into the large Snader living area. Once again, they saw hundreds, if not thousands, of Snaders moving about. The room filled with the roar of an engine from a nearby spaceship. Josh and Allison almost had to scream at each other to be heard.

"Why do you suppose they have a spaceship running?" Allison shouted

"I don't know, but we don't have time to find out," Josh hollered back. "The machine is located behind the training arena we were at yesterday."

"I hope those guys aren't practicing in the arena today."

They followed the path to the arena, careful to stay out of sight. Fortunately, the arena was empty. They ran across it as their excitement rose and their adrenaline spiked. They stopped behind the bleachers and Josh examined the map. He pointed. "It looks like if we go this way, the hall will lead us to the shop where they build and repair their robots."

They started sprinting again but froze when they heard behind them, "Stop right there!"

Neither one of them looked back.

"Stop right there!" they heard again as footsteps came closer.

Their eyes met and they slowly turned around. A Gude robot walked in their direction.

"Stop right there!" the robot shouted again.

They watched as the robot came within two feet of them and then walked past, shouting. "Stop right there!"

Allison laughed. "It must be a malfunction of some kind."

Josh gave a little nervous laugh. "That about gave me a heart attack."

They went through the hallway and found the shop. When they got close, they could hear voices coming from inside, so they peeked in through the open doorway. It was a very large room with robots and parts everywhere. Red Fox, Fungus and Dyson were each working on a robot. Despite the size of the room, the Snaders were close enough to them that Josh and Allison could hear what they were saying.

"Dyson, today is your day to run the course," Red Fox jabbed him.

"I thought I was going to get to go today," Fungus argued.

"You can go tomorrow or later today, if we have time," Red Fox said. "I want to see if Dyson has been practicing his fighting moves."

Dyson held a transmitter that was blinking bright yellow. "Hey guys, we have another robot roaming the arena somewhere."

"I thought we fixed that glitch," Red Fox sounded exasperated.

"Yeah, well, so did I," Dyson said. "We better go find it."

"I'm ready for a break anyhow," Fungus said, setting down a large tool.

Red Fox started in the direction of Josh and Allison before Dyson grabbed his arm.

"I think we need to go this way," Dyson said, nodding in the opposite direction.

They all left, exiting the room at the far end.

Josh and Allison entered the room. Josh looked around at all the human and Gude robots while Allison read the map.

Allison pointed to their right. "We need to go that way."

They ran through a long tunnel before they saw the wonderful sight of a large, twenty-foot tall machine that was as wide as it was high and twice as long. There were dozens of twisted pipes protruding from the front. Allison thought they looked similar to the drill bits her dad used to make holes. These drills were big, most of them bigger than her.

Allison's thoughts rushed to her parents, her dog Anna, French fries, root beer, chocolate chip cookies, fried rice. It had only been a few days but she couldn't wait to eat real food. Where was she going to start?

She was so wrapped up in her love affair with food that she squealed when she heard, "Stark, are you back yet?" She looked up and a red head appeared from atop the machine.

"Let's get out of here," Josh whispered with great urgency.

They took two steps before another Snader appeared at the end of the tunnel, cutting off their only route of escape.

"What the..." the voice from above shouted.

The Snader cutting off their escape route, the one supposedly named Stark, approached Allison and Josh. He stopped ten feet from them, stared at them for several uncomfortable seconds, then yelled, "Endu, you have your gun?"

Allison was so scared she hadn't noticed that Stark wasn't armed. They could make a break for it, but the Snader was bigger than them and there was no way they could both get away. Besides, there was nowhere to hide since their presence was now known.

Endu tossed his gun to Stark then climbed down to join them. Stark angrily grabbed the instructions for the machine from Josh and Dyson's journal from Allison.

They led Allison and Josh back to the room with all of the robots and lined them up against a wall. Endu casually tossed the machine instructions and Dyson's journal on the floor on the other side of the room. He took a rock and scratched lines in front and on both sides of Josh and Allison. He spoke as he worked.

"I'm programming these two robots to guard you." The robots approached. They stopped twenty feet away and aimed their weapons in the direction of Josh and Allison. "If I were you I wouldn't step outside of the box I drew." He snickered before he tossed a rock that landed just outside of the box. Both robots lowered their weapons and blasted the rock. Allison jumped and screamed and grabbed Joshes' arm as he turned away from the blast as pieces of rock scattered and pelted their lower bodies.

"Stark, you check the arena and I'll look in the supply rooms. Dyson's around here somewhere. We need to let the others know we have visitors."

Stark and Endu laughed as they left in opposite directions.

Chapter 39

"What are we going to do?" Josh asked as he wiped the blood dripping from his leg.

"I have no idea." Allison said in a monotone voice because her mind was trying to figure out what they should do. She didn't have any ideas. Soon they would probably be surrounded by Snaders, maybe tortured to find out why they were there. The Snaders would never believe the truth.

Her thoughts went to her favorite character—Annabeth Chase. She got herself and others out of worse situations than this. What would she do?

Annabeth was a great fighter, but that wasn't helpful. She was also a great strategist. She would figure a way out.

"We have to find a way to get away without getting shot," she said more to herself than to Josh.

"That's an amazing idea!" Josh said with sarcastic excitement. "Maybe we can ask the robots nicely not to shoot us, or convince them we're the good guys and the red freaks are evil, or maybe we should have asked Stark and Endu how we could escape."

"Josh that's it!"

"What!? You're going to say 'Pretty please, Mr. Robot, don't shoot us?'"

"No, no," Allison's excitement rose. "What you said at the end about Stark and Endu."

"You want me to ask them how to escape?"

"You don't have to." She turned and looked straight into his eyes. "They already showed us."

"What are you talking about?" Josh asked, confused.

Allison quietly mumbled to herself as she worked out her strategy. "Okay. We can't ask the robots not to shoot us, but I know how to turn them off. Remember, we saw Dyson do it in the arena."

Josh sighed. "I do remember, but the robots aren't going to let us flip the off switch on their back."

"No they aren't," Allison agreed. "That's why you're going to have to move quickly."

"Me?" Josh protested. "Why me?"

"You're a good athlete and a lot faster than I am."

"I'm not faster than laser fire."

"You don't have to be if they're distracted," Allison explained.

"How are we going to distract them?" Josh asked.

"Remember what happened when Endu threw the rock on the ground?" Allison asked.

"Yeah," Josh said anxiously. "The robots blew it to smithereens. I don't want to be blown up. I look better as one large piece." He raised his arms and flexed his muscles like a power lifter.

Allison rolled her eyes. "I'm going to distract the robots. I'll throw several rocks to the left and keep throwing rocks so the robots keep shooting in that direction. When they start firing you can run behind them and quickly turn them off."

Josh contemplated a moment. "It's not a bad plan."

"Thank you," Allison beamed.

"Except that I'm risking my life!"

"Josh, if we don't get away we're never going to see our families again. We don't have anything to lose."

Josh nodded his head in understanding.

Allison took a deep breath, let out a long sigh, then tossed a rock just outside of the box and continued to toss a rock every second, farther and farther away.

Josh raced around to the right and quickly shut off the first robot. He ran behind the second robot but before he could flip the switch it spun toward him. To avoid being in the line of fire he jumped onto the robot, wrapping his legs and arms around it's body. The robot moved and aimlessly fired as Josh held on for dear life.

Allison ran around trying to stay out of the line of fire, but there was no way to predict the direction the robot was going to shoot next. Josh lost his grip and the power of the robot's quick movement threw him to the ground.

The robot aimed the gun toward Josh. Without thinking, Allison threw herself on top of Josh. She squeezed her eyes shut and waited to be blown to bits.

They lay on the ground out of breath for several seconds. "Um, I think you can get off of me now," Josh suggested.

Allison's head had been buried in Josh's chest. She lifted her head and looked at Josh. He nodded his head in the direction behind her.

Allison rolled off of Josh, but it wasn't the still robot that caught her eye. A bright red figure disappeared from sight through the doorway.

"Who was that?" Allison asked.

"That was Dyson," Josh said. "He turned the robot off just before it shot us."

"Why would he do that?" Allison asked.

"I don't know," Josh admitted. "You said yourself he doesn't believe what the other Snaders believe. Maybe he was trying to help us."

Allison stared in disbelief.

"You can send him a thank you card later. Let's get out of here!"

They ran over to pick up the documents but only the machine's instructions were there. "Dyson took his journal," Josh told Allison.

She looked dejected. "Oh well, let's get out of here."

They ran back to the machine. In order to get inside they had to climb on and enter through the top, so Josh named it the 'tank'. It was made out of some type of hard plastic. He studied the map while Allison followed the directions to get the tank started. Allison turned on a monitor to show them what was in front of the tank.

"Here goes," she said.

She pressed a button and the machine roared to life. She pulled back a lever and they moved forward.

"Yee haw!" Josh shouted.

Allison followed the path about half a mile before it ended. There was nothing but dirt and rock in front of them.

Josh looked up from the map. "It's time to start going up."

"What do I need to do?"

Josh referred to the pictures. "The instructions say to push the lever on the far left until it reaches seven."

When Allison pushed the lever, the machine tilted back so that they were angled upwards.

She turned and looked at Josh. "Are you ready to go up?"

"Let's get out of here!"

Allison pulled the lever to make the tank move forward. It was slow, but not as slow as they expected, considering they were digging straight through the ground.

"This is amazing!" Allison said.

"This says that the front of the tank digs through anything in front of it."

"What does the tank do with the dirt and rock?"

214

"It goes inside the tank. It can be set to disintegrate the material or spit it out the back."

There were no windows but the tank had monitors that allowed them to see outside both forwards and backwards. Allison turned on the second monitor so that they could see what was happening behind them. "I don't see any debris flying out behind us so we must be on disintegrate mode."

The first hour or two went by slowly. Allison steered as Josh relaxed in the comfortable reclining seat and gave way to sleep. Allison's body yearned for sleep, but she was too afraid. She didn't trust her dreams or her dreaming ability. She knew she couldn't fight off sleep forever, but she was going to do her best. However, determination is simply not enough to deter sleep. She caught herself shutting her eyes twice. A minute later, her head dropped forward and she dozed off. Suddenly, the tank shook, and in that moment she went from the verge of sleep to alert.

Josh was wide awake too.

In her effort to fight off sleep, she hadn't been paying any attention to their surroundings. She looked at the monitor and saw the miniature spaceship that had just rammed them from behind.

CHAPTER 40

Josh nervously watched the monitor. They were in big trouble.

"What are we going to do?" Allison asked.

"I don't know."

"Is there a way to make this thing go any faster?"

"It's going as fast as it can. The tank isn't built for speed."

"What if they shoot at us?"

Josh was tired of being asked questions he had no way of answering. He yelled, "I suppose we'll explode!"

That was obviously the wrong thing to say. Allison was visibly upset and turned her head away. He felt awful. He looked at the spaceship again. It didn't have any windows, so they couldn't see who was flying it. Josh felt panicked as he anticipated being blown to bits. Suddenly, they heard another loud thud and the tank shook. It happened again. The miniature spaceship was now repeatedly ramming them from behind. Allison shrieked but still didn't speak or look at Josh.

He turned to her. He wasn't thinking, just talking. "Allison, I'm going to get you out of this, don't you worry." He sounded so confident that he almost believed himself. He didn't know why he said it, except that he wanted Allison to feel better. Josh racked his brain. "Okay, when I tell you to, slam on the brakes," He was surprised when she didn't challenge him. "Now!"

Allison pulled the brake and the tank slammed to a stop, jerking them both forward. The straps that secured them kept them safe, but they were going to bruise. At the same moment Allison hit the brakes, the miniature spaceship rammed into them. The increased impact to the spaceship caused it to flip backwards. It landed upside down.

"Now go!" Josh shouted.

Allison started the tank forward again. They watched anxiously to see what the Snader in the spaceship would do. As it had disappeared from their view, it still hadn't moved.

"Josh, that was awesome!" Allison exclaimed gleefully.

"That will teach them to mess with us," he boasted.

They high-fived each other.

"What's the first thing you're going to do when we get back?" Allison asked. "I mean, after you hug your parents and all that."

"I'm going to eat a large pizza, all by myself. How about you?"

"I want to take a nice, long, hot shower."

They both became very quiet.

"Are you thinking what I'm thinking?" Allison asked.

"I'm thinking about Flipper."

"Yeah, me too."

"Everyone will have to believe us about the aliens when they see this machine. And we can show them where the Snaders are. They'll surely help us find Flipper then."

Suddenly, they bolted forward. The spaceship once again rammed them from behind, this time even harder than before. Allison involuntarily screamed.

Josh grabbed the instructions to the tank and flipped through them. "Got it!"

He searched the control board for a moment. He pressed a couple of buttons and they could hear a faint grinding sound that started in the front of the tank and continued underneath them all the way to the back. They looked at the screen and watched as debris flew out of the back of the tank. The debris pelted the spaceship, causing it to weave and scrape against the sides of the tunnel. The tank continued to chew up dirt and rock and spit it behind them. They watched the screen closely as the spaceship once again began to disappear from sight.

"Josh, you're a genius," Allison said.

Josh smiled. "We aren't to safety yet."

The miniature spaceship was several hundred yards behind them and was almost out of sight when it started moving forward again, slowly gaining ground.

"Do you have another brilliant idea?" Allison asked, with her green eyes glued to the screen.

"I'm thinking!" Josh exclaimed.

Suddenly, they heard a loud boom and felt the tank rattle as the miniature spaceship exploded into thousands of pieces.

"Wow! What just happened?" Allison asked.

"I don't know."

They both sat back, stunned.

"I think we may be moving slower since we started grinding up the ground instead of disintegrating it," Allison said.

"I'll switch it back and keep an eye behind us."

Josh turned the disintegrator back on and Allison turned the speed to maximum. They held their breath. As the excitement diminished and the monotony of riding in the rumbling tank took hold, Allison felt herself falling asleep once more and decided it wasn't worth fighting any longer.

"I don't think I can stay awake."

"Are you going to try to find Flipper again?" Josh asked.

"I would love to find him," Allison mumbled with her eyes shut. "But I don't know how and I really just want to sleep."

"I'll keep the tank moving forward."

If Josh said anything further, Allison didn't hear it.

Chapter 41

Flipper waited until he was sure Malcolm was back upstairs. He opened his backpack and took out a two-foot long explosive strip. He stuck it across the opening of the door to prevent Malcolm from following him. Next, he took out a laser pen and placed it in the back corner of the room. When he pressed the button on the pen a small area of the floor opened up. He hopped down into the hole and the floor closed above him.

General Jaxxen had explained to Flipper that Malcolm was a double agent for the Snaders and had been for years. The Gudes knew all about it, but Malcolm wasn't bright enough to realize they knew. Malcolm had a room he used as a prison. General Jaxxen had built a tunnel from their headquarters to Malcolm's prisoner room without Malcolm's knowledge so they could secretly keep an eye on him. He knew Malcolm wasn't the mole because they never gave him accurate highly classified information. He had told Flipper he was confident Malcolm would lock him up in his prison.

Flipper had asked General Jaxxen if Malcolm might shoot him. General Jaxxen had said that he wouldn't for two reasons. One, General Jaxxen had written that Flipper was spying for the Snaders, so Malcolm would view him as being on the same side. Two, Malcolm was still accountable to General Jaxxen's authority in order to continue his image of fighting for the Gudes. Fortunately, General Jaxxen had been correct. General Jaxxen had said he expected Malcolm to eventually try to get the truth out of Flipper in order to work with him, but Flipper wouldn't be around long enough for that to happen. The explosive strip on the door was to keep Malcolm from following Flipper. His disappearance would give away the Gudes' knowledge that Malcolm was a double agent, but that was a small sacrifice.

Flipper turned on his flashlight. He climbed down a ladder into a small underground tunnel. Much of the time, Flipper had to stoop as he walked to keep from hitting his head and the tunnel was so narrow that one of his sides rubbed against the dirt wall most of the way. It was damp and musty, and water dripped on him the whole journey. At the end of the tunnel, Flipper climbed up a ladder that led to a dead end. He placed the laser pen on the panel above him and it slid open. He climbed into the room and the panel closed.

He was standing in a large room with stuff everywhere. It looked like a disorganized mess. He carefully made his way through the maze of junk and found the door. On the other side of the door were some stairs. Flipper walked up three flights and exited on the second floor. He found a window and looked out. He could see dozens of Snaders running away from the building he was in now—away from headquarters. General Jaxxen's attack was definitely causing a distraction. Flipper crawled out onto a ladder that went along the side of the building. He climbed four stories before he made the mistake of looking down. He hated heights and felt like he was going to pass out. He shut his eyes and told himself, "Just three more stories and I can go inside. Besides, the survival of the universe depends on me. Yeah, that's no pressure."

He climbed the next three stories constantly thinking he was going to fall or a Snader was going to see him and start shooting. Fortunately, neither happened. He opened a window, crawled in, and lay on the floor. His legs felt like rubber and he wasn't sure if he could control them any longer but he knew he didn't have time to enjoy the solid floor, so he talked his legs into cooperating and carefully stood. He peeked out the door. There was no one in sight, so he ran through the hall until he saw a set of large double doors. He opened them and was thrilled to see the room was empty.

General Jaxxen had told him the room was used for their top secret meetings. There was a secret elevator for the generals to use in case an emergency escape were necessary. Flipper found the wall that hid the elevator and used the laser pen to open it. He stepped inside. He pressed the laser pen into the slot on the elevator panel. The wall shut and the elevator went up. He exited the elevator onto the roof of the headquarters. He looked around but didn't see any Snaders guarding the generator. In fact, he didn't see the generator. He walked all around the roof, but it wasn't anywhere.

He heard voices from down on the street. There was a wall around the edge of the roof about six feet high. He had to step on a pipe in the corner to see over the wall. He looked down and saw more Snaders hurrying past the building. Something glowing in his peripheral vision made him look up. Floating in mid-air, between the headquarters and the building next door, was the generator. It was about the size and shape of a suitcase and it was at least ten feet away from the headquarters—too far away for Flipper to reach from the building.

He hopped down and found a long pole he had spotted a few minutes earlier. He carried the pole to where he thought the generator was and leaned it against the wall. He ran over to the pipe and climbed up onto the wall. The wall was only a foot wide and Flipper needed to walk twenty feet to reach the point closest to the generator. He had always been good at balancing, but had never tried this high. He was scared, but tried to stay focused on the pole leaning against the wall in front of him. He didn't look down but kept his eyes focused forward. It took him a couple of minutes, but he made it to the pole. His heart raced and he gasped for breaths, convinced that his fear was going to suffocate him. He breathed slowly and focused on the task at hand. He reached down and slowly lifted the pole. He turned and slid the pole through his hands out towards the generator, hoping he could hook it with the end of the pole and pull it to him. The generator wouldn't move. He tried pulling, pushing, jabbing and hitting it, but he couldn't get the generator to budge.

After several minutes Flipper was completely frustrated. He lifted the pole straight up in the air and swung it down as hard as he could. The pole hit the generator and ricocheted off the force field surrounding it. The force of the kickback knocked Flipper backwards. The pole dropped from his hands and plummeted to the ground below. Flipper fell off of the edge of the wall and landed flat on his back on the roof. The fall knocked the wind out of him and it took him a few minutes to recover. He climbed back up on the wall and slowly walked to the spot closest to the generator. His whole body shook with fear. He had no idea what to do next. He sat down with his legs on the inside of the wall and tried to think. He assumed he could get through the force field around the generator if he could reach it. He wasn't able to pull the generator towards him and without a spaceship he had no idea how to get himself out to it.

His thoughts were interrupted by a shout, "There's someone up here!"

He jumped to his feet, standing on the wall. He was no longer alone on the roof. Three Snaders ran around the corner to join the one who had yelled. The Snaders stopped and pointed their weapons at him.

Flipper raised his hands. "I think there's been a small misunderstanding here," he said sheepishly. "I'm just the repair man, here to do a little work on your generator. You wouldn't mind bringing it to the roof so I can fix it, would you?"

"Now!" one of the Snaders shouted.

They opened fire. Flipper was pelted with laser beams and fell backwards off the building.

Chapter 42

Flipper lay on his back once again struggling to catch his breath. He moaned and coughed twice before it dawned on him that if he was breathing, he wasn't dead. In fact, other than having the wind knocked out of him he thought he was fine. He sat up and examined his body. He didn't see any holes or cuts or bruises. He rolled onto his side and froze. He was looking straight down at the ground, floating in mid-air, ten stories high. He could feel something under him, holding him up. It felt solid, but it was invisible. He froze as terror filled every muscle. He heard a piercing scream and wondered if it came from him.

"Flipper!"

The sound of Allison's voice was enough to get him to move, although not much. He turned his head and saw his cousin standing behind him, also in midair.

"Allison?"

She was clearly distressed. "How are you floating in the air between two buildings? And why?"

"How are you standing in the air between two buildings?" Flipper shot back. "And why?"

"I-uh-well... Oh..." Allison struggled to articulate. "I'm dreaming."

"I wish I was!" Flipper screamed. "I'm scared to death and can't move!"

"Why are you out here if you're scared?"

"I was shot by some Snaders and fell off the building and landed here." Flipper tried to motion towards the building he had fallen off but didn't move anything other than his eyes. "I have to get the generator shut off so the Gudes can enter the city and fight the Snaders."

"Why you?" Allison asked distraught.

"Because I have Snader blood and the force field doesn't work on me," Flipper tried to explain quickly. "Wait! That's it!"

"What's it?"

"The generator must be creating a force field floor across the two buildings. That must be how the Snaders access it and how it appears to float in midair. It—and we—are standing on an invisible floor."

"How about we switch off the generator and get off of this invisible floor?" Allison suggested.

Flipper tried to move. In his mind he pictured himself standing up, but in reality he remained on the floor. "I don't know if I can."

Allison kicked his leg. Hard. "You have to! Get up!"

She reached down and pulled on his arm. Suddenly, he was more afraid not to move. She could cause them to stumble and fall off their invisible plank. He had no idea how wide it might be.

Suddenly they heard, "Holy snap!"

Flipper turned and saw the Snader soldiers looking over the wall at him and Allison in disbelief. He smiled and waved at them.

"How is he standing on our invisible walkway?" one of them asked in astonishment.

"We shot him several times. How come he isn't dead?" asked another with equal bewilderment.

"And who is that girl with him?" asked the third.

Flipper squatted down quickly and lifted the generator. The Snaders started climbing onto the wall, so Flipper walked across the invisible floor and climbed onto the wall on the other building. Allison was right on his tail.

He didn't have any idea how to turn the generator off. He didn't see any switches on it. One of the Snader soldiers stepped off of the wall onto the invisible walkway. The others followed behind him. As the Snaders started to run across the invisible floor Flipper raised both of his hands above his head and threw the generator into the darkness below. The generator crashed on the street into thousands of pieces. The force field vanished, and so did the invisible floor. The four Snader soldiers followed the generator, falling ten stories to the ground.

Flipper and Allison jumped off the wall onto the solid roof.

Allison looked at him. "What do you mean you have Snader blood?"

***

Gude soldiers on both sides of Timbuktu roared when the force field came down. They charged forward as General Jaxxen called in for more troops and for the air attack to begin.

Nicole, Jake, Chezlor and Alya also yelled with delight. They ran into the city and headed for The Freezer. They had over a mile to go, but it was too dangerous to get there any other way than on foot. They needed to go in undetected. Since Chezlor could run the fastest, he went ahead to scout out the area around The Freezer. He reached the park in a couple of minutes, hid behind a building and watched. There was a gated wall around the central area of the park. He could see large antennae-like structures rising high above the ten foot fence. It had to be The Freezer!

Two spaceships were parked outside the wall. Several Snaders ran out of the open gate and into the spaceships. Within a minute, both spaceships rose and flew away.

Chezlor could hear chaos in the distance as Gudes and Snaders began their combat. The noise from the battles increased. The Snaders had dozens of spaceships in the air and soon the Gudes would too. The fighting was about to take on a whole new intensity. Chezlor kept watch but didn't see any more activity around The Freezer. The others arrived and he updated them on what had happened.

He motioned to the park. "It looks like The Freezer is inside that fenced area."

"I see it," Alya said, pointing.

"That must be a big machine," Jake said in awe.

"It has to be to freeze the whole city," Nicole said. "And if they can power it up enough to use our satellites, they could potentially freeze our whole planet."

"Let's see if we can get closer," Jake suggested. "Chezlor, why don't you run to the other side and see if you can learn anything that could help us."

Chezlor was gone before he had finished saying, "You got it."

Nicole, Jake and Alya snuck up closer and hid behind some trees.

"It looks like the gate's open," Alya observed.

"I don't see any guards," Jake added.

"That's the good news," Nicole commented. "The bad news is that there are probably some inside. Let's sneak up and take a look. Are you guys ready?"

Jake and Alya both nodded and they ran toward the gate, weapons in hand. They made it without resistance. They stood against the wall and Nicole peeked inside. She waved for Jake and Alya to follow, and she slowly entered. There was one Snader inside the gate, facing away from them. He was too engrossed in his work to notice them.

Nicole, Jake, and Alya each aimed their weapons at him as Nicole shouted, "Hold it right there! We have several weapons pointed at you. Raise your hands and slowly turn around."

The Snader did turn around slowly, but he didn't raise his hands. He held a portable device with a screen.

"Ah, welcome! You have obviously come to see how our new little toy works." The Snader didn't seem concerned with the presence of the Gudes and their weapons.

"We've come to shut it down," Jake said with authority.

The Snader laughed. "How are you going to do that when you can't move?"

The machine hummed louder and faster.

Nicole yelled, "Fire!"

The machine popped and a bubble appeared around it. Nicole, Jake and Alya were engulfed by the bubble and were instantly frozen in place.

The Snader smiled evilly and walked towards them, unhindered by the freezing effect within the bubble. "As I said, you have come to see how it works. Rather nicely, I would say."

The Snader walked around them, admiring his work. "You know what my favorite part about this machine is? Even though you're frozen, you can still see, hear and think. That opens up so many fun possibilities for us, don't you think?"

The Snader let out a delighted laugh. They knew they were helpless to stop him.

"The battles going on right now mean nothing. When this machine gains full power it will surround the whole city. Within an hour, all Gudes in Timbuktu will be frozen and ready for slaughter."

CHAPTER 43

Flipper had been trapped on the building for quite a while before Fox and his men were able to fight off the Snaders and rescue him. Allison had disappeared almost immediately after they had destroyed the force field generator. He had so many questions for her and even though she hadn't been around for long, he was sure he could not have destroyed the generator without her. Heck, he might not even be alive. Flipper was with Fox, a couple of blocks from the headquarters, waiting in an open field as their escape spaceship approached. It landed a hundred yards from them. The spaceship remained running as the pilot quickly exited.

"Anyone else on board?" Fox yelled over the roar of the engine.

"No, Sir," the pilot replied.

"Fox! Flipper!"

They all turned around as Chezlor stopped in front of them.

"What is it Chezlor?" Fox yelled with concern.

Chezlor took a deep breath. "The Freezer's working! There's a bubble around it and Nicole, Jake and Alya are frozen. It will be fully powered in less than an hour and everyone in the capital will be frozen."

Fox gave quick instructions to the pilot and then turned to Flipper and Chezlor. "Into the spaceship. We have to get to The Freezer and shut it down."

They ran onto the spaceship and buckled in; Fox in the pilot's seat. "I'm going to fly low and try to avoid any Snader spaceships," he told them. "There's a lot of fighting going on, so hang on tight." With that, Fox flipped some switches and pulled back on the steering column. The spaceship lifted into the air and darted forward in a matter of seconds.

Although the Snader spaceships had been in the air for a while, the Gudes' spaceships were just approaching the city. Flipper looked out in the distance. Most of the fighting was going on around the edges of the city where General Jaxxen's troops were advancing. It appeared Fox had a clear path to the park.

Suddenly, a rocket hit a building in front of them. The building exploded and began to tumble over.

"Hold on!" Fox jerked the spaceship up to avoid the building, which crashed beneath them. Fox jerked the spaceship up again. A Snader spaceship went soaring underneath, just missing them.

"So much for going undetected," Chezlor said.

Flipper gripped the arms of his chair. Due to his fear of heights, he had never liked flying. Flying in the spaceship when they had left Rex hadn't bothered him due to the novelty of the experience, but this was sheer terror. He would rather be anywhere than on a spaceship being shot at. Well, except standing in mid-air between two buildings.

Fox continued to steer the spaceship towards the park while keeping a lookout for the Snader spaceship.

"Do you think we could just ask them to meet us on the ground to settle this?" Flipper asked with his eyes shut.

Shots whizzed by them again and destroyed another building. Fox pulled back and took them upward at a very steep incline.

"I'm leading them up high so they will quit destroying buildings," Fox explained.

"Going higher isn't what I had in mind at all!"

Flipper hoped the computer had been right about him. In school he had submitted a writing assignment making a list of all the things he wanted to do during his life. He hadn't listed getting shot down in an alien spaceship on another planet. Then again, he hadn't put down getting kidnapped by two different groups of aliens or fighting a dragon, either.

Fox was flying straight ahead now, with the Snader spaceship close behind. He flipped the spaceship over so that they were flying upside down.

"For the record, I am NOT having a good time!" Flipper shouted.

Chezlor looked at Flipper. "I always pictured a battle in a spaceship being more fun and less scary." Chezlor looked green.

"I never gave any serious thought to being in a spaceship battle," Flipper countered.

Fox made a couple more strong maneuvers.

Flipper turned to Chezlor. "We have rides back on Earth that feel a lot like this. People pay money to ride them. Sometimes I like those rides. The risk of death here is not adding to my sense of enjoyment."

Suddenly, there was an explosion in the back of the spaceship. They started swerving out of control, but Fox quickly straightened them out. He banked hard right and Flipper thought he was going to be sick. They heard another explosion from the back. The spaceship rocked as Fox lost control of it.

"Hold on tight! We're in trouble!"

"Hanging on tight is coming pretty easy right now!" Flipper yelled.

They heard more explosions outside.

"Is there anything we can do?" Chezlor shouted.

"I wish you were in the back so you could return their fire," Fox said.

"I think we would be in big trouble if we had been in the back," Chezlor said. "There may not be much of the back left."

"Good point."

"Is there any chance we can teleport safely yet?" Flipper asked Fox.

"It's pretty risky."

"So is this!"

"Touché."

There was another explosion and the spaceship went spinning in circles. All three of them yelled. Fox wrestled with the controls as the spaceship continued to drop quickly towards the ground.

"What if we didn't teleport very far?" Flipper begged.

"I have to take it down," Fox yelled.

"What?!" Flipper and Chezlor shouted at the same time.

"It's our only chance," Fox said. He pushed forward. They continued to spin and free fall. When Fox got the spaceship's nose down, he gave it everything. The spaceship rapidly sped up, heading straight towards the ground; Fox was able to gain control and stopped the ship spinning. He pulled back as hard as he could. The ground was coming towards them quickly.

"Have I mentioned I don't like heights?" Flipper shouted.

Just as Fox got the spaceship leveled off, they felt a bump beneath them.

"What was that?" Chezlor asked.

"That was the ground," Fox replied matter-of-factly.

Chezlor and Flipper looked at each other wide-eyed as the spaceship started to rise.

"Wow! That was close!" Flipper exclaimed.

"Sorry, I had to use the spaceship's momentum to regain control," Fox explained.

"Well, since it worked, we'll let it slide," Flipper quipped.

"I can see the Snaders in the distance. They're coming toward us. This spaceship isn't going to stay in the air much longer. I'm going to try to get us close to The Freezer and we are going to teleport down."

"You just said that was too risky," Chezlor said.

"It was, but I think now it is the least risky of our options. We are in no shape to fight and if we try to land we will be an easy target."

Fox directed the spaceship towards The Freezer. He flew as fast as he could, but the spaceship was losing power and the Snaders were closing in fast.

He yelled back to Chezlor and Flipper. "When I tell you to, unbuckle and run to me. I have to be holding onto you when I teleport or you will be left behind."

"Okay!" they readily agreed.

As they neared the park they heard another explosion just to their right.

"Get ready… Now!"

Flipper and Chezlor unbuckled and leaped forward. As Fox grabbed Flipper and Chezlor, Flipper felt the spaceship slam to a halt. The next thing he knew, they were standing on the ground a hundred yards behind the spaceship. They watched as the Snaders' spaceship slammed into theirs. There were several explosions and a big ball of fire engulfed what had been the two spaceships. The three of them stood in silence for a minute, catching their breath and processing what had just happened. Flipper dropped to his knees and kissed the ground. Chezlor chuckled and looked back at the destroyed spaceship. He paused, dropped to his knees and kissed the ground too.

"We have to hurry," Fox urged. "We're running out of time."

They were close to the park where The Freezer was located. Chezlor ran ahead but it didn't take Flipper and Fox long to run the two blocks. There was still no one around outside, so they ran to the gate and Fox peered in. He leaned back. "Nicole, Jake and Alya are still frozen. There's only one Snader in there and he's busy working on the machine."

"How are we going to get the machine turned off?" Chezlor asked.

"I have an idea…" Before Fox could finish, five armed Snaders ran toward them from behind.

"Hold it right there!" one of them said as they spread out in a semi-circle.

Fox, Chezlor and Flipper were trapped against the wall. Fox held up his hands and then slowly lowered his weapon to the ground. The soldiers took a step forward when The Freezer made a loud noise. The bubble expanded, gradually gaining momentum. Fox, Chezlor and Flipper stood against the wall—now frozen inside the bubble—as the soldiers raised their arms and hollered with excitement.

"Let's go wipe out the Gudes!" one of them shouted as they ran off into the distance.

CHAPTER 44

Flipper let out a huge sigh. Apparently, he had fooled them into thinking he was frozen like the others. He wasn't sure why the soldiers hadn't shot them, but he was thankful. Soon the whole city would be consumed by the bubble and it wouldn't take long for the Snaders to completely wipe out the Gudes. He had to stop the machine. But how? He picked up Fox's gun and looked around the corner. He was about to sneak up on the mad scientist when he remembered that the gun wouldn't work without the uniform.

He looked at Fox and whispered, "This is going to be embarrassing."

A few minutes later, he walked through the gate wearing a very baggy Gude military uniform. Seeing Nicole, Jake and Alya frozen was almost too much for Flipper. He needed to be mad, not upset. As he walked past his friends, he stared straight ahead and focused on the Snader. Once the Gudes were behind him and out of sight, he was able to steady his emotions.

The Snader must have assumed Flipper was a fellow Snader. He spoke without turning around. "The machine is almost fully charged. Within a few minutes all of Timbuktu will be covered and we can commence the takeover."

That was exactly what Flipper needed to hear to turn himself into a ball of rage. Through clenched teeth he said, "I'm not going to let that happen."

The Snader turned around and his whole body jumped when he saw Flipper. "Oh my!" He looked at Flipper curiously. "How are you not frozen? That's...that's...impossible." He showed no fear, which made Flipper even madder.

The Snader continued, "This is simply fascinating." He took a step towards Flipper to examine him more closely.

Flipper didn't have time for delays. "Take one more step and I will blast you."

"I simply must know how come you are not frozen," the Snader said, taking another step towards Flipper.

Flipper hoped the weapon worked. He closed his eyes, pulled the trigger, and the gun fired. Flipper opened his eyes. The scientist was on the floor, holding his leg. He had shot the scientist's foot.

Flipper looked at the Snader and tried to make himself very clear. "Now, put down the control module and slide it gently towards me."

Instead, the Snader lifted himself up so that he was standing on his good leg. Flipper pulled the trigger again and the Snader collapsed. Flipper had shot his other foot.

The Snader was on the ground in severe pain, clinging to the control module. Flipper repeated himself one more time, "Put the control module down and gently slide it towards me!"

The Snader held it to his chest, covering it by crossing his arms. Flipper shot the Snader in the arm. He dropped the control module but quickly reached down to pick it up with his remaining good hand. Flipper didn't hesitate. He fired once more and hit the Snader's hand. The Snader was now helpless. Flipper ran over and picked up the controller. He put the weapon's strap over his shoulder and went to work trying to figure out how the controller shut off The Freezer.

Flipper looked at the screen and saw a picture of a zombie. "What?!" he exclaimed. He touched the screen and the view changed. Now he saw two zombies. He moved it around a couple of more times and then said to himself, This isn't a controller. This looks like Minecraft!

He set the controller down and started searching the machine. If that wasn't the controller then there had to be something on the machine that would allow him to shut down its power. He couldn't find anything and started to panic. He thought about shooting The Freezer but was afraid that might leave Nicole, Chezlor and Alya frozen forever.

There was enough room to crawl underneath the machine, so he slid beneath it and began examining it. He was about to give up when he shouted, "No way!"

Up in a crevice of the machine, very well hidden, was a button. Flipper took a deep breath. "Here goes." He pushed the button and quickly slid out. He ran over to Alya and watched. The machine made a funny sound and began to smoke. The bubble quickly retreated and within seconds was completely gone. The smoke became dense as the machine melted from the inside out. Within minutes, it was a big pile of ashes.

"Flipper, you did it!" Jake shouted.

Alya hugged him, and soon Jake and Nicole joined in.

Fox and Chezlor came around the corner and joined in the celebration. Fox didn't even seem to mind that he was standing in his boxers and a t-shirt. Everyone gave him a funny look.

"Oh, sorry!" Flipper said as he took off Fox's uniform. "I had to borrow your uniform in order to use the gun."

They all laughed.

As Fox dressed he asked, "How did you destroy the machine?"

"Well, it was kind of complicated. I'm not sure you would understand the technical terms involved."

They all waited expectantly and he smiled. "It had a self-destruct button."

Everyone laughed again.

Once Fox had his uniform back on, Flipper handed him his gun. "Here, I don't want to have to use this ever again."

Fox took the weapon from Flipper and held it, then looked over at the Snader writhing in pain. "Did you do that to him?"

"You should have seen it!" Jake said excitedly. "He shot one foot, then the other. Then he shot the guy's arm, and when he reached to pick up the controller, Flipper shot his hand so he couldn't pick it up! It was awesome!"

Fox looked at Flipper and smiled. "Where did you learn to shoot like that?"

Flipper paused, not sure what to say, but decided to be honest. "Actually, I was trying to scare him, not hit him."

Once more, everyone roared with laughter.

Fox brought them back to reality. "Guys, we need to get out of here and to safety. The Snaders are still out there. This isn't over yet." He went to the gate to take a look outside, as everyone followed.

"Just a minute," Flipper said. He ran back to the scientist. "I know a good surgeon on Rex. His name is Dr. Needles. Tell him I sent you." The scientist looked at Flipper in astonishment. Flipper reached down and picked up the control module. "You won't need this for a while. Thanks!" Flipper ran back to the group and held up the controller. "Souvenir," he said, smiling.

"It's clear." Fox lead them out with Nicole at the rear to watch behind them.

***

There were air battles going on dangerously close to them. With all the spaceships in the air, Fox was concerned about his ability to keep the kids safe amidst the chaos. They had traveled a quarter of a mile when a loud explosion above caused them to stop and look. A spaceship had been blown to pieces.

"Everyone this way," Fox yelled as he ran towards the nearest building.

Debris from the explosion began raining down. Chezlor made it to the door a few seconds before the others. Fox stopped as a large red sheet of a spaceship displaying the letters NAD landed right in front of him. He turned to check on the others and saw another large piece of the spaceship falling towards Jake. He sprinted but knew he didn't have enough time. Suddenly, Chezlor whizzed by and tackled Jake, sending them both tumbling across the ground as the wreckage narrowly missed them. Fox and Nicole helped them up.

"Are you guys okay?" Nicole asked.

They both had severe scrapes and purple blood all over their bodies. They both said they were fine but it was obvious they were in pain.

Fox kicked open the door and they all scampered inside.

"That was amazing, Chezlor!" Alya said admiringly.

"Yeah, thanks Chezlor! You saved my life!" Jake said.

Chezlor shrugged his shoulders. "It wasn't a big deal. I just happen to be the fastest Gude on Vetrix. It comes in handy at times."

Nicole placed her hand on his shoulder. "That was really brave. You risked your life out there."

"If I had let that thing land on him, who would I have to play pranks on?" Chezlor said with a smile.

"Dude, you're not too good at accepting a compliment, are you?" Flipper said.

Chezlor looked down, abashed. "No, it makes me feel uncomfortable when people say nice stuff about me."

"Just say, 'Thank you,'" Flipper instructed. "You were awesome out there—good job!"

"Thank you." Chezlor playfully pushed him. "Now shut up."

Alya looked at Fox. "What are we going to do now?"

"We're going to stay here for a while," Fox said.

"I'll run ahead and see if I can find us a safe way to get out of town," Chezlor proposed.

"No, it's too dangerous to be out there by yourself," Nicole protested.

"We don't have a better option," Chezlor said. "We can't teleport, we don't have a spaceship, and we don't know if we can get out of town without going through a group of Snaders. Factor in the flying debris outside and we're trapped. With my speed, I can get past the Snaders and get help. Maybe find a spaceship to come pick us up and take us out of here." Chezlor had been replying to Nicole but looking at Fox. Fox was the ranking official and obviously Chezlor understood it was his decision.

Fox did not like the idea of Chezlor separating from the group but he knew they didn't have a very good chance of getting out of the capital without help. He looked around. They were in an old warehouse. It would provide protection from the debris falling from the sky, but the warehouse was large and empty. They couldn't protect themselves from invading Snaders.

He sighed. "You do everything you can to avoid the Snaders and at all costs, do not interact with them for any reason. If you don't see a safe way past them, get back here immediately. Do you understand?"

"Yes, Sir!" Chezlor said and, almost instantly, he was gone.

CHAPTER **45**

Nicole and Alya spent several minutes cleaning Jake's wounds. They stopped the bleeding but didn't have any medicine or bandages—those were going to have to wait until they returned to the compound. Fox and Flipper scouted the warehouse. They didn't find anything useful but learned there were four entrances. There was no way they could defend themselves if the Snaders tried to attack them from each of the entrances—which is exactly what happened next.

About a dozen Snaders came rushing through each of the doors to the warehouse. At first, Fox, Nicole, Jake and Alya drew their weapons, ready to fight, but they quickly realized they were completely surrounded and heavily outnumbered. Fox carefully laid his gun on the floor and the other three did likewise. They all raised their arms in the air.

Flipper and Fox recognized a few of the Snaders as ones that had them trapped just before The Freezer expanded and began freezing the city. It appeared, they weren't happy about their decision not to kill them when they had the chance.

One of the soldiers they recognized took a step forward. He looked right at Flipper and asked, "How did you get to The Freezer without it freezing you?"

Flipper shrugged. "Did you ever see the Doctor Who episode where Doctor Who and Rose are separated into two different universes?"

They looked at him with blank expressions. "Well, the two universes were separated by this empty area called the void. I'm no scientist, and I don't know anything about how your freezing machine works, but I think what happened in Doctor Who is what happened with your freezer thingy. Somehow, I got stuck in a void between this universe and another, and it allowed me to travel freely without being frozen."

Most of the Snader soldiers looked at each other; they weren't sure if Flipper was being serious or not.

Flipper continued, "Anyhow, I was just checking out the machine and accidentally pressed a button that said 'Self-Destruct' on it. I'm really sorry about that, and I can understand why you are all upset. I'm sure that it wasn't a cheap device to make, and probably took that professor guy several years to build. I would be glad to reimburse you for any damages, if you'll just send me a bill."

A Snader soldier had had enough of Flipper's rambling. He walked over to Alya and pushed her forward. He made her stand a few feet in front of the others. He put his gun to her head. Alya closed her eyes and tensed up; she started to cry.

"No more games. You are going to tell me how you stayed unfrozen. You can do it with the others listening, or I can silence them one at a time until you tell us the truth."

"Okay, okay!" Flipper pleaded. "I'm a Snader, so none of your weapons work on me."

The truth didn't satisfy the Snader at all. "You're a Snader? That's a worse story than the first one you made up. We aren't stupid, and we aren't patient. Say good-bye to your friend."

The Snader moved his gaze from Flipper to Alya. She still had her eyes shut tightly. She was trying to be brave, but couldn't stop the tears that flowed. The Snader took a deep breath. Suddenly, Chezlor appeared behind the soldier. He bent down and grabbed the Snader's pants. He pulled them down to his knees and disappeared again. He reappeared behind another one of the soldiers in the circle and de-pantsed him also. The two soldiers scrambled to pull their pants back up over their underwear. There was some whispering and several chuckles, enough of a commotion for Alya to open her eyes to see what was going on.

Chezlor appeared again behind another soldier. As he pulled the soldiers pants down, he yelled, "It's!" He vanished and appeared behind a soldier on the other side of the circle. This time as Chezlor de-pantsed him, he yelled, "Safe!" Chezlor did it a third time and yelled, "To!" The final time he appeared, he did so behind the soldier holding the gun towards Alya. He didn't pull his pants down, but grabbed his underwear and yanked as hard as he could, giving the soldier a painful wedgie. This time, he yelled, "Teleport!"

Fox shouted, "Let's go!"

The soldier in the middle yelled, "Fire!"

As the four dozen soldiers opened fire on the group, Chezlor, Fox, Jake, Nicole and Alya teleported away. When the soldiers saw the Gudes had gone, they all turned their fire on Flipper.

Flipper was getting really tired of all the laser shots hitting him. He shut his eyes, tilted his head back, and lifted his arms in the air. He let the shots hit him, accepting their barrage, since he couldn't do anything about it anyway. He didn't know what he was doing really, just trying to be dramatic.

"Cease fire!" the commanding soldier finally ordered.

The soldiers stared at Flipper in astonishment. He dropped his hands and opened his eyes. "Thank you. That was getting really annoying." He smiled and said, "Now, what were we talking about?"

The commanding soldier let his gun rest on the strap and walked towards Flipper, looking him over, not able to believe what he had just seen. "How did you…?"

Suddenly, Fox appeared beside Flipper and grabbed him. "Sorry guys—forgot one." Fox smiled at the Snaders and then disappeared with Flipper.

The Snader soldiers were left staring at each other. They really hated teleporting.

Chapter 46

The steady rumbling of the tank filled Allison's ears. She slowly opened her eyes and saw Josh staring at the monitor. She had just been with Flipper! It had been real!

She was so excited she shouted and caused Josh to jump and almost say a bad word. "Josh, I did it!"

"Holy... Shazam!"

She gave him a funny look before continuing, "I saw Flipper and I helped him!"

She told him how she had helped Flipper destroy a generator on Vetrix. "He says that the Gudes said they would bring him home after the battle."

"Wow! I hope he survives the battle okay." Josh sounded genuinely concerned.

"He said his part was finished and that Fox, the guy who kidnapped him, was going to pick him up and take him to safety."

"I hope we get to see him soon," Josh said.

"Me too—I can't wait to see him again," Allison agreed.

As the tank broke through the topsoil, their first glimpse of sun after several days underground was sheer bliss.

"Another beautiful, sunny day in Roswell," Allison beamed. "Or somewhere near Roswell."

The tank stopped as soon as they made it above ground. They crawled out and saw nothing but dirt. "I guess we have some walking to do," Josh sighed.

They were dirty, exhausted and dehydrated, but they were so excited that the two miles they walked before spotting a house seemed to pass quickly. They knocked on the door and a lady answered.

"Excuse me, ma'am," Allison started.

"You're the missing children!" the lady exclaimed, interrupting.

"What?" Josh said.

"It's been all over the news, and your pictures are up everywhere in town."

"We've been trapped underground," Josh said by means of an explanation.

"Come in, come in. I'll call the police and let them know you're here."

While they waited for the police and their parents to arrive, the lady gave them water and juice and fed them sandwiches. Josh agreed with Allison that they were the best sandwiches they had ever eaten. The police and their parents arrived at the same time. After several minutes of hugs and kisses and crying, their parents agreed to allow them to share their story with the police. Josh and Allison told the police everything, starting with Allison seeing the purple alien in her dream and then seeing him kidnap Flipper. They concluded by telling them about their escape and the big machine that they had left in the field after they had emerged from underground. They described where it was and what it looked like. The police radioed to have someone go out and take a look at the spot. Josh and Allison asked a lot of questions about Flipper and found out that he was still missing. No one believed the story of him being kidnapped by a purple alien.

The police got a call saying the officers out in the field were not able to locate the digging machine, nor a big hole in the ground. Josh and

Allison were so adamant about it that they finally insisted on leading the police to the spot. Josh and Allison rode with the police, and their parents followed. They led them right to where they had emerged.

"Stop, this is the place," Allison instructed.

The police car stopped and Josh and Allison jumped out. They walked around in disbelief—there was nothing there. The ground looked normal, undisturbed. There was no sign that anything had been dug up. Josh and Allison couldn't believe it. They walked around, stunned, talking fast, trying to explain how they had come from under the ground in that very spot, no matter what it might look like. Finally, Allison burst into tears. Her mom came over to her and held her tightly. Allison's mom walked her to their car and helped her into the back seat. As they started to drive away, Allison looked out her window and saw Josh, just a few feet away, looking at her. As Allison's dad pulled away, she turned around to watch Josh through the back windshield until he was out of sight.

CHAPTER **47**

Chezlor woke up. He felt like he had slept for a day. Every muscle in his body was sore. He lay on his side and felt like he hadn't moved from that position for hours. He wasn't ready to get out of bed just yet so he shut his eyes and rolled over.

The rooms in the hideout were a hundred feet underground, so there was no outside light. His room was always pitch dark until he turned a light on, but even with his eyes closed he could tell there was a dim light on in his room. He opened his eyes and fear surged through every inch of his body. There was a Snader standing by his bed. He screamed and jumped out of the other side of his bed. He ran to his door and threw it open. There was another Snader standing in front of him. He was trapped. In panic, he tried to run over the Snader, tumbling them both to the floor. He landed on top of the Snader, who burst, throwing red blood everywhere.

Jake, Alya and Flipper stood a few feet away laughing uncontrollably. Chezlor looked down at the Snader and realized what had happened. He smelled the blood. It was ketchup. He had been pranked. He walked back into his room and gently pushed the other Snader. It fell over.

***

Chezlor changed into some dry clothes then joined the others out in the commons area.

"We got you good!" Jake said, beaming with pride.

"You guys scared me to death!" Chezlor admitted.

"The whole thing was Flipper's idea," Alya boasted.

Chezlor looked over at him, "Good one, Flipper!"

General Jaxxen, Fox and Nicole entered the room. It warmed the three adults to see the kids laughing and enjoying themselves. Nicole sat down amongst the children. Fox stood behind them. General Jaxxen leaned back against the table, half sitting and half standing, and addressed the group.

"The Lizards who weren't killed in the battle have fled back to Rex. We did manage to capture a few of them, including the professor who invented The Freezer."

"Yeah, he couldn't escape because Flipper took both of his feet out," Chezlor pointed out. They all laughed. Chezlor continued,. "The first question you should ask him is why he put a self-destruct button on his machine."

Again, everyone roared with laughter.

Flipper was laughing so hard he could barely speak. Once he caught his breath, he added, "What's his name—Doctor Doofenshmirtz?" Flipper laughed but everyone else stopped. He was laughing so hard, it took him a minute to realize he was the only one still laughing. "Oh, you're kidding me! You guys aren't familiar with Phineas and Ferb? You've got to get cable here."

General Jaxxen continued as if he hadn't been interrupted. "We will interrogate each of them and try to learn what we can. We also have Sierra in custody, but of course she isn't cooperating. We may or may not ever know why she betrayed us."

The mention of Sierra brought a somber mood to the room, but the jubilation was too great for it to last more than a few moments. General Jaxxen seemed to understand and waited patiently.

"Flipper has indeed helped us to overcome the Lizards' attack on Vetrix, and all of you played a significant part in the victory. I was skeptical that a computer could select one person, especially a kid, to help defeat the Lizards. I underestimated both Flipper and my own son, Jake, as well as Chezlor and Alya. You will all be rewarded with medals at a special ceremony celebrating Vetrix's victory."

"Does that mean Flipper is staying for a while?" Chezlor asked hopefully.

"No, we must return him to his own planet," General Jaxxen said. He looked at Flipper and said, "I'm sure his family is very worried about him."

Flipper nodded as a wave of homesickness came over him.

"We'll bring him back to Vetrix with his family when the time is right, probably in a few weeks, for a grand celebration."

"How come the time isn't right now?" Jake asked.

General Jaxxen looked at Fox and then Nicole before answering. "I believe the computer's prediction about Flipper is accurate."

"Don't you mean *was* accurate?" Alya corrected.

"No, I mean *is*," General Jaxxen stressed. "I talked to Nicole and the exact question the computer answered was: 'How are the Lizards defeated permanently?' Flipper helped to save Vetrix from the Lizards, but the Lizards have not been defeated *permanently*. They will attack again at some point, either here or on Earth." Flipper sat forward when General Jaxxen mentioned Earth. "I believe the Lizards will try to attack Earth someday. We're constantly monitoring for that possibility and are prepared to act, but I believe our victory here will give us a respite from the Lizards' attacks and allow us to go on the offensive and attack Rex. I believe that Flipper still has a role to play—a significant role—in defeating the Lizards permanently. I will work with our top commanders to put together a plan to attack the Snaders on Rex. We hope that since we have them on the defense, we can keep them retreating and divert their attention away from Earth. At some point soon, we will need to bring Flipper back to help us in that fight on Rex," General Jaxxen paused to let that sink in. "I think that all of you—Jake, Chezlor, Alya—will be able to help us in that battle. We'll fill you in more as the plan develops. As for now, Flipper needs to get home and spend some time with his family. We'll bring him back when the time is right." General Jaxxen looked at Flipper. "Flipper, Nicole has something for you."

Nicole handed Flipper a device that looked a lot like a cell phone—the flip phone kind his dad still used.

"This is a communicator. It will allow you to keep in contact with us from Earth," Nicole explained. "You speak into it and record your message, then send it to us. It will also allow us to send you messages."

"No one on Earth understands the danger the Lizards pose to your planet more than you do," General Jaxxen said. "We would like you to send us reports, daily if possible, of any unusual or potentially unusual activity. We will keep you informed about how the plan is developing to attack the Lizards on Rex."

Nicole took a couple of minutes to show Flipper how to work his communicator. It was pretty simple and Flipper was excited to have a way to keep in contact with his new friends.

"How do I recharge it?" Flipper asked.

They all chuckled.

"It doesn't need to be recharged," Nicole explained. "It has a perpetual power source."

"Are you saying it doesn't ever run out of power?" Flipper asked.

Nicole smiled. "That's exactly what I'm saying."

"Wow! That is really cool!" Flipper said.

They took their time saying their good-byes before General Jaxxen declared it was time for Flipper to go. Fox teleported Flipper back to his living room.

"Flipper, it was very good to meet you. I'm sure we will be seeing each other again soon."

Flipper shook Fox's hand. "It was good to meet you too. Thanks for kidnapping me."

Fox smiled, ruffled Flipper's hair, then disappeared.

Flipper looked around the living room. It had only been a few days, but it seemed like an eternity since he had last been there. He heard a noise from the other room, so he yelled, "Mom! Dad! I'm home!"

ACKNOWLEDGEMENTS

I have to start by recognizing my mom, Phyllis Roth Lewis. Writing was her favorite hobby. Although I didn't start writing fiction until after she passed away, I realize my interest stems from her passion. She didn't teach me to write nor did she encourage or insist I do so. I simply "caught" the writing bug from her.

After years of lying dormant the writing bug has taken ahold of me. I have my daughter, Sydney, to thank for that. In 2010 we created a world, including crudely drawn maps and figures of fantasy characters. We researched names, brainstormed plots, and began writing a story. Unfortunately, that story has yet to be completed. I say yet because I hope one day she will finish what we started. Although we didn't finish the first book, it was that experience that steeled my determination to write a novel.

I decided to write a novel in the fall of 2013. This time it was my eleven-year-old son, Blake, who helped me create characters and a plot for what would become this book—Vetrix. I frequently threw ideas at him as I wrote and together we created a world where aliens are real, Gudes and Snaders battle for the universe, and twelve-year-old kids have a say in the outcome. Together we have created four books so far in this series. Yes, there are more stories of Flipper to come.

I would be remiss if I didn't mention National Novel Writing Month, or Nanowrimo.org. It was their vision, their website, and the other writers I met through the website that helped encourage and give me the tools to complete that first rough draft. I am now a four-time Nano winner!

I met my first beta reader through Nanowrimo. Anya Rousselle and I traded our Nano stories and marked them up for each other. She gave me lots of valuable insights and helpful suggestions. Without her help I never would have wondered far from my rough draft.

I had two other beta readers. My good friend Mike Walton took a pen to my manuscript and made many corrections to my early story. A friend and former high school classmate, Barbara Scheibmeir, gave me plot input, including one suggestion which turned into a major story change.

After several rewrites I sent the story to Jefferson Franklin Editing and Ashley gave me more constructive feedback than I was capable of expecting. I would not have been able to get over the hump and polish the story without her help.

I have three people to thank for proofreading my story. David Heffern, another YCHS alum and fellow baseball player, sacrificed a weekend and traveled to Newton to carefully read and fix several typos and grammar mistakes. I am thankful for his generosity.

My dad, Bob Bush, gave the story one final read before I printed the proof copy. He also was immensely helpful to me in getting my website set up and functioning as I wanted.

Once I had a proof copy of the book, Angel Charae graciously volunteered to read the entire book of Vetrix in three days to identify any final mistakes. She also proofread Before Vetrix before it went to print.

In addition, Joel Porter, also a YCHS alum, provided valuable insight by beta reading Before Vetrix.

I would like to thank Katharina Gerlach for formatting both Vetrix and Before Vetrix. Both books look professionally done because of her.

The beautiful cover was designed by my cousin, Debbie McLain, who has also designed most of my other covers. I am deeply grateful for her help in an area I have little knowledge.

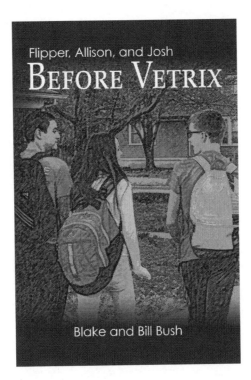

Flipper, Allison, and Josh

BEFORE VETRIX

Blake and Bill Bush

Three friends—eleven adventures—one good time.

Before Flipper is kidnapped in front of Allison and Josh (details in the book Vetrix), the three best friends had a relatively normal life, though these short stories show that even ordinary kids doing everyday activities experience extraordinary moments. What kind of fun lies inside these pages?

> Josh and Allison get kicked out of a field trip
> They each share their most embarrassing moment
> Flipper uses his best pick-up lines on a girl he has a crush on
> The kids play a prank on Christmas night
> Allison and Flipper help Josh deal with a bully
> An indoor activity sends one of them to the emergency room
> Flipper and Allison battle against a tarantula that is stalking them
> Flipper fights a goat
> Allison becomes a sleuth
> … and more

Experience the trio's friendship as they have a good time together, no matter the circumstances.

available in print and as eBook

ISBN 978-1-945871-23-8

Made in the USA
San Bernardino, CA
30 March 2017